KANE'S HUNDRED
AND THE HUNTER COMES

JANETTE ANDERSON

Published in the USA by:
BearManor Media
P O Box 71426
Albany, Georgia 31708
www.bearmanormedia.com

ISBN 1-59393-351-7

Printed in the United States of America.

Dedicated
To Sully and Kane,
Always in my heart.

CHAPTER 1

"Let's get the hell out of here!" screamed the running man. Kane Branson's thoughts jolted back to the present as Giles Harris became visible through the dense undergrowth, hurrying towards him…fast. Giles grabbed Kane by the vest.

"Why?" replied Kane. "Colonel Cheng is still inside the fort, isn't he?"

"Not anymore," Giles yelled.

"Where did he go?" Kane stared, his electric blue eyes piercing.

"He's coming after us, now, and this guy's got the whole fucking Chinese army with him!"

Kane spun around and bolted, the two men fighting their way through the dense undergrowth. Suddenly, the drone of helicopters could be heard overhead. They swooped by and circled back. Kane and Giles were their targets. Rounds of ammunition flew from the guns of the first craft. The two men stopped and hunkered down behind the trees. Kane bided his time. Raising his rifle, he rested it against an overhanging branch and sighted the pilot. With one clean shot from the 50 caliber the pilot was history. The chopper spun in midair and plummeted to the earth below spewing men from the craft like splitting peas from a pod. There was a sickening noise of metal and death. Screaming souls of men descended to hell. Kane turned to Giles, dropping the heavy gun on the ground.

"What the fuck happened?" asked Kane. "They knew we were here. Somebody must have tipped them off! Go, Giles get the fuck out of here. Tell Tony the same. See you back in Sydney…GO!"

Tony never made it. Kane came upon Tony's body some distance down the trail. Shot twice through the head…. Blood splattered the ground where he lay. Blood and what was left of his head. Kane stopped for a second. Bending down, and with bloodstained fingers, he touched the body of the man that had been his friend, smearing battle scars across his own face. "I swear to you, I will get the person responsible for this. You have my word." Kane Branson never broke his word.

Only minutes before Kane had been lying in the long grasses. Shadows fell across his face. Kane spun around, his finger tight on the trigger of the massive Heckler and Koch .50 caliber sniper rifle. Raw instinct and a lifetime of training took over. The gun completed the turn a second before he did. He aimed and was ready to fire. Smiling, he dropped his face to sight in the target of the rifle. He was staring at a huge eagle, wings spread, blocking out the sun as it hovered above, a small hawk zigzagging helplessly beneath the shadow, trying to avoid death. The hawk swooped and dove. The eagle stayed on steady course high above it, watching patiently.

Kane knew the eagle was toying with the helplessly outmatched smaller bird, delaying the inevitable as long as possible, enjoying the thrill of the hunt before the thrill of the kill. Still the hawk flew fast and furious. Kane watched as the eagle suddenly swooped up into the bright sun and disappeared. The hawk slowed and curved around in a tight circle. His pursuer was nowhere in sight.

"Know your enemy," whispered Kane to the hawk, as he continued to watch, as he lowered the rifle barrel.

Suddenly, a piercing screech filled the sky. Kane knew it was the hawk's death knell, the eagle's kill-cry, as he hurtled straight out of the sun toward its prey. Shielding his eyes, Kane tried to see. Nothing fascinated a hunter more than watching another professional at work.

The blinding sun prevented Kane from seeing anything but the hawk. A split-second later the eagle's razor talons came into view inches from the hawk's head. At the last second, the little hawk folded its wings to its side, dropping like a rock toward the forest below. Surprised, the eagle could not change course that quickly; it had to swoop to follow. Kane watched as the little hawk careered downwards. With only feet to spare before smashing into the forest canopy, the hawk suddenly unfurled his wings and rocketed laterally across the roof of the forest. In a moment, the small bird disappeared. The eagle circled, it curved, riding the thermals to another showdown for lunch.

"And know your prey," smiled Kane.

Suddenly the whistle of a tropical Mayan broke the forest reverie. To Kane's trained ear, it seemed a bit above the natural pitch. It was the signal that he'd been waiting to hear. "All Clear."

Kane's partner, Giles Harris, was somewhere nearby. After other missions together over the years, Kane and Giles had developed a wordless code for communicating during combat ops.

Giles, who was smart, and headstrong, was also a worthy partner in the heat of battle. Kane tolerated this man, this superb killer. He didn't have to sleep with him, and for this Black-Ops mission deep inside China, Giles was the perfect man to have as backup.

Kane returned the high-pitched whistle, making his way through the dense undergrowth. As much as he knew of the importance of the assignment, he hated the fact that if he were captured, the Australian government would have no choice but to disavow any knowledge of his presence there. The Chinese would not take lightly to the assassination of one of their citizens by a member of another country's elite police. It didn't matter that he made his millions from the suffering and pain of others.

'*Another day…another drug-lord,*' thought Kane, and that day was far from over. In fact, the day had just only just begun.

When her husband had suggested she join him in the Australian Federal Police, Kelly Branson had jumped at the chance. It was just another opportunity to forget her old way of life, the drugs and prostitution, and work closely with Kane. Lately she had been considering whether she had made the right choice. Kane was in charge of a batch of new recruits, and Kelly, not by chance, was in it. Kane's superior, Commander Buchanan, thought that he would be tougher on her and that tougher was good. Kelly's average training day included four a.m. runs along the beach, rushing back home to look after their child, then on to the academy for the day to train. The paperwork was hard and Kelly wasn't the brightest student. What she lacked in smarts though she made up in guts. Now she stood in the gym like the rest, waiting for their instructor.

Tall and blonde, fifty-four-year-old Kane Branson walked through the doorway, hair pulled back in a ponytail. Tight black vest and sweats only enhanced his virility. Bands round his wrists and his head. A stopwatch hung from his neck by a chain. Bare foot, with body lean and muscular, Kane stood there.

Kelly heard the women in the mixed class of fifty mutter at the sight of their new instructor. Some would make it through the class…some would not.

"I'm Special Agent Kane Branson. You will call me Sir. What I say, you do. All of you." Never looking Kelly's way, he continued, "First line, step forward. Each one of you, call out your name starting from the left." Kane glanced quickly across the lines assessing the likely candidates.

"Ty McLeod, sir." Blonde, athletic, eager and willing to be taught the trade.

"Brent Prince, sir." Cold, a dead fish.

Each one called out their name until the whole row had finished.

Kelly stood in the second line waiting her turn.

"See those ropes? In twenty seconds I want you all at the top of them. The last one up is out of the class. Go!" Kane started his stopwatch.

Some of them struggled to gain height up to the top. A chubby, geeky looking guy with spectacles was last. They hung there, hands burning with new course rope on fresh skin."

"Down!" Kane demanded.

The geek dropped to the floor last. Not even trying to excuse his actions, he turned and walked to the door, his head hanging in shame. A feeling he was used to having.

"You… Ben Grey. Where do ya think you're going?"

Kane folded his arms and stared at the geek.

"Last one up, sir. Out of the class, sir," replied the young man.

"Only if I say you are. Back in line along with the second row. Try again. Second line, forward," and Kane shook his head.

Kelly looked dead ahead. She had more to prove than the others had.

"Genna Ingram, sir." An intelligent mind and she sported a strong body. Hair pulled in bunches, and seemingly nothing going for her in the looks department. Yet, the girl was determined.

"Paul Mann, sir." Good looking, almost pretty, and set to win at any cost.

"Kelly Branson, sir." She never hesitated.

"He's your father?!" whispered Mann, leaning towards her.

There was a startled look among the line. The row finished speaking.

"Go," ordered Kane, while holding his stopwatch. Seconds ticked by.

They grabbed at the still twisting ropes. Kelly went up hers as though her life depended upon it. In a way, it did. She was third up the rope and Ben Grey was fourth. A slight smile spread across the geek's face.

"Everyone down, except for Kelly," boomed Kane.

They dropped, and went quickly back to their lines. Kane walked to the bottom of Kelly's rope. Holding the end of it, he twirled it slightly.

"This is Kelly Branson. She's," he looked slowly around the room, "my wife. And before you go thinking I'll be lighter on her than the rest of you, you should know that I'll be twice as hard. You can bank on that."

The whole time that Kelly hung from the ropes her hands burned fiercely. Kane looked up at her.

"Okay, Kelly Branson, you can get down and return to your line."

"Sir, yes, sir. Thank you, sir," replied the young woman's voice.

Kelly slid down to the floor. She was tiny next to Kane and scurried back to her group. The arrogant Mann stared.

"You're *married* to him?" His voice wasn't so quiet.

"Someone say something?" Kane boomed, his eyes fierce as he searched around the room.

Kane kept his word. Kelly worked twice as hard as anyone else did. When they went through the hoops, she went twice. When Kane wasn't looking, Kelly shed a tear, but she never flinched. Kane knew. Not only did she come in fifth in her class, she made a friend of Genna from the first line.

At twenty-seven, Genna was only a few years older than Kelly was. Tall, plain, a crack shot, bright, and willing to teach Kelly the math she could not grasp; also a young woman who wanted to speed through the ranks of the AFP for her own reasons. What better way than with Kane's wife? She was right. They were going straight into the drug-crazed world of Hong Kong.

Now was the time to weed out the chaff, and truth from the lies. To go back and finish the mission that Kane and Giles started a year ago in Hong Kong. Kane had failed and that he could not tolerate…not for any reason. And he had a score to settle and a death to justify.

Right now, Kane's little group was finishing their training in one of the hottest and steamiest place in Australia: Alice Springs and the Finke River, and it served as a good double for Hong Kong's steamy settings. Pine Valley nestled on the outskirts of Alice Spring. The days were long and tough and served as a taste of what was to come on foreign shores. Survive here and a person could probably survive Hong Kong.

Commander Buchanan gave Kane free range to do with the recruits as he pleased. Kane always had permission to do what he thought best for his people. His knowledge of foreign locals, and how to deal with them, was coming in handy. The first mission he had taken had been to the island of Hong Kong.

It was the departments hope that Kane knew how to smooth the rough edges of these youngsters and turn out polished pros. After all, Kane had ninety-nine missions under his belt. Kane was supposed to know what he was doing.

Sitting alone by the campfire, he watched the hot white flames dancing on the brisk night air. Dressed in T-shirt and pants, his body glistened in the light, sweating from the day's workout. He watched as the party fought over the sparse number of tents. Some of them would have to double up.

Kane could hear noises in the distance, and, at closer quarters, he could hear the women laughing in the canvas tent. The girls flipped a coin to see who got the one single tent. Kelly won. In the lamplight, Kane could see Kelly's shape, the outline of her breasts as she pulled off her T-shirt. Within seconds, she climbed into a nightshirt, one that resembled something like a sack. Kane also saw her turn his way taunting him through the canvas. She pulled the sack down slowly. Kelly knew he'd be watching. Giggling, she tossed her light brown hair back behind her. He called out to her.

"Agent Branson," yelled Kane. "Mind stepping outside here a moment?"

Kelly stepped out of the tent and into the night. She walked seductively towards him, her hips swinging. Licking her dry lips, she focused her eyes on Kane.

"Sir, yes, sir." His wife stood in front of him.

He looked up at her. Even in that sack she was sexy.

"What the hell are you trying to do to me?" Kane rubbed his dusty palms together.

"To you, sir? Nothing, sir." She winked at him.

"You know when we get back to Sydney we have two days at home, don't you?" He bent his head slightly as he spoke.

"Sir, yes, sir," Kelly replied.

"Well, Agent Branson, just be prepared for me," and he looked up and stared hard at his wife.

She looked down at his tight black pants. One part of him was already prepared for her.

"For you, sir? You have some plans for me, sir?" Kelly asked coyly.

"Oh, you bet that sweet fanny of yours I do!"

"Oh, I hope so, sir. Anything else, sir?" Her round, full eyes gleamed.

"You know full well there is and I can't do a damn thing about it. I could get arrested for what I'm thinking right now. Get to bed and, Kelly, sweet dreams, darling."

"You too, sir. Think of me in your arms, nestled onto your chest, my legs wrapped tightly around you, and your…" She whispered low.

"Stop right there!"

Kelly laughed, turned, and walked away from him. Glancing back over her shoulder, she blew him a kiss.

"Fucking stupid rules of no mixing with the opposite sex," he growled, and Kane scuffed his boots on the barren earth.

Kane Branson never played by the rules. He waited till the fire was just embers, dumped the rest of the extra-strong coffee on it and walked purposefully away. Creeping into his wife's small single tent, he sat on her fold-up cot and stroked her hair. It was soft and silky to his rough fingers.

"You awake, Kel? Wake up. Spread your wings, little butterfly," he whispered.

He slid his hand under the course military blanket. She moaned in her sleep. As he touched her, she wriggled. Sliding his hand along her thigh, he could feel as her legs parted instinctively. He felt her push back against his hand.

"Even in sleep, little Kel."

"Sir, yes, sir," she happily murmured only half awake.

Kane left her before dawn, before the skies filled pink with morning sunlight. Pulling on his pants, he pulled the T-shirt back over his head. He slid his gun and holster back on again. Only he was carrying out of this little group. The rest of their guns were stashed ready in hiding. He stood in the entrance to the canvas home and watched her sleep. Kelly turned over and felt the emptiness of the cot. Her eyes flickered.

"Kane?" she asked for him in a whisper.

"I'm right here, darling," and he bent down beside her.

"I thought I was dreaming. I thought that I could feel your arms around me," and she brushed the stray hair from her eyes.

"You did, darling. I hope that's not all you felt?" Kane sat back down on the cot. Kelly tuned to face him. The covers slipped down and revealed her naked breasts.

Trying to concentrate, he said, "Baby, if you don't want to go on to Hong Kong I'll understand. It's not a place…"

"Till death do us part, is that not what we said the day we married?" She sat up in bed and the blanket slipped even further.

"Yeah, that's what we said, but…" He was distracted.

"No buts. Where you go I go. Come back under the blanket with me," she whispered and revealed the rest of her body.

"Can't, darling. I could be fired for sleeping with an agent even, if that agent is my wife."

Giggling again, she could not help but ask, "Since when has that stopped you? I'll make it worth your while."

He looked wistfully at her. "Yeah, I bet you would."

There was a discreet cough from outside the tent.

"Just a moment," muttered Kane.

He held Kelly's face in his hands, kissed her pouting lips, stood up and pulled back the flaps of the temporary home. Stepping outside into the warm morning air, he looked and listened.

"Good morning, Agent Ingram. You come to look for your friend? She's just waking up at the moment…said she'd been dreaming. Can't make sense of a thing she says." Kane smiled at her, turned away and disappeared to his own quarters.

Genna stood watching him for longer than was necessary, then crept inside Kelly's tent. She saw the glow her friend sported.

"I envy you, Kelly. You have someone who cares what happens to you. But then look at you…and look at me. I'm good at everything except getting myself a man." She stood by Kelly's cot.

Kelly pulled the blanket tighter around her naked body. "Are you jealous of me, Genna?"

"No, not jealous. Envious, yes. You and Ka…SFA Branson have a bond. Everyone can see it. He's harder on you than anyone, but when you can't see he looks at you in such a way…" Genna stopped speaking. "He's proud of you. And obviously is so in love with you. Even airhead Blair notices it." There was a hint of sadness in her voice, and she turned and left Kelly alone.

Kelly knew how much Kane loved her, but having a friend to confirm it helped. Kane would die for her if he had to. She lay back on the cot for a few moments longer and thought about what Genna had said.

"Any more eggs, Agent Mann?" yelled Kane as he scraped the last pieces of the fluffy yellow stuff from his plate. The food tasted good and he was hungry.

"Sir, yes, sir." He took the steaming hot pan of sizzling eggs across to his boss. "Crispy bacon also, sir?" And delicious aromas filled the morning air.

"Anything. For some reason I'm extra hungry today," and his eyes gleamed as he remembered last night.

Kelly blushed. Genna saw it.

"Sir, yes, sir," replied Paul.

Kane took head position at mealtimes. Sitting where he could watch everyone at the same time, his eyes focused on the complete picture.

"Okay. That's it!" Kane stood up and set his plate down on the hard ground. "Chat time. From this second on, we're on a first name basis only. I can't stand this *sir* thing. You all got it? What's my name, Genna?"

"Kane, sir," she replied somewhat startled.

"What?" Kane screamed at her.

She jumped. "Kane."

"That's better. In the next few days, some of you will leave us. Only seven of us will actually go on this undercover mission to Hong Kong: three vets, three of you, and me. Commander's orders. There are reasons, as you will see. No discrimination. You pass or fail right here in Alice Springs. And if you fail, it's not because you can't make it; just that you don't qualify for this mission." He glanced around him. "Eat now, because this is the last meal any of you will be served for two days. Any food you want, you find for yourselves. You'll be allowed water. You'll carry backpacks. You will sleep on the ground, and you will wash downstream. The only people you will see will be each other. In a half hour, three vets will join us. They go with us. If anyone thinks they cannot make it, now is the time to drop out of the plan. The chopper will take you back to base. I can tell you this. So far you are all equal on points. This last test is the one that will decide who goes on this mission. Is everyone clear?" Self-elimination was more of what Kane had in mind, and what better way than back to nature. Let her decide.

Kelly didn't look up from her breakfast. She had been told back at base that she was designated to go with Kane. This was unfair and she knew it. She also knew that she had to prove to the others that she could do it on her own merit. Their answers in unison brought her back to reality.

"Ready to go in one hour," barked Kane.

Kane pulled his belongings together and waited for his old comrades to arrive. He was looking forward to seeing them again. In one hour, everyone would be on equal footing. He glanced at Kelly. She saw him and smiled.

The whirring of engines heralded the silver AFP choppers arrival. It landed on the parched earth, creating a windstorm of dust that swirled around the group gathered near the trees. Three men dressed similar to Kane disembarked from the helicopter, all dragging backpacks behind them. Kane stepped forward. They mockingly saluted him, hands raised to their temples. The chopper departed with the same flourish that it entered with.

"Forget that crap of saluting," and Kane reached forward and hugged his friend.

"Kane, it's good to see you. Been a year my friend." Gray-haired Giles Harris reciprocated the gesture. "It's been a long time since we first were on a mission together. Remember it as if it was yesterday. You even look the same as you did back then. Must be all those pretty girls that agree with you." He looked across at the women.

"Just one girl, my wife. The very pretty girl with the long curly hair," and Kane pointed at Kelly.

"That's your wife?" Giles exclaimed. "What the hell have you got that we don't? No… don't answer that. Don't think we want to know. You never mentioned anything about her last year."

"True…I didn't." Kane declared. "I guess I have something you guys don't." He laughed, and he arched his eyebrows.

A long slow whistle came from Alex Power's mouth. "Trust you, Kane. Always could pick them." The lithe, dark skinned man reached forward and shook Kane's hand.

"So could you, my friend." Kane grasped Alex's hand tightly and shook it vigorously. He turned to the third man. "You didn't tell them I was married again?"

"Nope, thought they needed a surprise." Dan Lord now followed his father-in-law wherever he went on a mission. He had retired once when he had married Kane's daughter, at Kane's request, but rejoined the AFP when he couldn't take the civilian life.

"How's my daughter?" asked Kane.

"You know the same old mother hen." Dan laughed. "But I love her."

"You damn well better had. Someone pull strings to get you on this mission?" Kane laughingly glanced sideward. "How are Star and my granddaughter?"

"Both of your daughters are fine. Star misses you. She told me to tell you that."

"Is this a family affair?" Giles looked surprised. "Didn't know Lord here was your son-in-law," he complained. "And you have another kid? God-damn, Kane. Don't you ever plan to grow old?"

"No chance." Kane slapped him on the back. "Let me introduce you to the agents. Remember, no favoritism to my wife and you, Powers, no flirting with her either."

They walked across the hard terrain toward the new recruits. Four proud and just men.

Kane introduced each one. "Dan Lord, my son-in-law. Alex Powers and Giles Harris, both long-time friends. All decorated vets. Now known as Dan, Alex and Giles." Kane turned to the young group. "Names."

"Genna." She smiled revealing pearly white teeth.

"Ty." Proud and assertive.

"Ben." He looked embarrassed at being there, his spectacles slipping down his nose.

"Paul." A bold and belligerent tone in his voice.

"Blair." She flashed her blue eyes at Alex. Blair Cotton had been the third girl for the group's trials. Kane had chosen her himself. Alex could see why he'd picked her. A vivacious blonde.

"Kelly." Her smile was only for Kane.

Dan moved forward to hug his stepmother-in-law. Kelly looked at her commander for approval. Kane nodded his head very slightly. Her hair hung down her back, and moving forward, she gripped Dan tightly round his waist. He reciprocated the gesture, and then whispered in her ear.

"How are you holding up under all this?" Dan asked.

"I'm just fine," she whispered.

"You tell him yet?" asked Dan.

"Nope. He wouldn't let me go along if he knew," she reminded him.

"You plan on making this an ongoing thing? Not telling your husband you're pregnant?" Dan emphasized.

"No. However, you know he would stop me and you won't tell him either. You promised," she whined in his ear.

Kelly was as tough as ever in Dan's eyes. He carried on hugging his stepmother-in-law, a woman ten years his junior. "Yeah, I promised… unless it gets to be too much for you."

"I'm only six weeks gone. Nothing's going to happen to me," and Kelly clung to Dan.

"What the hell are you two whispering about for so long?" asked a quizzical Kane.

"Just family stuff," replied Dan. He turned away from Kelly, and devoted his attention to his father-in-law. "So, when do we leave?"

"A half hour from now," replied Kane.

Breaking camp was done with military precision, with tents coming down easily. They were stacked with great rapidity into the stationary truck. Each person carried only what they needed. Kane ordered the rest of the gear to be dumped for the chopper on its return. The party set off in single file and walked in the afternoon sun, the deep rays giving more tan to their already glowing bodies. All sported black T-shirts and tight fitting black pants that tucked into the black, laced-up military boots. On their backs, they carried bedrolls and not much else except an odd shovel or two, and canteens of water. One-after-another they proceeded. One vet went forward, and one new agent followed. The walking on the cracked, parched ground was intense. Their aching feet craved rest. After several hours, cool water was all the entire group could think about. Still, they walked. Three young women and seven men. Not all would make it the team. Alice Springs sucked the absolute life and soul from their bodies. At last, on Kane's instructions, they paused for breath. The girls collapsed next to each other.

"Goddamn, I'm tired," Paul stated to Ty. "The girls look done in, 'specially his wife. The man pushes really hard." He sat down on a gnarled tree stump and wiped the sweat from his brow onto his black pants.

"His job to," Ty said. "Can't take us if we can't make it. If we were in Hong Kong, he couldn't wait for us," replied his companion.

"Couldn't wait or wouldn't?" returned Paul.

"Couldn't." Ty couldn't figure out why all these questions from Paul. The answers were obvious enough.

"He'd go back for his wife, though," muttered Paul.

"Would he? Not so sure he would. Kelly knows more about him than you think. Remember that she sleeps with the man. Kelly didn't get here without knowing him. Watch her very carefully. She may teach you a few things. The girl's tough. Rumor has it that she went through a lot before Kane married her. And don't underestimate Kane. He's all for his group. Even when you think he's not watching you, he is." Ty sat down on the boulders.

Paul stood up from the dry stump and joined him. "How come you figured all this out?"

"'Cause he's smart," interjected Blair. Unnoticed, she'd sauntered across to the guys.

"Who asked you your opinion? We all saw you flash your eyes at Alex," Paul was quick to point out.

She blushed. Her pretty pink lips curled on her fair skinned face.

"You have a problem with that, or you jealous, Paul? And I don't mean of me. Genna and I wondered about that. Kelly's taken and no one would dare cross Kane. Genna, well, she's nice but plain and you didn't even look my way. Even little old Ben made a pass at me…"

"Blair! That's enough!" Kane's voice was not to be denied. "Go and sit with Kelly. Paul, Ty, move. Arrange your sleeping quarters, instead of just taking up breathing space. We'll camp here for the night. Start again tomorrow."

Nevertheless, the same thought had crossed Kane's mind and that could be a problem. Thinking about it Kane had never seen Paul flirt with any of the girls, even Kelly. Kane could not fault Paul for his sexual preference, but he could keep an eye on it.

Kelly stretched out her bedroll just a few feet away from the other girls. She didn't want to talk; instead, she wanted to think. She lay down on it and soon discovered how cold and hard the ground was. Even last night's cots were better than this.

When the sun dropped, so did the heat. Her stomach rumbled and her feet ached. She watched Blair and Genna talking. Seeing the boys over to one side, she knew they no doubt were talking about her husband and his policies. And in the embers of the firelight, she could see the older men, four men on a mission. Kane's profile was one of courage and determination. He turned his head slightly towards her. Kelly saw it in slow motion. Winking at her, he then looked back at his colleagues. Why had she come with him? What did she have to prove? On the other hand, was she just afraid he wouldn't come back this time? Ninety-nine missions under his belt. One more to go for Kane's hundred.

CHAPTER 2

Five a.m. came abruptly.

"Everyone up. Rise and shine!" Kane yelled at the top of his voice, and kicked at the bedrolls in his path.

"It's not even light yet," muttered Kelly, while turning her back to him.

"You have a problem with that, Agent Branson?" retorted Kane peering through the half-light at his wife.

"What's up with him?" Giles whispered to the guys next to him. "Did he get out the wrong side of his bedroll …or someone else's? On the other hand, perhaps that's the problem. Maybe, Kane can't get by without fucking his…"

"Keep that thought to yourself if you would like to keep breathing," Dan intervened and rolled over onto one sun tanned arm.

"He's still as tough, huh?" asked Alex.

"More so. He became that way after his first wife's death." Dan sat upright. "Then he met Kelly."

"How did they meet? I mean there's such an age difference," remarked Giles casually.

Alex was listening. He'd heard most of the details.

"Long story. She's the daughter of one of the men who killed my wife's mother. Sometimes, I wonder if he ever really forgave himself for not being there when Sage died. We were out celebrating on the night that she was murdered. Kane was drunk, as he often was back in those days. Never touched a drop of it from that day on… but, you know all about that, right?" asked Dan.

"Not exactly. Was never sure quite what happened. It was all hushed up outside of your department. Top secret. He never told me anything." Giles stopped. Only months before he'd been with Kane on a mission and Kane said nothing about this new family. Giles continued. "No wonder that the girl came with him. I'll give her one thing, Kelly has guts. He's got guts too," replied Giles. He'd always admired that in a woman.

In the early morning light, Kelly gathered her things together. She knew Kane's moods very well, and she felt it best to keep away from his current one. She was ready first. Blair was last; too busy with her own needs to notice how much time that she was taking. Blair, flush-faced, looked up and the imposing figure of Kane stood right in front of her, his feet spread apart, and his hands on his hips.

"Lady, if you're goin' to finish this course, you stay with us. If you don't, you'll be sitting back there in the dust." He pointed down the road. "Let's go, unless you want to walk on your own in the boiling sun."

"Sir, yes…I mean, Kane, sir." Blair was flustered and it showed.

Kane went back for his gear with Giles following him.

"Man, what's wrong? You weren't like this last night?" Giles tapped Kane on his arm.

Kane looked down fiercely. Giles removed his hand from Kane's sleeve.

"Nothing…yet." He swung his pack onto his back and slid the holster over his shoulder. "Rest of you, let's go."

Kane strode into the morning light. Early morning rays cast shadows across the dew. Lizards strove to find warmth on the desert blasted rocks, and the scream of the eagle heralded a new day. Blair was last in line. Dust blew in her face and grime set in on her sweaty body. Paul walked in front of her, and he was conscious of the comments she had made last night. He was also aware that Kane had heard. Paul wanted to make this team. It was imperative to beat someone out of a place. His easiest target was Blair or maybe Ben, the walking disaster. Nevertheless, Ben had a brain that Kane could use. Blair, Paul thought, after spending the morning with Kane, was not so smart, but she had a body that most men could use. And Kane would be no exception.

At ten a.m., Kane stopped the group, and dished out the water. He wet his bandana from the canteen that hung from his belt, and replaced the cloth back on his forehead. Holding the canteen in his hands, Giles approached him with a certain caution.

"Have a question for you, my friend. Why are we going back to Hong Kong? Buchanan must have told you."

"Know as much as you. All I have to do is complete these people's training, take them back to base, pick which ones I want, and get on that damn plane. Then, and only then, will all be revealed. If you happen to find out sooner, be so kind as to let me know," and Kane took a swig of water, which went down in one go. He took another, tipped some onto his hand and soaked his face with it.

"Is it drug-related like last time? You must know that, and we both know what kind of terrain we're going into or we wouldn't be doing all this crap," Giles gestured at the stuff around him.

"We go to the city first. Some things we need to find out really soon. Then, it's off to the mountain regions of the island. There won't be a bar or even a watering hole to run to when we get thirsty. There will be times when there won't be food. We only get what we carry or what we find to eat. That's it." Kane kept an even tone throughout his explanation. He was careful not to give anything away. Kane knew the answer to Giles' questions. As far as Kane was concerned, the discussion ended.

"You sure that you're working for the AFP, not the commando hit team? Next, you'll have us in combat fatigues and berets." He saw the stony look on Kane's face. "No, you can't be serious? Combat clothes? You're joking, right? How far are we going to take this with these people?"

"Until we reach what we're searching to find," replied a serious Kane.

"What *we* are searching for…or you're searching to find?" asked Giles.

Kane thought that a very odd statement.

"I sort of volunteered for this mission. And, I gather, so did you. I have what I want. It's standing right over there," and Kane stared long and hard at Kelly.

Giles more than glanced at Kelly. "Then, why let her come along?"

"I can't…" Kane stopped. *Not smart to admit that he couldn't be without her.* "Kelly is gonna make a great cop. She's tough and I can keep an eye on her. Good practice for her. Make sense to you?" asked Kane.

"Yeah, it does. But don't let her presence cloud your judgment."

"Nothing clouds my judgment, mate." Kane snapped the cap back on his canteen, and hung it on his belt. Giles watched Kelly, who couldn't help but cloud a man's mind. Kane saw Giles watching Kelly, which worried him. Maybe, the selection here wasn't such a good idea. "Something else bothering you?" asked Kane.

He was interrupted by a ruckus behind them.

"Get lost, Blair. You carry your own stuff. You're no-one special." Paul's loud voice was attracting the attention that he desired.

"I didn't ask you to do…" Blair never got to finish the sentence.

Kane turned away from Giles and moved to the rest of the group.

"What the fuck is going on here? You two, step aside. What's happening?" Kane's tone was anything but subtle.

Ty intervened. "She…"

Kane cut his eyes to him. "Is your name Paul or Blair?"

"No, sir." Ty stepped back.

"Blair, what's the problem this time?" Kane was beginning to tire of this ritual.

"Nothing, sir." She brushed her clothes down and pushed back her hair.

"Look, lady, this isn't Sydney. No one cares what you look like… no one, do you hear me?" He peered down into her face.

"Kane, that's not fair. It wasn't her fault. I didn't hear you pick on Paul like you did her," interjected Kelly.

Kane spun around and stared at her. Kelly realized she had just undermined him. He didn't even give her the courtesy of a reply. His eyes narrowed in anger, and he turned back to the two culprits.

"Let's get this straight right now. There are ten of us. Only seven of us go forward. At this rate, it will be easy to drop one, or maybe two, of you. Paul, you stay away from Blair. Dan, keep her with you. That way she can't provoke any *man's* feelings." Kane saw Paul flinch. "Now that that's straightened out, let's get this show back on the road. Kelly, a word."

Kane put his hand on Kelly's shoulder and together they walked to a thick clump of eucalyptus trees. Alex watched them leave. He, too, was aware that there was already a problem brewing. Walking Kelly a good twenty yards from the rest of the party, he stopped, faced her, and put his hands on her shoulders. Kelly thought she really didn't want to hear what he was about to say.

"Kelly, don't you ever do that again. I know that you were standing up for what you thought was right, but those people must respect and obey only me. You understand?" His hands were tight on her shoulders.

Kelly fought back her emotions. "Yes," she whimpered.

"Darling, it has to be like this. I thought that you understood this before we left home. This is my job. This is who I am. You know that better than anyone, baby." He tried to tone his temper down a notch.

"I was wrong, Kane. I'm sorry. It's just that, well, those girls aren't like me. They didn't come up the way I did. They don't know about drugs and alcohol. They're good women," her words came pouring out together with emotion and meaning.

"And what do you think you are? You're just as good as them, and Kel, you seem very upset over this," and he stroked her face. Her outburst concerned him. This wasn't the Kelly that he was used to being with… something was wrong.

"You're yelling at me," she blurted.

"Baby." He leaned down to her height and kissed her. "Think of Sydney, darling, and the motorbike rides. Think of the Harley. Think about what we do together, you and me. Think of the two of us riding out to the ocean with the wind in our hair. You pressed to my back, your arms 'round my waist. When things get tough, think of how much I love you and…" Kane paused, "I would die without you."

As quickly as he held her in his grasp, Kane let go of her, and walked back to the group, his long hair blowing in the breeze. Kelly clasped her hand to her mouth, so that the words, which stemmed from her brain, would not reach her lips. *She should not have come along*. Kane didn't look back. Kelly was the chink in his armor, and she realized if anyone found that chink, Kane was dead.

"So what's next, Kane?" asked Alex, his feet kicking the loose rocks on the ground.

"Let's camp here." Kane moved his backpack down on the ground under the trees. "Plenty of shady trees for us, and it's fucking hot. And I have something for them to do, anyway. They're going to refresh in the good old fashioned art of self-defense. And then they're going to get supper. When they find it, that is."

"You son-of-a-bitch. You really gonna make them find their own food?" Giles laughed, and ran his hands through his sprawling hair.

Alex sat in silence watching the whole show. He moved slightly on the boulder.

"Oh, not just them…you, too." It was Kane's turn to laugh.

"You fucking bastard. Go to hell!" boomed Giles, dropping his backpack next to Alex's boulder.

"Probably I will, but you'll do it. While I'm in charge, you will," Kane didn't falter.

Dan studied his father-in-law. One day, he hoped to be like him. Dan put his backpack on the ground next to Ty.

"Dan, you were in Kane's station back home. Was he always this tough?" whispered the young man.

"Do you mean tough? Or, do you mean unpredictable? Yes. That's why we would follow him anywhere. You think he's hard now, wait 'til he gets you to Kong."

"How do you know that I'll get there?" Ty asked his face expectant.

"You'll get there." Dan smiled while unpacking his bedroll.

Dan knew whom Kane wanted. He'd been his undercover partner too long not to know.

Kane paired the group off... Dan and Blair, Kelly with Ty...the arranged combination of Giles and Genna, Ben with Alex... and himself with Paul. It was *make-or-break-it* time for Paul. With his fingers, Kane drew a circle in the dirt. He motioned Giles and Genna to get inside it. They obliged him uncertain as to why they were doing it.

"Okay Giles... attack Genna."

Kane's statement was simple and to the point. He stood with his hands on his hips waiting.

Giles hesitated. His first mistake was not a Giles-type failing. Kane watched.

"No? Not man enough to...okay. Genna attack Giles."

Kane said the statement with force. Genna braced herself, brought her foot up, and kicked Giles with everything that she had hard in the stomach. Doubling over, he held his gut. He had not expected her to follow through with such force and strength.

"Goddamn, that hurt. Why you..." He straightened up as best he could clutching his stomach and his pride, and looked the girl in the face.

"Well done, Genna," and Kane openly applauded her.

In Kane's mind, Genna had just earned a place on his team.

"What the fuck do you mean?" He starred at Kane. "The woman just decked me." Giles' breath was labored.

"That's what I told her to do, to attack you. Now, get in there and hit her back."

As a seasoned vet, Giles wasn't happy. Kane was making a fool of him. Giles made a fist and looked at Genna, but aimed his swing at Kane instead. Kane caught Giles' arm as it touched his chest. Turning him around, he bent the arm back behind the man's body. Giles yelled in pain. Giles was slipping. Moreover, he didn't expect such force from Kane.

"You broke my fucking arm. Goddamn you, Kane!"

Kane pulled him back against his own chest, displaying him. "This, ladies and gentleman, is how not to get caught. And if I had wanted to break his arm, it would be done by now." He released his grip.

Giles clutched his aching arm. Dan smiled. *Kane was still Branson.*

"Rest of you try it now," demanded Kane.

Giles stared at Kane. "You made your point, Kane. I thought we were friends."

Giles was in stark contrast to Kane: tall, gawky looking, and bushy gray hair that seemed always to be unkempt.

"Were? Mate, if we weren't *still* friends, you wouldn't be able to use that arm right now. Want to try again, with me?" He egged him on.

Kane laughed and offered Giles his outstretched arms, his chest ready to take jabs.

"Go, fuck yourself," retorted an unhappy Giles.

Kane not only could hear the annoyance in Giles; he could see the annoyance in Giles' eyes. Perhaps, he had pushed him too far too soon. However, Kane had to set a plan into action. Giles walked away shaking his head in total disgust.

"You think that was wise?" whispered Dan.

"Maybe not, but, still, it's done now. How are the others doing? Are they all working together okay?" Kane had one eye still on Giles. He sat down on the ground.

"Fine. You made your choices yet, Dad," asked Dan and followed suit.

"Call me that again and you'll be seeing stars. Yeah, I made my choices, some time back. This is just to confirm them."

"So, share," demanded Dan.

"Uh-uh. You'll wait, right along with the others. And, by the way, when it comes to your time… to turn on me…remember what we planned back in Sydney?"

"I know…look as hurt as the others. What about Kelly?"

"What about her?" Kane asked while putting his hand in his pants pocket to pull out his cigarettes. Within seconds, he realized that smoking wasn't a wise decision.

"Kelly knows she's going, right…but does she know the rest?" asked Dan.

"No, figured the less that she knows the better. Why this sudden concern?" Kane turned his head to look at the other man.

Dan was his son-in-law. Yet, at times, he wondered if his brain was in gear.

"No reason. I know how close you guys are and I thought you may have told her," Dan lied.

"Told her what? About the mission? No. No one knows the whole plan…not even you," and he smacked Dan on the back. "The group has no need to know anymore than they do already. We have to find out who squealed on us in Hong Kong. I have my suspicions. You probably do too." Kane sucked on a blade of thin grass instead of smoking. He smiled and sat cross-legged on his Australian turf.

"You son-of-a-bitch. You already know who it is, don't you?" laughed Dan.

"Maybe," and he winked at his partner.

"God damn you, Kane. You had all this figured before you ever even left for Sydney. Buchanan in on it too?"

"Most of it," Kane replied. "Blair is gonna become a prostitute. She'd make a good one. Long legs, pretty pink lips…" He paused. "Kelly goes as the tutor. That's all. She's not my choice for the leading role…my own wife? Hell no."

"This, from the man who doesn't let anything cloud his judgment?" Dan turned his head towards Kane.

"She's my wife, damn-it. Blair can do it," and Kane averted Dan's gaze.

"You know damn well that Kelly can do it better," argued Dan.

Kane ignored the comment. "We have to find out who betrayed last year's team and got my man, Tony, killed." Kane paused as he remembered Tony. Looking down at his hands, he still expected to see the bloodstains. "That same person is letting the China white run through to our country. It is that very person that is here in this group. That's why these men were picked. They thought that they volunteered. They didn't. Enough bait was down for the rat. Find the man who is spearheading the operation, and you find the informant…and a good way, as any, is to find a good drug deal going down and then buy into it."

Now, it was time for Kane to retrieve the cigarettes. Sliding one cigarette out, he pushed the packet back into his pocket. Dan offered him a light from the book of matches that he carried in his kit. Kane cupped his hands around the tiny flame. The cigarette caught light. With the cigarette between his lips, he inhaled deeply. Smoking was one of two vices he could not give up doing. The other was Kelly.

"Whose rules are we playing by, here, Kane?" asked Dan.

"Mine!"

"That figures," Dan muttered, shaking his head slightly. "What about Ben and Paul? Ty, I know is going. You'd be stupid not to take him. That man's bright; easy to get along with…" Dan stopped, mainly because Kane had gotten a look in his eyes that bordered on dangerous. "And stupid doesn't seem to be one of your attributes."

"Ty goes. Kelly goes. You, Alex, Giles, and me… leaves two spaces. One goes to Genna; that leaves three people. In the next two days, they will fight for that right. My money is on Ben. But it's Blair whom I need." Kane blew smoke into the warm air, polluting it just a little more.

Dan wondered what Kane meant by his comment. He looked over at his father-in-law, his hero. Dan was nothing like him in stature. Dark and short, he came from a broken home. Maybe that's why he picked Kane to be his hero. Not only had he gained a wife when he married Kane's daughter, he had also gained a whole family.

Kane watched them all. Maybe it wasn't necessary to have them do this kind of workout on such a hot day. Still, these people were his to do with…what he pleased. He was making them all work, just the same. Time he showed that leaders worked out also. Squashing the cigarette, Kane stood up and returned to workout with the others. Paul was still standing…waiting…Blair was also waiting. It was by Kane's command that these two were not supposed to be together. "Okay, that's enough. Giles, Alex, come over here and stand here by Dan and myself. Rest of you go, find everyone some food. Berries, snakes, lizards, anything that moves we'll eat it." He paused and looked at the statue like people around him. "What the hell are all you waiting for, now? Go!"

"Thought I was going, too?" Giles sniped.

"You knew… you fucking well knew that you weren't. Cigarette?" and Kane asked, pulling the carton from his pocket, and lit another one.

Giles was suspicious. One hand was giving the other… and he declined the cigarette.

"Couple more days, we'll be out of this shit-hole. It's so damned hot. Don't know why they just didn't let us meet you in Sydney." Giles sat down, then lay back on the dry earth, pulled his khaki hat down over his face, which left his bushy hair sticking out a quarter of an inch.

Kane kicked Giles feet. "That's why. You need to lose a few pounds before we go hiking. Good way to do it out here."

"You're still the hotshot that *we all loved* back in the old days. Guess that you'd have to be somewhat of a hotshot in order to keep up with a twenty-four-year-old-woman. Maybe she could handle someone younger."

"Think you're up for the job then, Giles? You're nearly my age. But I'm sure a forty-year-old man like Alex could fit the bill. He's so good with women. Right Alex?" Kane brought him into the conversation on purpose.

"Hey, you said that, not me. Nah, Kane, I'm not going near your Kelly," retorted Alex.

"You know, Kane, you're a lot more pushy and irritating than I remember. You're more of an individual now than team player, except where Kelly is concerned. That true?" Giles said it jokingly.

"Fucking stupid question," replied Kane. "We're about to set out on a mission. A team, not individuals. Stupid fucking idea." Kane smiled and squashed the cigarette beneath his boot. His plan was working. Giles was becoming irritable. It was hard to believe one of the members of his party was a double agent. But unfortunately, one probably was. He wondered how the girls were faring.

Kelly and Genna picked things from the fruit-bearing bushes.

"This one?" asked the innocent Kelly, holding out some red, round-looking goody from a bush.

"Yeah, it's great if you want to poison us all," laughed Genna.

"How the heck do I know what's poisonous or not? Kane taught me a lot of things, but picking berries was not one of them," and she dropped the berry on the floor. The fruit splattered at her feet.

"We would never have guessed that," retorted Blair. "Think Kane could teach me some things, then. You wouldn't mind would you, Kel? You know…just one or two things," and her mouth turned up at the corners in a smile. She flashed her eyes at Kelly.

"Course not. I wouldn't mind, provided you don't mind me teaching you how to hold your head under water afterwards." Kelly began scratching in the earth, pretending to look for anything that crawled.

Blair smiled nervously and moved away from the other two girls, her hair bouncing behind her.

"Where's she going?" asked Genna turning her head to watch her.

"Away from us, I hope," replied Kelly, and stretched her back.

"You don't like her too much, now, do you?"

Kelly stood up, and wiped her brow. "No not really. Especially, when she makes jokes like that. I've seen her watch Kane and Alex. It's as if she's trying to weigh up which bloke that she's going after; and when she going to go after them. If she, or anyone, goes after mine, they're dead." Kelly noticed the looks that Genna occasionally shot Kane's way, and it applied to her too.

"Lizards and snakes…anything that moves. How are we supposed to catch those and then kill them? What does he think we are, anyway?" Paul said as he groveled around in the undergrowth.

"He thinks that we are capable of fending for ourselves. We're supposed to know these things by now. You obviously never belonged to the Boy Scouts." Ben pushed his glasses back up on his sweaty nose.

"And what the hell do you know, Ben? You couldn't catch a cold, even if you set out to do it. All you know is computers. I still can't work out why you're here. Ben the computer nerd," and Paul laughed a cruel laugh.

"My knowledge may just save your life one day," answered Ben, pushing hair back from his face, and his glasses higher up on his nose.

"Yeah, right, mate. Like a computer is just going to jump up and catch dinner," mocked Paul.

"You know, Paul, you have an attitude that would cost us our lives if this was for real. Why did you join the police? Someone else could be on this mission. Or, did you just want to prove a point?" asked the now irritated Ty. He was tiring of Paul's incessant banter.

"I don't know what…" Paul stopped.

They could hear Blair scream from the bush. She had wandered too far from the party. Then they heard Kelly.

"For god's sake, someone help!" Kelly screamed.

Blair's screams pierced the evening wind. All Kane heard was Kelly's cry.

"Kelly!" Kane yelled. "Dan, stay here," and he was gone though the brush.

Night had descended fast and so had the dingoes, which had caught Blair's scent as she strayed from the other girls. Kelly told her to stay in sight.

Blair had made a kill, a small lizard, and was taking her prize back to the others unaware of her four-footed companion. Blair heard the branches crack behind her. She partially turned and saw the Australian wild dog behind her. It was then that she screamed and the female dingo came to join its mate. Blair dropped the lizard, but not quickly enough for the starving animal that had young to feed. The dingo caught her hand and in the evening shade, it ripped open her fingers. She kept on screaming, which certainly was the worst course of action, causing the animal to become excited at the smell of fresh warm blood.

Kane ran through the brush in the direction of the bloodcurdling screams. Ty and Kelly were there ahead of him. Ty reached for his gun. Reality set in that he wasn't carrying. Kelly looked at the ground, grabbed the largest branch that she could find and brandished it at the dog. The animal let go of the girl's bloody hand and moved a few paces back. Ty saw the other dog move forward, teeth bared and ready for the kill. On his hip, he carried a knife. He pulled it, lashed out at the dogs, howling and screaming as he did, trying to distract the dogs from the girl.

"Both of you get back!" Kane arrived with his gun in his hand shooting at the ground under the dingoes' feet. "Get out of the way, Kelly!" Kane let off a round from his .38.

The animals squealed in fear and fled back into the brush. Kelly dropped the branch and ran to Blair. Ty still had the blade in his hand. Kane moved to Ty.

"Ty put the knife away. Ty, I have it. You can stop now." Slowly, Kane lowered Ty's arm. Taking the knife from the young man, he stowed it in his own pocket. Ty had shown no fear. Kane turned to his wife. "Kelly, how's Blair?"

Her fingers were in shreds where the dog's teeth had buried deep. Blair's hysterical shrieking didn't help, nor did the flaying of her arms.

"Blair, quit! Blair, shut up." Kelly shook her, without any luck. She turned to her husband. "Kane, I can't control her," Kelly cried.

Kane took over for her. "Blair, stop it! You want the whole pack on us?" He grabbed the screaming girl by the shoulders. "Blair!" He raised his hand, hitting her hard across the face.

There was total silence and she fainted into Kane's arms. He picked her up as if she weighed nothing. Blood dripped down his legs from Blair's open wound.

"Guess there's more than one way to get a man," Genna dryly observed from behind them all.

Kelly turned to face her. "Took you long enough to get here. She could have been dead." Kelly was angry with her and she didn't hide the fact. She looked around her to see who was with her. "And where are the other two?"

"I don't know. Thought that you hated Blair," Genna replied flippantly.

"Not that much, I don't!" screamed Kelly back at her.

Kane heard. "Let's get the hell out of here. All this noise will bring the whole goddamn pack down on us."

"Too late, sir." Ty's eyes were wide.

Kane looked in the direction of Ty's intense focus. Yellow eyes stared back through the falling dusk. Kane counted one set, then two, then three pairs of eyes glaring in the darkness. He could hear the dogs moving slowly through the grasses. Kane needed to reload and carrying Blair had caused that to be just a little impossible. Kane realized that Alex and Giles had caught up with him.

"Alex, you got your gun?" asked Kane with a low voice.

"Yep," and Alex held the gun straight. He was right behind Kane.

"Fire over their heads. If that doesn't work…shoot the fuckers!"

Alex fired high in the air. The dogs stood their ground, teeth bared.

"Kelly, Ty, Genna, get the fuck out of here. Now," Kane whispered, even in his anger. "Alex, Giles, you two guys know what to do!"

One after, the other, Giles and Alex mowed down the enemy. There was a sickening thud of bodies dropping. Alex shot the first and second dogs. Giles got the other two. Then, he did a strange thing. He fired the rest of the bullets into the two already dead-dogs. Alex watched him in dismay. To shoot once, with purpose, was all it took. To keep on shooting was something else, altogether. Alex made a mental note to let Kane know.

Running, Kane carried Blair in his arms, her body hanging limply. He strode across the earth making sure that they put space between themselves and the onslaught behind them.

"You three, keep up with me. The guys can look out for themselves."

Kelly could not help wonder how Kane could carry Blair, run and talk, all at the same time.

Back at the camp, the others waited. Dan spread a bedroll on the earth and Kane gently laid Blair on it. She was losing far too much blood. One of the teeth had caught a vein. Kane grabbed Kelly by the hand.

"Kelly, put your fingers right there. Keep pressure on the vein. We have to stem the flow of blood."

Kelly squatted on the ground next to Blair and applied the pressure where she was told. Kane pulled the bandana from his head and made a tourniquet for Blair's arm. The bleeding subsided somewhat. Blair cried. The pain had to be intense, and Kane knew that.

"It'll be okay, Blair. They'll have you back home in no time. You cry if it makes you feel better," and she cradled Blair in her arms. "It's okay… shush," she whispered. "Kane, help her," Kelly begged.

Kane pulled the radio from his backpack, turned away slightly, and crouched low on the ground. His voice was almost a whisper; yet, the radio crackled and hissed. Eventually he got a line.

"Home base. This is Hunter. Home base. Do you copy? Hunter… to Home base."

The radio crackled again. "Hunter. This is Home base. What's the problem? You're not supposed to contact us for three more days."

"Problem. One of the girls is down and we need you to fetch her. Losing a lot of blood; send chopper now. Over."

"On its way. Be with you in an hour or two. Give us exact location." The radio hissed and crackled repeatedly. "You got painkillers with you?"

"Yeah, over." Kane's voice was still low, but not low enough.

Kelly stared in disbelief at her husband. Hunter? She'd heard that term before. She'd heard Commander Buchanan and Kane discussing it some time back. When she'd gone to look for Kane one evening after class, she had quite accidentally heard the two men talking. Kelly remembered. The Hunter Project: hunting down heroin coming into Australia. Now, she knew what type of mission in which they were involved in. Listening, as Kane gave their location, she looked down at Blair and her arms tightened on the girl's body. Blair hadn't heard. Then, Kelly looked at Dan. He saw her reaction, one of sheer disbelief.

"Shit! Kane, she heard you." Dan turned to his boss, his eyes like slits. "Kane, talk to her." He looked back at Kelly. "You can't say a word, Kel." Dan put his hand on Kelly's shoulder.

Kane replaced the radio in the backpack. He pulled what resembled a first-aid kit from the front of his pack. Shaking a bottle, he pulled a syringe from the kit and stuck the needle in the solution. He squirted the needle in the air.

"Blair." Kane tried to make her focus. "Blair, I'm gonna give you this shot. It will help you with the pain 'til the chopper gets here. Dan, you hold her."

Kane plunged the needle in her arm. Kelly felt Blair pull back against her. She quieted down almost instantly. Discarding the needle back in the kit, Kane looked at Kelly. He viewed the situation closely. Everyone else was out of earshot.

"Planned on telling you at some point. Baby, I'll explain later. Just trust me, okay?"

Kelly nodded. Now she realized why Kane had tried to dissuade her. Her husband was the Hunter. This was not the AFP's usual kind of mission. The reason for this mission was to find a traitor. As a rookie, she never thought that she would be part of it. Now, she wondered why she was. She looked up at Kane, her eyes wide. Kelly sat on the hard dry ground. She was going into Kong. She'd known that all the time, but now, she knew the reason. The Commander of the AFP had sent her with Kane just in case…in case Kane didn't return.

Kelly sat there cradling Blair to her, while the girl slipped in and out of consciousness. Still, Kelly sat almost comatose by what she now knew. Kelly didn't know how long that they waited, but suddenly, chopper blades hovered overhead. Brush parted in the helicopter's wake. The glare of the behemoth was obvious in the night sky, its drone echoing on the wind. The beam highlighted the group underneath it, and the chopper landed safely. Two paramedics disembarked.

"You can let her go now, Kel. They'll take over," and Kane took his wife's hand and raised her up to him. Kane held Kelly against his bloodied clothes.

The AFP paramedics shot a larger amount of morphine into Blair's arm, and lifted her up between them. She was partly conscious.

"I'm sorry, sir," she blurted through tears and pain. "I'm not as tough as I thought." Her speech was slurred. "Kelly…"

"It's okay, Blair." Kane patted her on the head. "You'll make another mission," reassured Kane, and he took back his bandana.

Kane held Kelly's hand and together they watched 'til the chopper light was just a blob on the horizon. Dan stood next to Kane.

"Well, that made your decision simpler."

"Dan!" and Kane cut his eyes to Kelly.

They hadn't noticed Giles move up behind them.

"Got rid of one. Who's next, Kane?" Giles asked sarcastically. "That is the idea, isn't it? Self-elimination, 'til you find the thing you're searching for."

Kane let go of Kelly and turned to face Giles, his face displaying anger.

"You know you're getting to be a real fucking pain, Giles. Suggest that you and I stay apart as much as possible. Pity I can't get rid of you."

"Go to hell. The famous Kane Branson will just have to put up with me," he smirked.

"That's what I thought you'd say." Kane turned to Dan. "I need some time with Kelly. I need to…"

Giles grabbed his arm. "Yeah, we all know what you need. Rules, Kane. Remember those? I know that you think they don't apply to you. Why should you go getting laid when the rest of us can't?" Giles' mouth twisted as he spoke.

"That's your problem, Harris. You should have thought of that before you came along."

"Yeah, like you did? Brought your own personal sheila."

"I think I'd let it go, Giles," Alex intervened. He'd wandered back to join Kane.

"You're in your forties, Alex, but I don't see you with any twenty-four-year-old that's young enough to be your daughter," snarled Giles.

This time Kane couldn't let the comment go. He let go of Kelly, punched Giles out with one blow to the jaw, and watched Giles land on the floor. Giles had gone too far. Kane shook his hand. It hurt.

"When he wakes up, tell him to wash his mouth out with soap and water. Kelly."

He strode away with Kelly in tow. The group watched them leave. In the dark, Kane was wary how far he moved from the camp. Under the eucalyptus trees, he found a place for them, took his holster and gun off, and laid it on the ground. Kelly sat down next to him, her body leaning against him. Kane pulled the cigarettes out and lit one. Kelly took the cigarette from his fingers. Taking one drag, she handed it back to him. He looked surprised.

"So, how do you feel about the situation now? Remember, I asked if you really wanted to go through with this. I'm sorry you had to find out the way you did. Someone is helping the Chinese get a nice clear path into Australia. It has got to be someone with power. We have to find out just who…the drug traffic from Kong, back to Sydney, gets worse, by the day. It's probably someone of high rank on a different payroll. That's part of our mission…to find out *who* it is. All we know is that it's likely that one of our team has connections. And the other part of our mission is to find who betrayed me last year. But that's tomorrow, Kel." Putting his arm around her, he pulled her to him.

"Back up just a minute. It's one of us? That what you said?" Kelly inquired.

"Did I? Guess I did. Here, rest on my body. You know how brave you were tonight?" He pulled her T-shirt down from her neck, and fingered the butterfly on her breast trying to distract her.

"Not brave, just instinct. And don't change the subject, Kane." She tried to pull away but didn't succeed. She hadn't tried too hard.

"You're gonna make one hell of a good cop, Kelly Branson. With, or without, my help. But that's enough talk, for one night. It's late, and you should sleep. Gonna be a long day tomorrow, and who knows what might happen?"

She leaned against his chest and put her fingers on his lips. "Don't talk like that. Kiss me."

"One thing, Kelly. You do understand what will be expected of you now, don't you? Blair was supposed to be the... well the one who..."

She tried to stop him from speaking. "I know what to do. And I make a great prostitute. You know that!"

"Yeah, I do. But for now, Blair's off the team. That only leaves Genna and Ty who will go. Paul was off long back… Ben, I would like to take. Gonna ask if we can take him at least part of the way. I didn't want you to go, darling, not for that reason."

"You gonna make love to me, Kane Branson? I'd like to prove that Giles was right for once!"

"Right in what way?" asked Kane.

"That you brought me along for your own personal use. You did, didn't you? You better say yes, Kane Branson."

"Ma'am, yes, ma'am!" 'And that of the Australian Federal Police,' he whispered under his breath.

CHAPTER 3

Kane lay awake and watched the sun rise. He marveled at the shades that Australia had to offer in her morning glory. Sunlight bounced off Kelly's dog tags and reflected against him. Rubbing his hands up her tan arms, he slid them across her shoulders. He held her to him protecting her from her near future. A few more minutes' sleep wouldn't hurt. Kane pulled his jacket up around her and nestled into her hair. Even in the dust of the desert, she smelled good. Kane cast his mind to the journey ahead of them. Each had their role to play. Soon, he would tell them exactly what the roles might be. Buchanan was going to allow him to add Ben to his list, even just for a short spell. He needed Ben's talents in order to get into the computers of the capital. It was one way of finding out who was financing the ventures of the China white gangs. Overhead, the eagle screamed, its shrill cry waking the girl.

"Hi," she murmured, rubbing sleep from her eyes.

"Hi, yourself. Sleep well?" responded Kane.

"Always, next to you." Kelly nestled in closer to him. "What will the others say?"

"Who cares? I'm the boss out here," and Kane shrugged his shoulders.

"You know, if I didn't know better, I'd believe that you wanted to upset them." She looked up into his face and studied his reaction. She squinted her eyes. "You do want that, don't you? That's the whole idea."

"Bright girl. Maybe your talents are wasted." Kane smiled at her, raising his eyebrows as he did.

"On whom? You're the only one on which I want to waste my talents. But, you're not going to be the only one now, are you?" She viewed him suspiciously.

"We'll find a way round that, baby. There has to be another way. Gambling is big out there, too. Maybe Buchanan will let us take someone else…" Kane pulled her tighter to him, trying to protect her.

"You know that's not gonna happen. It was Blair, or me. I can take care of myself. I'm a big girl," quipped Kelly.

"No one knows that better than me." Kane once again slipped his hand under her vest.

"Makes his own fucking rules, doesn't he? Son-of-a-bitch. Why the hell doesn't he just come down here and do the girl?" Giles looked up toward the trees.

"What's the matter? Think he could show you a few moves?" Alex laughed. "Man's more accomplished in most things than you'll ever be." He rolled over on the hard ground.

Dan turned in his bedroll and stifled a noise that sounded like a snigger.

"Something funny, Dan? You're his son-in-law. Don't you find it strange to have a mother-in-law younger than your wife?" asked Giles.

"Actually, it makes life interesting. His daughter and Kelly are the best of friends, just as Kane and I are. Yeah, mate. We're just one big happy family. Just like here," Dan laughed and gathered up his gear.

"Oh, sure we are. He just wants to pit us against each other. Well, it doesn't work like that. From now on, I'm keeping more to myself. You two do what the hell you like, as far as I'm concerned. I'll go on with you all, but with one eye upon Kane. Alex, perhaps you should do the same. After all, nearly the whole damn Branson family is here." Giles picked up his stuff and moved away from them.

Genna sat up in her bedroll. It was strange being the only woman right now with all the men. She'd actually be glad when Kelly was back with her. She had heard the comments from Kane's friends, and had stored them away. Genna liked Giles. He was similar to a father figure, yet he wasn't. He was plain looking like her, and that fact she found somewhat attractive. They both did things by the book. Besides, it was Kane who had really caught her attention. He was all man and did things his way, which was a complete contrast to her. Therefore, she continued watching Giles as he moved his things away from the others. He sat down a few feet from Genna, and smiled at her. Giles had noticed Genna's grit and determination. He liked it. And he liked Genna. She, like Kelly, was a much younger woman. He offered Genna some water.

"Would you like some?"

"Thank you," she replied and took the canteen from him.

At the riverbed, the three young men sat on the banks. Ty washed away the night with the cold fresh water. He splashed it over his tough young body. Stripped to the waist, his vest hanging round him, it was obvious that Ty had worked out long before his admittance to the AFP. Ben dipped his feet in the water and last night's events were the focal point of discussion.

"So, who do you think is out next?" asked Ben, already knowing the answer.

Paul figured he would not be the one picked. It didn't take a genius to know that Kane disliked him. He had the feeling that Kane had figured out where his sexual preference really lay. Paul knew Ty was in solid. Ty was tall and blonde like Kane was. Paul stared at Ty. He looked even better this morning, muscles flexing in the sun…clever, athletic and handsome, Ty. Then, there was chubby Ben. Good old Ben. Sickening Ben. Genna came up behind them just ahead of Giles.

"Good morning. Anyone caught breakfast yet? I'm starving." She dipped her hands in the water, splashing the crystal-clear waters onto her face. The coolness felt good.

"Why don't you catch breakfast, Miss Hang-on-to-the-boss'-wife," quipped Paul. "You're good at everything."

"That's enough, Paul. Genna, I'll do it. I'll catch and you cook," stated Giles who had followed Genna down to the river. His hair stuck out even more this morning, causing him to look unkempt. The tight black apparel didn't do much for his physique.

"Sounds good to me. I'll get a fire going." Genna smiled at him and she scampered around in the clearing finding some firewood.

Ty saw it. "Now, they would make a good pair," he mused. "Didn't see it before. Seems that the women on this trip like older men. Guess I have some growing up to do."

The thought amused Ty and he waded out into the river. Ben followed, and Paul wandered farther down the riverbanks alone.

Kane watched from the clearing as Kelly took off down to the river-bank. Pulling his holster over his shoulder, he made certain that his knife was still secure in his boot. He felt a little lost without being able to use his usual mobile phone. Radio contact was not all that he had with home base. His well used cell was tucked away safely in his boot.

Kelly reached Genna.

"Need some help?" Kelly offered and began picking up dry kindling wood.

"Sure, that would be really nice. Giles went to catch fish." Genna's eyes flashed toward the river.

"Nice man, huh? Not married, you know," Kelly said mischievously.

"Kelly, stop. He could be my…"

"You mean like Kane, could be mine? You can say it. You can't offend me. I'm used to it. But Giles is a nice man."

It didn't take long to find wood, build a fire and construct a spit. Giles returned with several fish. Ty even caught a couple, much to his own amazement. Kelly laid the fish down and gutted them, tossing away the entrails. Genna was amazed at her friend's dexterity with a knife. Cleaned and pierced with sticks in their scaly bodies, Genna and Kelly held the fish on the spit. They sizzled and spat and the smell of hot food fetched them all to the fire. The fish smelled delicious by any standards. Ben leaned back against the tree patting his stomach.

"Any more?" asked the overstuffed geek.

"Ben, you'll burst if you keep on eating. Here, you can have mine. Not hungry this morning." The smell of cooking had made Kelly want to vomit.

"Eat up, Kelly. You'll need all of the damn energy that you can get today," stated Kane and with his fingers pulled the last remaining breakfast apart.

Dan covered for her. "Guess some people live on love. Right, Kel?"

She responded appropriately. "You should know, Dan. You're married to a Branson!"

"Yeah, guess so. Say, you want to help me with the dishes then, mom?"

She flashed her eyes at him. "Why not."

"Dishes?" asked Kane. "We only have knives."

"Well, then, we'll wash the knives." Dan needed to talk to her. "Please come and help me wash knives."

Kelly picked up a couple of the blades and followed Dan to the edge of the river. She sat down on the muddy bank.

"You doing okay, Kelly? You look somewhat sickly. You didn't eat. Kane knows that you're able to eat with the best of them. He's gonna get just a little suspicious, if you don't, especially after a whole day of not eating properly." Dan sat down on the muddy bank. "Don't you think you should tell him? So, what if you don't go on this mission… they'll be others."

Kelly turned to him, her face perplexed.

"I have to go. You know that. Especially now that I know what the mission is. How long has he been the Hunter?" she asked. "I knew about the project. I overheard Kane and Buchanan talking about it some time back. I didn't know it was in operation."

Dan looked at her face. There was a glow about her. If Kane couldn't see it, he would never see anything about his wife.

"Best let him tell you. He told you some, right?" Dan dipped the knives into the swirling current of the river.

"Yeah, he told me some, but not…"

She stopped speaking. Her eyes fixed on the object that had just come into her field of vision. Although her mouth opened, no words escaped. She stared at the water. Dan was still watching her face.

"Kelly, Kel? What's wrong?" He followed her eyes and saw in which direction that she was staring. "Oh, my God!" Seeing clearly, what she was envisioning, he yelled, "Go get Kane!" Dropping the knives, Dan dove fully clothed into the water.

Kelly cleared the ground between her and her husband in a couple of minutes. "In the water," she screamed. She doubled over, a cramp in her side. "Body…in the water."

Kane grabbed hold of her arms and held her upright. "Kelly, you're not making sense. A body?"

Then he remembered that Paul hadn't been at breakfast. Kane let go of her, shed his gun and holster, and took off running. Kane slipped down the bank into the water. Dan already had a hold of the arms of the out-stretched body. Together, the two of them pulled Paul to the side. Kane took Paul's weight, while water swirled around them.

"There's no pulse," yelled Dan, his fingers searching the boy's neck.

"He's been in the water too long. Don't even bother searching. He's already turned blue!" screamed Kane. "I'll get out of the river and onto the bank. Push him up to me."

Dan held Paul in the current. Kane tried to pull the body upon the bank, but the body, wet and heavy, slipped in the mud. Ty rushed to Kane's side and grabbed one of the lifeless arms. Together, they retrieved the young agent from his watery grave. Kane lay back, exhausted. Paul was no lightweight. Ty helped Dan from the swirling current, and then sat beside Kane.

"Thanks…I'll remember that. I owe you one, you hear," Kane said.

Ty nodded. Kane brushed his bedraggled hair out of his steely eyes, and sat upright. Mud slithered down his muscular arm, and he wiped it away. His eyes looked at Paul. Then the cold, steely blue eyes shifted across to his son-in-law.

"God all fucking mighty!" he yelled. "This wasn't supposed to happen. Fuck!" His outrage shocked Dan. The rest of them gathered around gawking at the body…and at Kane.

Kelly stared at her husband. "Kane, I don't think…"

"That's right, Kelly, you don't think! I do it for all of us." He cut his wife dead. "Dan, go radio them to come get him." He stood up, wet clothes clinging to his body. "Don't just sit there, do it! And all of you stop staring like you've never seen a dead person before."

"Kane, maybe one or two haven't? They're not all hard like you," Giles retorted.

Kane turned on him. "Then, I'd like to know why the fuck they're here? If they can't handle looking at a dead body, what can they handle? What good are they going to be to me?" Kane turned on his heel and walked away.

Genna burst into tears. She didn't know why. Nevertheless, it seemed a good idea to gain Giles' attention.

"It's okay, Genna. His bark's worse than his bite. Still, I have to admit this is an unusual situation." Giles put his arm around her.

"Kelly, go after him. Ask him to radio in, would you?" Dan cut his eyes at her. Kane wasn't thinking clearly.

"Yeah." She turned and ran up the path to where Kane stood.

She found him leaning against a tree, muttering to himself. "Two down already, just like last time. Be lucky if we get there with seven. Fucking hell!"

Kelly approached her husband a little cautiously. Her love for him causing emotions and confusion to mix, she decided to take a risk and talk to him.

"Kane, Dan wants you to radio in the latest. Guess he thought it best."

Kane looked at her for a second before it registered what she was saying.

"Yeah, I'll do it. I should do it. What the fuck was I thinking…" Kane turned to Kelly. "Why aren't you crying, Kel? Why aren't you shocked? They just stood there as if hell had frozen over, or something. Goddamn." He thumped his fist on the tree. "Who is it? Who's working with the informant? Someone is a betraying son-of-a-bitch. Now, I'm not sure who it is."

Kelly jumped. Kane's temper had turned up a degree higher than usual. She waited, looked around her, and gave him time to compose himself. This wasn't the usual Kane. Kelly broke the silence.

"Blair was an accident, right?" Kelly brushed the hair from her face. From her pocket, she produced a band and pulled her hair into ponytail.

"Was she, baby? You said you two were arguing. Someone could have gone after her. And the others could have gotten to her, just as quickly as you could and Ty did. It might be nice and convenient for her to be out of the way. Let's see, that took the numbers down one…which put you in first place."

Kelly shivered. Through the trees, came a cool wind. Kane sat down on the ground and reached for his pack. Pulling the radio out, he called Home base. The line crackled, and then spluttered into life.

"Home base, this is Hunter. We got ourselves a body here."

There was a pause. "Hell, Kane, what are you doing out there? You're not supposed to get rid of them like that." Commander Buchanan was not happy.

"Getting rid of them? You arranged this little fishing expedition. Maybe, you have someone watching us, getting the numbers rounded down a little at a time. That it?" Kane snapped.

"You know that's not the way. Think maybe we'll bring you all back a day earlier. I'll send the chopper in later today to get Paul. Over and out."

Kane had never mentioned the dead person's name. He glanced at Kelly, reflecting on his new awareness and on what he would do next.

"Kelly, from now on in stay near me. Tell Genna to stay close to Giles, even if he's a pain in the ass right now. In fact, Giles is just about to make a play for your little friend. I've seen him look at her. But then, I've seen him look at you, too." Kane went back to his original thought. "Well, now he has a big chance with Genna, I mean."

Kane's clothes still clung to him. Kelly could see his outline clearly. She wanted her husband. Sitting on the ground next to him, she leaned against the tree.

"Can I ask you a question?" She looked into his face knowing he wouldn't lie to her.

"Sure, darling." He was back to his normal self.

"We gonna make it back from Kong in one piece?" she asked tentatively.

Kane took his wife's face in his hands and kissed her full lips. Stroking her hair with his rough hands, he gently whispered something in her ear. Then he rose up and walked away.

Going back to the scene of the crime, Kane saw Dan sitting with the body. The others had drifted down stream a little. Kane tried to change the tone of the day. He stared at the sky.

"The chopper will be here in a couple of hours to get him. We're being pulled out a day early. Therefore, now you get to go home to my daughter. Make the most of that time, Dan. We may be gone to Hong Kong longer than we think." He paused. And he thought. "Time we had another baby in the family. Slipping aren't we, boy?" Kane sat down next to his son-in-law.

Dan wondered how Kane could joke at a time like this. Or was he joking? He watched Kane light up a wet cigarette with some difficulty, a kind of a smug smile on his face. One of the members of Branson family wasn't slipping. Dan realized that Kane knew Kelly was pregnant again… the glow was hard to miss.

"Kelly's going on with us, then?" Dan inquired.

"Any reason why that she shouldn't?" Kane puffed on the weed.

"Damn you, boss. Sometimes, I don't think you're for real."

"Sometimes, I'm not." He smacked Dan on the back. "Okay, now back to work. Cover Paul up with his bedroll. We still have to get through the next few hours. Watch out for Ty and Ben. Alex…he's just Alex. Gonna have a man-to-man talk with Giles, although he's a pain in the butt right now. Still, he needs to keep Genna occupied for a while."

As he spoke, his eyes darted around the landscape. Dan could see that he was worried. Aside from losing two members of his party, events cast aspersions on his credibility as a leader. The turn of events had not been good for morale.

"You think we're being watched, even now?" asked Dan.

"Yeah, I just don't know by whom," replied his boss, and Kane rose up and walked back down to the river towards the others.

Kelly waited 'til Kane was out of range. Zooming in on Dan, she said, "You look like you want to tell me something, Dan. Do you?"

"Not a damn thing," came his fast reply.

Kane reached the group. Sidling over to Giles, he put his arm around his shoulder. Giles stared at him.

"We need to talk. There's something that I need you to do for me. Think

you can take Genna under your wing? I mean like…way under your wing?"
Kane winked at him.

"Are you suggesting what I think you are insinuating? I don't believe
you, man. You're suggesting I…"

"Why don't you just tell the whole fucking world? For God's sake,
man…shut your mouth! There's a reason. Will you trust me? How far you
want to take it is up to you. I *can* trust you to do that, can't I? I can't watch
everyone. She likes you." Placating Giles was hard, even for Kane.

Giles stared at Kane as though he was insane. "Think she likes you a
whole lot better… but, yeah, I'll do it. Mainly, because I like her. I wouldn't
want you hitting on her, Kelly or no Kelly. She's a nice girl. Intelligent, strong,
good body, and isn't it against the rules…you remember rules, Kane?"

"She's never had a serious boyfriend, so go gently. After all, this isn't
the usual kind of game playing rules here. Oh, and remember, she tells
Kelly everything," Kane laughed.

"That figures. Kane's law!" Giles stopped speaking. He held back his
thoughts. "Still, it wouldn't be the first time… us sharing bedroom secrets…
now would it? Remember our first trip to Hong Kong? Then again, last
year is mainly why I volunteered to go back with you. Just one more time
together on a mission."

'*One more time,*' thought Kane. '*The last one for whom?*'

"About Kelly…"

"What about her, Giles?" asked Kane.

"You have a cute woman there. Then again, you always did have all the
luck with the women. She's in place of Blair now, isn't she? Or, was she
always the leading lady?" Giles asked.

"How do you know all this?" Kane was on his guard.

"Buchanan told me more than I let on to you. I was waiting to see
if you told me, and, in true Branson fashion; you didn't. I was pushing
you when you hit me. Trying to get you to bend. I also know that there
is an informer. I know that Paul's death was no accident. He didn't just
fall in the river, hit his head, and drown like you told them. I heard your
words, knew what you were saying. Panic is the last thing you want, now.
And Blair? Accident, maybe. Avoidable, definitely. Buchanan thought you
might need help. I'd already planned on looking after Genna. The only
thing I don't know is why we're going, aside from the obvious. There has
to be another reason other than finding out why so much China white is
flooding into Australia. But you're not going to tell me, are you?"

Kane looked deep into his friend's eyes. Was Giles Buchanan's errand boy? Was he the double agent? Was Dan the only one on his side? Kane chanced it. Better to know your enemies and your prey.

"There's someone working for both countries. Passing on the information about the drops. Money changing hands that the government can't trace. Got to be someone in an official capacity. Buchanan wanted me to find out who it is. Figured that I had the experience. Answer your question?" His hand tightened on Giles' shoulder.

"I'm on your side, pal, not against you." Giles expression never changed.

"Yeah, sure." Kane dropped his arm, but not his guard.

Again, Kane reached for his cigarettes; a move, which Giles noted, was performed every time that Kane felt anger or distrust.

"Dan knows also, right?" asked Giles.

"Most of it. Cigarette?" Kane shook the packet.

Giles shook his head.

"Nasty habit. Then, I have to have some vices," his voice a little on the edgy side.

"Yeah, I know that. I know you. So what's next?" Giles hid his feelings well.

"You're gonna take them for some exercise. Next, you'll take them swimming for the afternoon. Then we'll eat. Stay close to the girls. If they need the latrines make 'em go together. Nothing else can happen before we get back. Nothing, you understand?"

"Sir, yes, sir," he mocked and gave a slow salute with his hand.

"This is backbreaking. Giles must have trained under Kane. How you doing, Kel?" Genna asked as she rose up again from the ground.

"Like you said, backbreaking. If I have to do another pushup, I'll die. And how come it's only the four of us? Don't the *grownups* need exercise? I know one man who is going to get some later."

Genna whispered to her, "And exercise," and she laughed. "I swear that Giles, he keeps smiling at me."

"Nooooo." Kelly turned her head away to hide the amused look on her face.

Giles looked down at his watch. The seconds ticked by.

"Fifty. Okay, you can stop. Take a break." Giles stopped his stop watch.

"Thank God. I thought that he was trying to kill us. My gut is killing me. Period due any day," and Genna straightened up while holding her stomach.

"Oh great! That squashes Kane's little plans for you and Giles," Kelly mumbled, and she flopped down in the long grass.

"Say something, Kel?" Genna asked.

"No, nothing," Kelly replied.

"Anyone fancy a swim?" Giles pulled his T-shirt off and tossed it on the ground.

Genna could see his tanned body. For some reason, today it gave her feelings that she'd never had before. Kelly watched her with interest. *Deja vu.*

"I'm game," Ty yelled. "Come on, ladies. Let's all go."

Ty ran down the bank into the river where only hours before, one of their comrades had been found murdered.

"Not me. I'll stay here to guard the clothes." Ben sat on the bank looking miserable about his appearance. He knew he was chubby. His skin was white. He wasn't handsome like Ty, and he certainly wasn't anything like the men on this mission.

"Come on, Ben. We can't all look like Kane and Kelly," and Genna took his hand. She was endearing herself to Giles more by the minute with her concern for the other members of the group.

The girls pulled their tight black pants and boots off, dropped them, and ran to join the people already splashing water in the river.

Kane sat under the trees and smoked two cigarettes before he felt the need to join them in the water. He watched Kelly, clad in regulation underwear of black vest and black underpants. Even in those, she looked great. Dan sat alongside him with a wistful look on his face.

"You miss Sage?" asked Kane.

"You read minds now? Sure, *Dad.* I miss your daughter. I can't wait to get back to her. You miss Star?"

"Course. And I know Kelly does. Sage will be spoiling your kid and mine to death. Still, seems strange having two daughters so far apart in age. You ever think about our strange family?" asked Kane nonchalantly.

"Sure. If ever anything happens to you, you know I'll look after the girls. You do know that, don't you?" asked his son-in-law.

"Yeah, I know. By the way, did you tell Kelly that I know?" He considered a third cigarette and decided against it. *He should really give it up.*

"Know what?" Dan turned his brown eyes on Kane.

"Thanks." Kane slapped Dan on the back. "You're okay for a son-in-law."

"That's between you two. But you do know you're both crazy?"

"Yeah, that's what makes the relationship so interesting. That and a few other things." His eyes never left Kelly. "Now I think I'll join her and partake of one of those other things."

"You son-of-a-bitch, Kane," and Dan laughed.

Kane left the gun and holster with Dan. He pulled the laces out of the boots and kicked them off in haste. Last, to go was his vest. Striding down the clearing to the river again, he had a kind of cold feeling as if they were being watched, and not by any four-legged animal.

When Kane reached the water, he whispered to Alex and then waded out further. Kelly watched Kane approach her. He took her hand, leading her through the swirling current, away from her friends.

"Hey, *boss*. Thought we were here to swim?" Giles yelled.

"You swim! I have better things to do," Kane shouted back.

"Yeah, we see that. God damn him. Really rubs it in, doesn't he? He just asked me…"

"Asked you what, Giles?"

"Nothing, Alex. Just nothing… maybe the guy believes that he's giving me some pointers," Giles mumbled to himself.

Kelly's hair lay wet and flat against her body. Her giggles had long since subsided. Her suntanned body glistened with droplets of water from the cooling river. Kane pulled Kelly along with him. Out of sight from the prying eyes, he stopped and pulled his wife to him. He felt her body tense as her breasts touched him. Reaching around her back, he slid his hand into her underpants, pulling them down past her thighs.

"Don't change, do you Kane?"

"You want me to change?" he replied huskily.

"Never," Kelly murmured.

Her arms circled his neck and she kissed him as the water surged around them. Cold vibrant water buried their entwined bodies beneath it. Their legs floated together. She felt down under the water for him. Kane grabbed her hand and stopped her, and at the same time, she felt him thrust inside her. Gulping, Kelly tried not to swallow water. His grip tightened on her, and her legs clung to his body as if they were leaches. The two of them exploded up through the water together and Kelly gasped for breath.

"You okay?" Kane whispered in her ear.

"Yeah." She clung to him. "You just never cease to surprise me. Just when I think that I know you, you find something new, Kane Branson."

"Go, go back to them. Make certain that Genna knows exactly what she is missing," he said, and laughed at her girlish charm.

Kelly wrinkled her face at Kane. She thought for a moment. "Oh, I get it. I'll make certain that she knows every tiny detail."

He winked at his wife.

Kane let her swim back to the group. He saw her and Genna exchange words. Now, it was Giles' turn to follow his lead.

The party sat around the glowing campfire, waiting for the chopper. It was very late, not the usual AFP style. Evening came in fast. It was now their last night in Alice Springs. It was cool, and the girls huddled close to the flames.

At last, the chopper arrived for Paul. The glaring light and relentless whirring noise of the chopper blades heralded its arrival, blowing dust about them. This time, Buchanan flew in with the gear. He didn't disembark from the chopper. Instead, he called Kane over to him. Kane left his group to go and meet with him.

In the fading light, Kelly watched the two men shake hands. Buchanan perched on the side of the helicopter. The conversation seemed to start pleasantly enough. Suddenly, it wasn't so pleasant. Both of Kane's and Buchanan's voices were raised. Kane turned away from Buchanan. He called Kane back. The argument became more heated. The chopper lights highlighted the two men, causing the whole group to be able to see them arguing. This time, Kane walked away with Buchanan still making his point.

"Alex, Giles, get that body onto the plane, so his mightiness can get the fuck out of here," Kane growled at the two men.

They did as they were asked, carrying the bed-rolled body to the craft. Buchanan acknowledged both of the men. Paul's body was arranged, with care, into the back of the helicopter.

Kane watched from a distance while Paul took one last chopper ride. Whether he cared for Paul or not Kane did not want him dead. The helicopter lifted off, leaving them standing in a flurry of propeller winds.

"What were they arguing about?" Alex asked as he stood back from the chopper's swirl.

"It's none of our fucking business," Giles replied brushing his clothes down from the propeller dust.

"Since when have you taken Kane's side? Oh, since he set you up with Genna. I saw you talking with her. Planning some little rendezvous later?" Alex asked.

"Goddamn, you do have a one-track-mind. Girls need looking after. I can hardly look after Kelly, now can I?" retorted Giles.

"Who are you kidding? You would, if you could. Sure, I know when a man is goin' after a woman. God, you only to have watch Kane. He wants that girl twenty-four hours a day. And you, it's gonna be that way with Genna, cause you sure the hell can't have Kelly," Alex flashed his eyes at him.

"Pity you're on this mission, Alex. If I were Kane, I'd find a way to get rid of you. Never did care that much for you. You and Kane could always get what others couldn't," Giles said with contempt.

The pair had reached the campfire.

"That a threat?" Alex looked across the firelight at him.

"No, that would be a promise. But then, I'm not Kane Branson, am I?"

"No, you sure the hell are not," Alex said in a less-than friendly manner.

Giles sat down and warmed his hands over the crackling fire.

"What's that all about?" Kane sat next to Giles.

"Forget it. Not worth talking about at this point; but watch out for him… think he fancies your wife."

From where Kane was standing, that wasn't what he'd heard at all.

The group waited for someone to fix dinner… and they waited. Genna sat near Kelly on the other side of the fire next to the men.

"Be glad to eat something other than fish, after tomorrow. Grilled fish, baked fish, raw fish, burnt fish…did I miss anything?" Genna asked.

"Sickening fish?" murmured Kelly.

"You didn't eat any of the gourmet fish. Just those berries that you keep picking. By the looks of today, you need strength," Genna whispered to Kelly.

Underneath her surly façade, Genna did have a sense of humor. Kelly thought that Genna might have another side to her.

"Oh you mean…" Kelly blushed in the firelight.

"Yes, I mean just that." She became serious. "Kelly, what's it like? I mean…with Kane?"

"Genna, you still a virgin?" Somehow it didn't surprise her. She'd watched Genna staring at the men…and mainly at her husband.

"Course not." Genna looked into Kelly's face. She grimaced. "Well, yes. I believe in saving myself for the right man. How do you know when it's him?"

Kelly looked across the firelight at Kane. As a one-time prostitute, she had known many men. That was, until Kane.

"You don't have to answer, Kelly. It's written all over your face. You just know, don't you?"

Kelly nodded. "It's a wonderful feeling. Like today at the river. Never the same twice… Kane is exciting. Life is an adventure with him. It was hard for me to go from my old life to living with him, but the man stuck by me, him against the world. Things you only read about in books, Genna. When we get to Kong, you'll see; he'll be a totally different man. All business. When he pulls the strings, we jump. And that's the way it will be. Even Giles will jump."

"I'm going with you?" She was excited.

"Oh, yes, Genna. You're on his list."

Genna's eyes gleamed fiercely in the light. She had made it, one way or another.

With the fire burning brightly, the night didn't seem as frightening. Safety seemed to be in numbers but those numbers also seemed to be dwindling fast. In the distance, noises on the evening wind were playing tunes in their minds. Ty began banging a rhythm on his canteen with his knife. Genna began to sing along, with a slow melodic tune. Winds whistled through the eucalyptus trees. The night was almost eerie. Without warning, Kelly rose from her sitting position. In slow, almost hypnotic, and rhythmic timing, she moved her body in twisting turns to the captivating music of the night. Kane saw a side of Kelly that he had never seen before.

Kane looked around the spellbound faces. His eyes settled on Giles' face. The man was looking at Kelly with such a wanton look in his eyes, that Kane was frightened for her. Kane knew then that he had found the right girl for the job that he never wanted Kelly to do. If he had not been so obsessed with his own observations, he would have seen the enemy within.

CHAPTER 4

As they stood waiting for the huge service chopper to come for them, Kane thought back to the previous night. Kelly's dancing was indescribably seductive. Her lithe and slim body weaving about in the tight black clothing had caught all of the men's attention. Yet, the whole time, her eyes had held Kane's in a hypnotic gaze. The image stayed with him throughout the night, almost taunting him. Sleep had not been his friend.

Kane's thoughts were disturbed as the chopper's blades created a rushing noise in the morning air. Dust, once more, swirled the barren earth. As the craft descended, Kane was able to see Buchanan clearly. The look on his face spoke volumes. Kane hadn't yet recovered from the last tongue lashing. Almost arrogantly, the Commander stepped out of the silver aircraft and approached Kane.

Kane strode giant confident steps to meet the Commander. The conversation between the two men was low and intense, continuing for several minutes. Each man stated his view. Suddenly, and without warning, Kane raised his arms, turned on his heel, and moved a few paces back towards his group.

"Branson. Get back here. Now!" Buchanan's angry voice echoed on the wind, his face reddened by his temper.

Glancing at his group, Kane first stopped; then he turned, and walked back to his boss.

"What's all that about?" Giles whispered to Dan.

"Figure they're discussing Paul again, and the loss of this party," Dan added

"Didn't just fall into that river, did he? Someone wanted him out of the way. There's a person that really wants to see your father-in-law disgraced, Dan," added Alex.

Someone…somewhere, had it in for Kane and wanted to see him put in his place, or out of it. The question was did they want it enough to take a life? Right away, both Branson's and Buchanan's voices were raised.

"Harris! Get over here," yelled Buchanan.

Giles Harris raised his eyebrows, but went in double quick time. He saluted Buchanan. Buchanan returned the gesture. "Branson is out and you're in charge." Buchanan was crimson red. He matched only the ribbons on his highly decorated AFP khaki jacket.

"Excuse me, sir, but I don't think so. If Agent Branson's out, so am I," replied Giles.

"I said in case you didn't hear me, that you're in charge. You going to disobey an order?" Buchanan became angrier by the second. Standing on the edge of the clearing, he stared down Harris.

"This isn't the military, sir; and, I repeat, if he's out, so am I. Get Powers to take over; after all, he's next in seniority." Giles actually didn't want out, and the mission would be no good without Kane along.

Kane turned away, but Giles caught him by the jacket sleeve and slid his arm across his friend's chest. Kane stood still and held by Giles' arm. Giles continued pleading Kane's case.

"Why did you do that, *sir*? Kane Branson is the best."

"Best at what? Losing his people?" Buchanan roared, his face turning red with anger.

Kane pulled against Giles' arm, his muscles flexing. "Let go of me," he growled.

"No, damn it! This isn't right." Giles' grip tightened on Kane. Turning back towards their boss, he continued his speech, "Buchanan, you know he's the best. Whatever the differences between the two of you might be… you both should shelve them. This isn't the time or place. The whole group is watching. You are undermining your best man. They are supposed to follow him, not you, sir, or me."

Buchanan looked around him. The whole group was staring in disbelief. It was a bad move. It was his move to make, his game to play. Buchanan realized Kane could not see his face.

"Okay, forget it. Branson, you take them on, but you better come back with seven," Buchanan puffed out the words.

"Eight." Kane stared defiantly at the ground.

"What? The team is only for seven. One has to go. I don't care who goes, just make the decision quickly," Buchanan demanded.

"Then, we don't go as a team, I don't go. I want them all." Kane pulled violently away from Giles and turned to face Buchanan.

The eyes of the two hotheads met. Kane's stare never faltered. Buchanan blinked, unable to withstand Kane's icy gaze.

"Okay, you win. Now, let's stop talking. You get them all in the chopper, and let's get back to the airport." Buchanan turned away in disgust and headed for the aircraft.

One by one, the group piled in the giant bird. Glad to be inside the huge airy AFP helicopter and away from the extraordinary heat, Genna and Kelly sat side by side. Kane's wife knew… Kelly knew by looking at him that it was better not to say anything. All she had to do was see the glaze in his eyes to see he was angry. Kane's face was of stone, the features less than tempered, and his eyes fierce. No one spoke. Kelly watched the other passengers.

Ben looked totally uncomfortable. He still wasn't certain of his future with the team. Ty looked hot and tired. Genna with obvious stomach cramp watched Giles, who was bland and unreadable. Dan sat next to his boss, proving himself, as always, loyal and devoted. Alex had an expression on his face of total disbelief. It was besides him, how their last few minutes, had even been allowed to transpire.

Next, was Buchanan, her eyes hesitated there. *What was happening?* Finally, Kane suppressed his anger…for now. When Kelly's eyes landed on his, Kane stared a hole through her with a look of fierceness, which only they understood.

The helicopter made good time to the airport, touching down with an hour to spare. Standing on the runway with their backpacks, the group could see the aircraft waiting to take them back to Sydney. Eight little Rambo's were waiting to go home.

"Kelly, you and Genna stick with Dan. I need to talk to Buchanan, in private. I'll be with you before the plane lifts off; and, that won't be long. Trust me, baby." Kane leaned forward and gently kissed her lips.

"Is everything okay?" Kelly asked tentatively.

Although he was in a hurry, gently, yet forcefully, Kane put his arm around her and kissed her again. "Will be when we get home." Afterwards, he strode off along the shimmering tarmac in the same direction that Buchanan had gone.

The group waited nervously in the airport lounge. One of them would be dropped. Ben had a feeling that he would be shortly saying 'goodbye' to his companions.

The group was conspicuously dressed all in black. It probably would be better if they changed back into the civilian clothes. The girls disappeared into the ladies' room and the guys, to the men's. A few minutes later, they all emerged.

Genna donned comfortable grey shorts and a buttoned-up blouse. In total contrast, Kelly came out in tight cutoff denim shorts with a bright yellow T-shirt. With her hair pulled up in a ponytail, she looked nothing like a cop. The guys came out of the men's room wearing jeans and T-shirts. Kelly turned the guy's heads, and popped gum at the same time. There was still no sign of Kane or Buchanan.

"Will all passengers for Flight 169 to Sydney, please board now. This is the last call for passengers for Flight 169," boomed the loud speaking voice of Ansett Airlines. Kelly had heard the first call while in the ladies room.

"We better get on the damn plane. Kane will be on this plane, Kelly. Said he would." Giles looked her up and down, investigating her. "No one would believe you're a cop. No one in their right mind, that is."

Giles ushered the group down the gangway and onto the now-crowded jet. Kelly kept turning her head to see if she could see Kane, much to the annoyance of the rest of the group. The group members found their places, and took the left over room in order to store their bags in the luggage holds above their heads.

Kelly shared the three-seated row with one missing husband and with Genna. Kelly wiped away the window mist with her palms and peered out, hoping to get a glimpse of her man. Crossing her legs, she slumped back in the seat, her high-heeled sandals dangling from her feet. From her pocket, she retrieved another piece of gum, having discarded the most recent piece, as they boarded the plane.

Kane would be here. He'd said so. She heard Genna gasp, and Kelly turned her head in order to look in the direction that Genna was staring. Strolling down the aisle walked Kane. His gray suit fit well on him and the off-white shirt and gray tie enhanced his color. Shades, hair tied back, and a swagger that was noted by the women that he passed. Kane stopped by the girls and leaned across Genna. He aimed his speech at Kelly.

"'Scuse me, darling, think you're in my seat. My ticket says I get the window seat."

Kelly blinked. "No, this one's mine. But if you want it, I'll move."

Genna sat open-mouthed.

"Thanks, I'll take you up on that offer," and he squeezed past Genna, allowing the cut of his pants deliberately show the lines of his body.

Kane followed through on the charade. Kelly moved and Kane sat down next to the window. Kelly wasn't sure what she was supposed to say. One thing she did realize was that she was in an all-too-familiar scenario from a lifetime ago. From across the aisle, the others watched.

"What is he playing at, is something I'd care to know." Alex was still dressed in black, but in jeans and an open necked shirt complimenting his dark features.

"Oh, he's not playing. He's dead serious," replied Dan.

Kane read the magazine as the plane took off without any problems. Dozing a few moments refreshed him enough that after awakening he began a pleasant conversation with Kelly. Not far into the chat, came the proposition.

"Want to get laid?" Kane asked her matter-of-factly.

"By you? Who wouldn't? But I'm married. What if my husband finds out that you're talking to me like this?" She scrunched up her face in mock gesture.

"No problem. Have a place in Sydney. We can go there," replied Kane nonchalantly.

"Sounds good to me. What about my friend here?" She inclined her head toward Genna.

"She can come, too; no problem. I can entertain you both." Giving the girls a wink, Kane rested his hand on Kelly's bare leg. "Nice sun tan you have. Go all the way up, does it?"

"Yeah. Yours?" asked Kelly.

"You wanna find out how far?" he asked, lowering the shades onto his nose.

"Sure," Kelly replied.

Genna gulped. Did they mean what she thought they did?

Those in the row behind them heard everything. Especially, the man right behind Kane. Ty and Ben were in the row in front of Kane. Nothing that Kane did surprised Ty…not a damn thing.

The trip was uneventful enough, by Branson standards. Kelly dozed. Genna dozed. The guys sat talking. Kane sat thinking. Two drinks and a very plastic airline snack later, Flight 169 landed. Kane thought the flight number was a good choice.

Sydney was still Sydney. Still bold, and daring. Still, hot.

"You girls got any luggage that you'd like me to get for you?" asked Kane.

"Yeah. Backpacks from our hiking trip." Kelly stretched up to get her gear.

"Allow me," he said, and with ease, pulled the girl's gear out of the luggage rack. His pants pulled tight against him and his shirt strained over his muscles.

Like lambs, Genna and Kelly followed him off the plane. The rest of the team followed at a safe distance. Dan knew all about Kane's little scams from being his partner for so long.

"I'll have my chauffeur get the car," and Kane clicked his fingers. From nowhere, Buchanan, dressed in a chauffeur's uniform, false moustache and shades, appeared, "Go get the car."

Buchanan must have been on the same flight, somewhere.

"Yes, *sir*," he mumbled. "Taking this too far," he murmured to himself. "Thinks I'm his fucking chauffeur."

Outside the airport, the limo arrived. Tinted window job with all the works. The little group piled in and the car pulled around the corner of the road.

"Okay, stop! Much as I like this, we have to get the others. Not bad, though, for a dry run." Kane laughed, and propped his snakeskin boots on the leather seat.

"Get your damn feet off there. Game's over for now," yelled a disgruntled Buchanan.

"You bastard, Kane. You played me at my own game," giggled Kelly.

"Worked though, didn't it?" Kane laughed. "As long as the guy in the seat behind me bought it, that's all that matters to me right now; and, judging by the look on his face when we left the flight, he did. Someone gonna give him a ride home, Buchanan?"

"Commander to you. Yeah, they're gonna get him." He threw his chauffeur's hat onto the seat. "Rest of your little group is on their way to the department. We'll meet there and then decide where you're going to stay for three days. Best if the three of you hang together, just in case. 'Specially now that Kane is your pimp."

"Our what?" Two pairs of popped eyes stared at him from the spacious back seats.

"Pimp, Genna. You know what that is?" asked Buchanan.

"I wasn't born yesterday, sir. Kelly, I can see. But me?" Genna looked astonished.

"Gee thanks, girlfriend," cut in Kelly. "Thanks for that statement, you really know how to make a friend feel," she added sarcastically.

"I didn't mean it like that. But look at me and then, look at you." Genna was flushed pink, and nervous that she still wasn't explaining herself well.

Commander Buchanan had his doubts that Genna could pull it off, and he had even bigger doubts about Kane Branson. He might have been better off if he had not hauled Kane up like that in front of his team. But right now, even Buchanan didn't know whom to trust.

Kane lounged back in the car, knowing that he shouldn't trust Buchanan, either. Something wasn't right. All that he could trust was his gut instinct and his wife.

"So, we don't have to pick the others up…so, why don't you just drive, man." He pulled Kelly to him, kept his boots propped on the seat, and closed his eyes.

"You just keep pushing and I will have you removed from this mission, Branson," Buchanan threatened.

"Try… but you'll lose the best team we've had in years and you damn well know it." Kane didn't even open his eyes.

Kelly curled up beside him. She knew Kane's game. On the other hand, Genna didn't have a clue, which was the way that Kane wanted it.

At the Sydney branch of the Australian Federal Police, Kane took Kelly's hand and walked her through the department like he owned it. Kelly, with a huge grin on her face, scurried along beside him like his prized trophy. Kane raised his shades in acknowledgement. Cheers and whistles went up for him amongst his comrades. Kane flexed his muscles. The department was not accustomed to seeing this side of Kane Branson. They certainly weren't accustomed to see that much of his wife. The pair entered Buchanan's office, sat down, and Kane put his feet on the desk. Buchanan brushed them off with a swat of his hand.

"Like I told you, don't push me too far, Kane."

Kane smiled. He had far more pushing to do. Buchanan gave Kane center stage as the Rambo's filed into the office.

"Gee, Kane. You going into Hong Kong dressed like that?" asked Alex as he stepped from the outer offices into Buchanan's official lair. His eyes looked Kane up and down. He whistled.

"Cute, Alex. Sure am, and you guys are gonna work for me. On my left, you see my two *working girls.*" He waited till Ty and Ben entered the room. "On this side, the guy who's going to be my accountant. Ty, well, he's gonna wish that he'd stayed at home by the time all of this is said and done. Ground rules for the capitol. After we have established ourselves and found out the sources, we are to move on through Lantau. Nice new airport there; easy to get in and out of with low amount of security. The department is somewhat certain that's where the heroin factory is located. Nevertheless, we'll find that out when we get there. The prison would be a good cover for such illegal activities as drug smuggling. Anyway, that's the basic plan. All of you are in now. Ben, you only go so far. When we leave the main city, you'll be pulled out and that's a detail that won't change. Alex, you and Ty, will end up inside the prison as inmates… if that's our final destination. Giles and I will operate from the outside. You girls will be on a flight home by then."

"Agent Branson?" The man in the plane, one row behind Kane, came into the room. "You had me fooled. I don't know you, except by reputation. You're damn good, sir."

Kane nodded his head. "Thank you. I try." The stranger proudly shook the cop's hand.

"Oh, you're trying alright," muttered one of his team members under their breath.

"You met my wife, yet?" Kane ushered Kelly forward with a pat on her backside.

She moved towards them shyly.

The AFP agent gulped and stood with a boyish grin on his face. Buchanan sent the bloke on his way.

"Okay, back to business. Dan, you want to go home for the three days? You know your part better than I do, so get the hell out of here and give Sage our love." Kane hesitated. "Tell Star that we'll be home in a couple of hours. Don't tell her it's only for a day. Kelly and I have to be back here before any of you. Ben and Ty, you two kids have fun. Maybe, Alex can show you the night life," and Kane mischievously winked at the younger men. "Genna, you have to be where we are. Sorry, but that's the way it is. Giles, too. Maybe, you two can keep each other company." Kane smiled politely and turned to his boss. "We'll be back here tomorrow at 23.00 hours. Giles, keep your eye on Genna for a couple of hours, okay mate? Let's go, Kel. We have something to do. See you two later. Sir," and Kane mockingly saluted Buchanan. Kane grabbed Kelly's hand, led her out of Buchanan's office. The two of them headed back the way that they came. He turned and gave his squad an opportunity to have one more look at himself and his wife.

Outside, in the AFP lot, he persuaded an off-duty agent to lend him his motorcycle. He slipped the bloke a hundred and assured him he would bring the cycle back in one piece.

Kane sat astride the motorcycle and turned to face Kelly, who stood next to the machine.

"I'm sorry if this prostitution thing brings back bad memories for you. It was to be Blair's job. Kel, I promise to be with you at every turn. Pimps with prostitutes have a better chance of scoring with the people out there. It's an easy way into the drug market. Hong Kong is not Sydney and prostitution is the game. I asked Buchanan if I could take in someone else and he politely told me to go fuck myself. He said we could try the gambling houses, maybe go that way, but as far as female company, you and Genna are it." Kane pulled Kelly into his arms and she leaned against the bike. "You can still back out of this. You don't have to go, especially now." He stopped.

"Why especially now? Someone tell you something?" Kelly was too quick.

"No one said anything. Should they have? You know, Kel, I'm really busy, but I'm not blind or deaf. I did hear you throwing up a couple of times. And, I saw you eating fruit when everyone else ate that stinky fish. Maybe just some food didn't suit you, right?" He looked into her face.

She blushed and dropped her eyes. "Maybe I have food poisoning?"

Kane could see her moist eyes in the lamplight as his hand slid down to her stomach. "Maybe. Take it easy though, okay?"

"Yeah, I will… nothing serious, honest. Come on, now let's ride. That's what we both like to do best…well second best, anyway. That is why we're doing this bike ride, right?" Kelly joked.

"Yeah, baby, that's why," he reassured her. Kane kicked the motor over and revved it a couple of times.

She climbed up behind him on the bike, wrapping her arms around his waist. He left the parking lot doing a screeching seventy and headed down the coast road. Kelly felt that same thrill that she always had when she rode with Kane. He felt the cold steel between his legs and the power of the throttle in his hands. Kelly snuggled behind him, and as her stomach touched his back, she felt the gun tucked in the waistband of his pants. He was always carrying and sometimes that worried her. She could smell the freshness of him. He felt her hand slide down under his belt. Glad as he was that his wife was an expert at seducing him, he tried to concentrate and failed. Kane almost made it to the beach and stopped the motorcycle under a narrow bridge. It ground to a halt, with a screeching noise from the brakes.

"Off." He dismounted the bike.

"Me, or my clothes?" Kelly laughed.

"Both." Kane led her down under the bridge, picking a safe way to his destination.

They were not the only ones there. The homeless lay there, too. There was also a smatter of teenage guys with girls. One of them looked up from his date.

"Rich bloke, huh. You makin' out behind your wife's back?" shouted a longhaired youth.

"Could say that, mate. Could say just that," and Kane laughed.

It was the break in the tensions of the day that he needed the most. Kane looked at Kelly, who was shivering. Taking off his jacket, he handed it to her.

"Here, pull this on and you won't be so cold." Kane pulled his jacket around her. "Too crowded down here. Guess we'll just have to wait. I wanted us to have this memory to take with us to Hong Kong."

"I know that. And, honestly, I'm not cold. Not really, but it is too crowded. So, where now?" Kelly pulled his jacket tightly around her body. Actually she was freezing. She knew what he was trying to do.

"Back to the office; take Genna and Giles home with us. Giles rides a motorcycle. Bet you didn't know that." He laughed.

"What's funny?" Kelly asked curiously.

"Can't imagine Genna doing what you just did on a Harley. Let's go get them and head back to our place. I know you're anxious to see Star."

"For you, Genna just might," muttered Kelly under her breath.

Kane held Kelly's hand and pulled her back up the bank.

Respectful of its power, Kane mounted the silver dream machine.

"Sometimes, it scares me how well you know me." She slid her arms into the jacket sleeves and sat on the machine, and once more clutched him in her arms.

Back at the department, Genna and Giles waited, an awkward silence hanging in the air. Genna sat on the table, her legs swinging backwards and forwards. She was getting impatient. The other members of the group left long ago.

"They will be back soon. Kane had something he wanted to do." *'And he always gets to do what Kane wants to do.'* Giles continued. "Then we'll go with them. He'll have borrowed a motorcycle by now. I should go get one."

"A motorcycle?" Genna looked amazed.

"You can ride one, can't you?" asked Giles.

"Of course I can ride," replied Genna. *'A bicycle!'* she thought.

Buchanan's office door opened. Kane looked around for his companions. Buchanan had obviously left.

"You two ready?" yelled Kane, looking at Genna and Giles.

"Been ready for two hours, mate. Thought you two had gotten yourselves lost," Giles joked; nonetheless, underneath he was agitated. He picked up both his and Genna's packs.

"Kelly wants to see Star. You know…the motherly thing. You both can stay with us. We have two spare bedrooms," laughed Kane and nudged Giles' arm.

Kelly kicked Kane.

"That hurt," yelped Kane, while rubbing his supposedly bruised leg.

"Supposed to hurt," Kelly said, pleased that she had hurt him.

"You'll pay for that later, young lady."

"I hope so," and Kelly turned her impish face up to Kane, her eyes seducing him where he stood.

Outside, in the cool night air, Kelly stayed in Kane's jacket. They waited while Giles acquired his own transportation. Kane sat astride his motorcycle, and kept it revving. He didn't like to be kept waiting. Kelly leaned forward against his back, and when she whispered in his ear, Kane laughed aloud.

Tightening her arms around her husband's chest, she smoothed the creases of his shirt. He loved the power that even these motorcycles gave him, and he loved to feel Kelly behind him. Kelly kept glancing around her. She could sense Kane's patience was gone, and she began to wish that Giles would hurry. Finally, Giles pulled up beside Kane. The two bikes sat side by side on the lot. Kelly looked at Genna, who appeared to be terrified.

"Kane, take it slow. We'll follow you. Don't you guys wear helmets?

It's the law you know…but forgive me, I forgot. We go by Kane's law. Just give me the address in case we lose you," Giles said sarcastically, and donned his helmet.

"I'll go slow," Kane teased. "60 Manor Way. Just stay with me."

"Be the first time ever for him if he does go slow! Genna you better wrap yourself around Giles. Especially if he wants to keep up with Kane!" and Kelly's words were lost on the wind.

Slow meant eighty. Keeping up with Kane was just possible. He actually stopped for red lights. That's when they caught up to him.

"Do you have to go this fast?" yelled Genna to Giles, her voice just about reaching him.

"You want to lose them? Hold on tighter if you're scared," and Giles pulled Genna's arms across his stomach.

"Not scared. Just don't want to die right now," Genna mumbled her voice lost in the drone of engines.

Kelly snuggled into the back of Kane. It was good to feel her so close. Just like old times on his Harley. Road racing when he was young gave him the speed he still had. He'd kept his old silver Harley, complete with Australian flag on the gas tank all these years, polished and ready for action.

Pulling into the driveway of 60 Manor Way, Kane sat waiting for Giles, counting off the seconds as he lingered. It wasn't long before he heard a screech of brakes as Giles shot by the driveway to the house. Giles turned the bike around making a very illegal U-turn as he did, and pulled in behind Kane.

"Man," yelled Giles, "you still ride fast. Genna here was having a heart attack." He pulled off the helmet.

"Was not," she muttered and scrambled with some urgency to get off the bike.

"You just break the law, there, Giles? No U-turns …" Kane boomed.

"Fuck you, Kane…" and Giles parked the motorcycle.

Kelly stood on the gravel, near the front door and waited for Genna.

"Gen, want to come up with me to see Star?" Kelly asked excitedly. She still had Kane's jacket wrapped around her.

"I'd love that, Kelly," answered Genna as she followed her into the house.

Giles stared up at the house. Not a house, more like a mansion. Manor Way did the house no justice. He was surprised that it wasn't gated. Kane watched Giles' expression with some humor. He'd omitted to tell Giles anything about his luxurious lifestyle away from the AFP. Fact was that the last time out, Kane had omitted to tell Giles anything.

"What the hell are you doing on the side that affords you to have a house like this one? Even a senior agent doesn't make the kind of money it would take to own this place." Giles looked at the building. Large and spacious, he was certain that the house was something he could never afford.

"Sold my apartment block in Woolongong." He paused for effect. "AFP moved us up here after I came back from the States. Became too hot to stay in the same place. I picked the house myself. We all live here…me, Kel, Dan, Sage, and the kids. Just the way it worked out…cozy. Nice though, huh?" He could just about see the envy in Giles eyes, which interested him.

"You could say that," replied Giles.

"Want a cigarette? Kelly won't let me smoke inside of the house."

"Did I hear that right?" stammered Giles. "Kelly won't let you…"

"Yeah. Says it's bad for the kids." He pulled out the packet and was almost ready to slide a cigarette out, when Dan appeared at the door.

"Heard you were here from outback of the house. Only *Dad* rides at those kind of speeds and lives…"

"Tell me about it," echoed Giles.

"Girls go upstairs with the kids?" inquired Kane.

As Kane spoke a child with long blonde hair, and a toothless grin, ran through the door. "Daddy, she cried."

He picked the child high into the air and hugged her to him. "This is Star. Light of my life. Isn't she cute? She's missing her three front teeth. Fell off the bed."

Star returned his hugging tenfold.

"Good, God…no doubt whose kid she is," Giles replied.

"Sorry, Mr. Branson, Star got away from us." A tough looking sheila, with hair pulled back in an old style bun, burst through the doors, and strode out in brogue shoes onto the gravel.

"It's okay, we're really glad to see one another." Kane was still hugging his kid. The child clung to him as if she hadn't seen him in months.

"Maggie, this is Giles Harris. He and the young lady are staying the night." Kane turned to Giles. "Maggie comes free gratis from the AFP. For the safety of the agents, as they say. Maggie carries a .38 in her back pocket. Right, Maggie?" Kane said while smacking her on the back.

"Right, Mr. Branson. Are you coming in to see Sage?" As she smiled, a gold tooth twinkled.

Supplied, and paid for, by the AFP, this lady posed a threat to the whole of mankind, and looked as if she could take out anything single-handed. Star snuggled in close around Kane's neck. She allowed no one else to touch her. Her Daddy was home. Maggie went back inside.

"I guess we should go inside too." Kane was enjoying the night, and his child.

Giles looked around him. Something didn't seem right. The property was very splendid. There had to be countless numbers of rooms, both upstairs and downstairs… probably even room service. The cost of everything was definitely too much for Branson's pay packet. Somewhere down the line, Kane had done the AFP a favor. The AFP had paid him back. Kane said he sold the block, but this house and its accompanying security was more than required for even a special agent like Branson.

"Someone still looking for you, Kane?" asked a skeptical Giles. Something didn't smell right.

"Mate, if they were, do you think I'd leave my family here?"

Kane pushed the already opened door farther. He could hear the noise of excitement from the hallway.

Girls and children were tumbling down the stairs. Kane set his little girl down on the ground. The child clung to his leg with her small chubby arms just making her hands meet round his calf.

"Dad," Sage threw her arms around her father and kissed him. Finally, she let go of her father, and turned to the other man. "You must be Giles. Dad told me about you when I was a kid. He said that you were on his first mission."

"Hope it was all good." Giles thought Sage had Kane's blonde coloring but she seemed to be short and just a little chubby. He put his hand out to her.

She shook Giles hand. "You know how Dad lies," and Sage rested against her father.

Giles was beginning to believe that. Another small child was scrambling down the stairs. Giles Harris was beginning to wonder how many more Branson's there were hidden away. It looked as if this one seemed to belong to the Lords, which made the little girl, Kane's granddaughter… another blonde.

Kelly flopped down on the black suede couch. She rested her head back on the pillows. Pulling her long tan legs up onto the soft cushions, she let her high-heeled sandals drop to the floor. Giles was only too aware of Kelly. Genna he liked… Kelly he wanted. Kane noticed the look and smiled. Plan was dead on track but maybe the train was running faster than it should have been. Kane sat down beside her and let his hand rest gently on Kelly's legs. Slowly, his practiced fingers slid up to the end of her shorts.

Star climbed up on her father's lap and rested her small head on his chest. Her long blonde hair mixed in with Kane's tresses. Genna viewed from side stage, a place from which she would always be watching.

"Sage, you want to take the kids upstairs? I just need to keep Dan a little longer, then he's all yours, baby," Kane laughed and he handed Star over to her stepsister.

The little girl protested. She attempted hanging on to Kane. "I'll be up soon, baby. Daddy will come and tuck his little Star in bed."

Giles squirmed. He'd never heard Kane talk in such a way.

Kane waited until only the five of them remained. He offered all of them a drink. Giles noted that Kane only had an orange juice. Kane handed out the alcoholic beverages and sat down next to Kelly.

"Okay, now we're all here. Four of us will go back tomorrow to the department. Dan, you have an extra day. The four of us are going to pay the Ocean View Club a visit tomorrow night. Genna, Kelly or Sage will fix you up with some clothes. Giles, you can find something in my wardrobe to fit you. Tomorrow night, we'll stay at the base. Buchanan wants Giles and me to know a few more details. We need to know how to handle the explosives that we're picking up over in Hong Kong. Seems it's some new stuff that will come in useful for this trip. Afterwards, we wait till the dawn flight." It was all set, all arranged; just like that. "Kelly. Let's get to bed."

"Not tired," Kelly pouted, her legs dropping to the floor.

"Said bed, darling. Not sleep."

Giles coughed. "Guess we should turn in, Genna. Long day tomorrow."

Giles watched them all go up the stairs in front of him. Just one big happy family living there. Kane disappeared into Star's room and closed the door. Kelly went straight into the bedroom that she shared with Kane.

"Kelly showed me where our rooms are located." Genna interrupted his thoughts as she and Giles climbed the stairs together. Outside his door, Genna stopped. "This one's yours. Mine's right over there."

Was she coming on to him? He didn't think so.

"Goodnight, then. See you in the morning," Giles paused. "Genna, what do you think is going on here?"

"Just a happy family," she answered. Turning, the handle of her door, she also disappeared into her room.

Kelly lay back on the sheets and waited for Kane. With a quiet approach, Kane entered the room. In the half-light, Kelly saw him undressing as he slid in beside her. He leaned across the bed. Kane was naked and she could feel his body pressing against her. Once, he wore an S around his neck on a chain. Now he wore a K. She touched the jewelry. Sliding the straps down on her nightgown, he kissed her shoulders. In the lamplight, she could see the muscles in his body. Working out continually made his body great. She pushed his hair back noting the silver shades creeping into the blonde.

Kane's hand slid under her nightdress and up along her thighs. He parted her legs with his fingers and she waited expectantly. She bent her tan legs in anticipation and raised them up either side of him, her feet sliding on the soft white sheets.

Kelly moaned gently. With more urgency, her body then moved in time with his. She could feel him inside her, a feeling that she never wanted to stop.

Giles could hear through the wall. He listened to every moan that the couple made. Genna was on his mind, but Kelly was creeping very successfully into his heart. He pulled a pillow over his ears, which didn't help any.

Their hands met as Kane held Kelly to the bed. Kelly moaned louder. Kane encouraged it. One final last expression of satisfaction reached Giles' ears. He couldn't stand it. Getting out of bed, he headed for his door. Suddenly, everything became quiet in the room next door.

In her room, Genna stared blankly at the white ceiling. What would happen in the next month? She thought of Giles; afterwards, she thought of Kane. Her jealousy for Kelly increased every time she was around her. Even if there wasn't a Kelly, what would a man like Kane want with someone like her? Finally she dozed.

Daylight came too early for Kane. He was comfortable. Kelly's legs were still wrapped around him and he didn't want to move. Running his hands through her hair, he realized how silky soft to his touch it was. He pulled her hair to his face and the sweet smell of her lingered in his nostrils. The thought of his child inside of her excited him. Little Kelly, his Kelly, not some damn undercover cop picking up johns in a club in Hong Kong. That was beyond comprehension. He made a decision. She wasn't going and that was final. He would tell her when she awoke. Slowly, he pulled apart from Kelly and her long eyelashes fluttered.

"Kelly, I don't want you to go on this mission. Giles was correct when he said that I brought you along for my own reasons. I have and now, I'm beginning to feel…" Kane didn't get to finish.

"Feel what? Like you're using me to get the right response from your team? I know the truth, Kane, and that's all that matters. I know how much that you love me, and if you have to screw me in order to prove a point to the others, feel free. I know, Kane…and that's what counts."

Daughter number two disturbed her parent's conversation. Star came bouncing through the doors, wanting to be part of the grownup world. She tumbled onto the bed and giggled along with Kelly. Star jumped on Kane, and together with Kelly, tickled him until he laughed along with them.

Breakfast became a scramble of people fighting for food, except for Kelly. Bacon and eggs were more than she could handle. The smell of fresh sizzling bacon and the sight of runny yellow eggs went way over the top for her stomach. Kelly settled for some dry toast, and even then, she pushed more of it around the plate, than into her stomach. Even fresh brewed coffee smelled uncommonly bad to her today.

"You okay, Kel?" Sage inquired, noticing the hardly touched toast.

"I'm fine. Does everyone in this house know?" asked Kelly impatiently, picking up a glass of orange juice, then setting it down hard so that some spilled over the glass top.

"Know what?" interrupted Giles spooning more scrambled eggs onto his already packed plate.

"Know that I don't like bacon in the mornings," she replied, too quickly.

Kane sat at the end of the huge oak table and pondered. Surveying the big picture, Kane decided that he didn't want Kelly to go, but she obviously had advantages. Knowing the situation ahead of time, she was probably even more aware of it than he was. Yet, if Kelly had this effect on Giles, what would she do to the Chinese? Still, it was no comfort to him to be using his own wife. Kane finished his breakfast and excused himself. He needed some space from the whole situation. Stopping at Kelly's chair, he whispered in her ear and disappeared from the room. Kelly wouldn't see him again until nearly five. The afternoon passed and the four made ready for the long night ahead of them. Kelly spent time with Star in the well-groomed gardens... another little gift from the AFP. Maggie and Sage's child joined them. Kane watched from the dining room window. He wanted a son next. The door opened and Sage entered the room. Within seconds, she rested her head on her father's chest.

"What you thinking, Dad?"

Kane put his arm around her and pulled her close. "Nothing, baby. Just watching them all playing out there. God knows where we'll be two days from now. Watch out for all of you. Maggie will be here, but you're my daughter and so is Star." He pushed the drapes further apart and opened the window a fraction to get a better view of his family. "Did you know that Kelly was pregnant?" he looked down into her face.

"Is she?" Sage tried to look shocked, her cheeks turning red.

"Cut the crap. Why didn't she tell me herself?" He let go of the drapes.

Sage replied, "For the very reason that you're angry now. You wouldn't let her go with you and that would kill her. She begged us not to say anything. Kelly's only six weeks... could be a mistake. She has been under some stress..."

Kane looked at her as if she was stupid. "Stress makes you not want your favorite breakfast and throw up, does it?" He faced Sage and pushed her long hair behind her ears.

"No." She was red. "Take her, Dad. She doesn't want to be apart from you." Sage hugged him tighter.

"You girls have come a long way in these few years. Thank God that I found you both," and Kane showed far more emotion than he was given.

Kane hugged her tightly, and if Sage had not known better, she would have thought her father had shed a tear. He turned from her and left the room to face the night ahead.

Genna fidgeted by the front door. High heels, short black skirt, and one of Kelly's T-shirts made her a whole different woman. Makeup was a definite improvement. Giles was the first to notice.

"Well. What do we have here? Seems to me that we've got Kelly mark two," he stated. He was dressed in black slacks and a crisp white shirt that, until today, had belonged to Kane; it probably still should have.

"Thanks," replied Genna. "I don't feel right like this. Hope Kane knows what he's doing."

"Kane always knows what he's doing." Giles said, and thought back on the previous evening.

Down the stairs, came Kelly, in the tightest leather pants that had ever been Giles' good fortune to see. She wore a white, camisole top and black high heels to complete the picture.

"You forgot your jacket, darling." Kane carried it on his arm.

Dressed in a black leather jacket and blue molded-on jeans, Kane reminded Genna of someone out of a biker movie. He slung his gun-and-holster over his shoulder, and handed Kelly her jacket. Kane stopped his wife on the stairs.

"Here." Very slowly he opened a couple more buttons of her top, revealing a lot more cleavage.

Kelly's breasts became much more visible to the eye, especially to Giles' eyes. Very clearly, he could see the shape; soft and round. As Kane touched them, Kelly responded, her nipples becoming erect in her camisole top.

Dan surveyed the scene. He knew what Kane was doing. It was a good way to lure any enemy.

Kelly shed a tear as she kissed her child goodbye. Kane didn't let any emotions show, but he did notice that Kelly was much more sensitive now. Kane ushered Kelly out of the door to the motorcycle, one he would soon be returning to its rightful owner. Kane donned his shades, and impatiently waited for Giles and Genna. They were taking too long. He revved the throttle and Kelly wrapped her arms tightly around him. At last, the group was ready.

They flew down the highway to the club. Kane tested the smaller bike to its maximum and was impressed. The second bike was barely able to keep pace. The whole time, Giles thought about Branson's prosperity. It bothered him. Something just didn't seem right. Kane pulled in first to the club. The parking lot was packed with cars and people. Nevertheless, Kane found a couple of spaces at the back of the lot, and lingered awhile by his bike. From his jeans, he pulled his cigarettes. He lit up his usual brand while Kelly played with her hair. Pulling her lipstick from her purse, she daubed bright lips onto her face.

When Giles dismounted his bike, Kane made a suggestion. "Why don't you take the girls inside? I'll be just a minute." Kane was looking around him as if he was expecting someone.

"Okay. I'll get us a table. You better hurry, or I may run off with your wife," laughed Giles. Nonetheless, Giles wasn't joking.

"Yeah, sure you will. Take her. She's yours," and Kane smacked Kelly's rear.

Kelly blushed.

Giles accompanied the girls towards the club entrance. There were throngs of people everywhere and Giles glanced back to look for Kane. He spotted him talking to a shady looking figure.

"Friend of yours, Kelly?" asked Giles.

"Who?" Kelly's reply came quickly.

"Bloke with Kane."

"Never seen him before," she lied, without even turning around to see.

Inside the club, Giles could smell the sweet pungent odor of grass. Smoking grass was usual for a club, and a smell that Giles had been very used to at one time in his life. The table that Giles' obtained made it easy to watch the girls' picking up men.

"Watch and learn, Genna, for when we get to Hong Kong. This is what you and I will be doing seducing men… well one of us will be, anyway!" Kelly licked her lips as if she was looking forward to the fact.

"Are you serious? I can't do this. My mother would have killed me."

"But your mother won't know, will she?" quipped Kelly.

She laughed and tossed her hair back.

"That she won't," Genna mumbled, and slumped down in the red cushioned chair.

Giles turned his head to search for Kane. In the shadows, Giles spotted Kane by the back wall. He was talking with the same guy from the lot. Kelly noticed them also. She realized that it was a setup.

"Giles, why don't you buy us both a drink? You may as well get in practice for your role. Starting tomorrow you'll be Kane's right-hand man." Kelly smiled at him and hung her arm over the back of the chair. She leaned back and the buttons on her blouse pulled tight across her breasts, exposing the butterfly once more.

"Yeah, how can I forget that? Man, how the hell did I get into this mess anyway? Should have stayed home." Giles didn't look happy at being Kane's right-hand man.

"Come on, Giles, there will be some perks of the job out there," whispered Kelly.

Kelly slipped her other hand discreetly onto Giles' knee. Giles responded and closed his hand over hers. Laughingly, she tossed her head from side to side, her hair swung seductively behind her. She moved her hand carefully from under his, and patted his hand.

"Now, that wouldn't be any fun, would it? You not coming with us." She glanced back at her husband.

Kane realized that Kelly had had enough time to pursue the plan. He left his red herring by the back wall. The bloke was just that: a red herring. But doubt crept into Giles' mind.

"Okay. So we all set here?" Kane sat down between the two girls. "Everyone okay?" Kane deliberately put his arm around the back of Genna's chair and his other he let rest on Kelly's shoulder, while his fingers lightly touched the top of the butterfly. Genna noticed, and so did Giles. *So that's the way it was to be.* Three drinks later, and with a couple of lithe dancers two feet from him, Giles relaxed in his seat. Kelly stood up to use the restroom. Kane saw Giles' eyes fix onto her butt. Things were moving a little too quickly. Time to slow it down.

"Say, baby, you think you're getting the hang of this again?" asked her husband.

"Sure. Seducing men is my specialty. It can't be much different to my old way of life, can it? Genna, you want the ladies room?" Kelly picked up her purse, swung it over her back and walked away.

Genna collected her purse and joined her.

"You think that my wife is a looker, don't you?" Kane's question to Giles was direct and matter of fact. He needed to know if the mission was accomplished.

"Hell, Kane. What man wouldn't think that?"

"I agree, and I saw her hand on your knee. She did it on purpose. Told her to practice on you. Kelly does everything I tell her to. Worked though, didn't it? You get the picture?" He paused. "I asked you to look out for Genna, and by God, you'll do that, but make even the slightest little pass at Kelly and you're dead." His voice was totally under control.

"Fuck you, Kane Branson," Giles retorted.

"No, Giles. That's Kelly's job." He smiled sardonically.

CHAPTER 5

Giles' unusual display of anger didn't help. He sulked. On the contrary, Kane was flying and he loved it when his scheming paid off for him. Sitting in the corner of Commander Buchanan's brightly lit office, Giles' tension apparent. He tapped on the desk with his fingers until the Commander's icy stare stopped him dead.

Buchanan explained about a new chemical explosive called ONC, "It's a strong contender against TNT."

"So what does this ONC do that TNT can't?" asked Kane.

"It's twice as powerful as TNT, twice as dense as water, and it releases a large amount of energy, but in a small volume. When it burns, ONC almost instantly turns into a very hot gas of nitrogen and carbon dioxide," replied Buchanan.

"Well, that could come in bloody useful if we want to explode something. Point is how do we get it there?" Kane asked, as he perched on the end of Buchanan's desk at two o'clock in the morning. His shoes repeatedly kicked the desk leg.

"It will be made available to you when you're in Hong Kong. Just make certain that you get everyone there in one piece. Your flight was to leave at dawn tomorrow. There's a slight change of plan. Instead of a military flight, you'll all fly by regular aircraft. We thought that this would end up being a better cover for the mission. You go in two groups straight into HK International Airport, then through Lantau. I suggest that you get yourself some sleep, make the most of the day, but keep yourselves ready. The rest of the group gets in," he hesitated and looked down at his watch, "later this evening. I need to talk to Branson before you turn in for the night. There are some cots upstairs. Yes, actually there is just about anything that you'll need…clothes for Hong Kong, passports, money, everything… all there, upstairs, waiting," Buchanan said with some finality.

Kelly, who had been sitting quietly at the back of the room with Genna, took the hint. She jumped up out of the chair.

"Let's go take a look, Genna. We just might see something nice for bed. Plus, it will be fun, no telling what we'll find." Kelly laughed…turned back around and looked at Kane, then blew her husband a kiss.

"Cots are all together, Kelly," added Buchanan looking Kelly in the face.

"Since when does that stop Kane?" retorted Giles.

Kane didn't respond to Giles. However, he did respond to Buchanan. "Why the change of plans? Seems kind of strange the way that you're doing it. And who's this, *we* bit? Don't you think that we'll be a little bit obvious? Or, is that the reasoning behind those plans?" Kane pulled the cigarettes from his back pocket, and lit one.

"You read, Branson?" asked his boss, pointing at the NO SMOKING sign.

"Very well, actually. That's the sign I've read many times. Now, my question is, do you answer questions? Why the change? I don't like big changes in mid-stream." Kane posed the inquiries.

Buchanan didn't answer his agent's questions.

"You can all go. Just need Branson for a while longer." Buchanan sat back in the chair. "Close the door behind you, Harris."

Giles obeyed. The rest of the party left the room.

"Think they bought it?" asked the commander.

"Sure the fuck hope so. I'm beginning not to trust myself. Besides all of that, I was starting to doubt you. You made some slips that even I couldn't figure. You almost gave it away knowing that it was Paul, even when I had not told you. Fortunately, only Kelly heard. They must not have figured out that we keep in regular contact. But yes, I think they all bought it. Even Kelly's wondering though, and Genna thinks that I'm a tough guy. The lady even wants to get into my pants. Giles' anger was apparent, and he wants into Kelly's pants. We'll wait and see how Ty and Ben handle the rejection. This will be kind of fun."

"This actually what you see all of this as, Branson, fun?"

Kane squashed out the cigarette between his fingertips. "Not in the slightest." Opening the office door, he left the room. Kane climbed the stairs to the makeshift dormitory, and fumbling around in the dark, he found Kelly's cot.

"Move over, baby," Kane whispered.

"Kane, we can't, can we?" Kelly asked timidly.

"Why the hell not, baby? Both of them are asleep. And, if they're not, too bad. I'll leave before they wake." Pulling the covers back from Kelly, he climbed in beside her.

However, one of the members of the group wasn't asleep that night.

"Pass the muffins, someone," asked Ben.

Ben arrived just in time for breakfast. Ben always seemed to know when there was food. Ty was close behind his pal. Only Alex was late, still traveling on his own agenda. Alex was the sleeper of the group. Alex only let people know what he wanted them to know. His position in the team still remained a closed book. Still, he was willing to agree with Giles that Kane had changed. Kane no longer was the team player that he used to be.

The team found the morning exhausting. Kane put them through refresher paces both physical and mental. They had to be razor sharp. Kane paid special attention to Kelly. Now that he knew that she was pregnant, he didn't want anything to go wrong. He also kept his eye on two of the men with him. Giles had a tendency to turn to Alex for companionship. Although Giles and Alex had their differences, Alex made a better traveling companion for Giles than Kane did, just as Kane and Giles had made a good team in the past. Dan finally joined the crew. As the sun set over Sydney, they, at last, had their final briefing. Kelly watched the sun sink behind the opera house when her husband started speaking. Kane sat on the end of Buchanan's desk looking around the room at his final choices. There wasn't one that he questioned. They were each there for very specific reasons, ones that would slowly reveal themselves.

"As some of you may already know, there is a change of plan. The rest are getting ready to find out what is happening… Giles, you can fill them in."

Giles nodded. Dan could sense the tension between the three older men.

"Go through your things carefully, especially you two. Anything in the paperwork that you don't understand, you let me know." Kane inclined his head toward Ben and Ty. "Tonight, we'll have dinner together. You go and get yourselves some good sleep. I need you to arrive at the airport for the first departure flight. Ty, you and Alex will be traveling separately from us, just in case someone is watching. You two girls are with me. Giles, you and Dan come and go with us. Ben also. A pimp needs a good accountant…so does a legitimate businessman. And that's what we deal in, the good old honest trade of prostitution. Who knows? We may even take up gambling while we are there. Okay, so any questions?" Kane looked around the room expectantly.

"Yeah. What happens if something should befall you on this trip?" asked Giles.

"Nothing is going to happen to me on this or any other trip. So you just mind your own business and leave my business to me."

Kane's steely eyes flashed at his companion. It was a public warning and the rift between he and Giles widened.

As the evening shadows shortened, so did the tempers of the team. Even Kelly felt that Kane was riding her. She took off with Genna and Ty to watch some game on Ben's computer. Kane and Dan sat outside on the department steps and watched the world go by. Kane puffed on his cigarette and Dan drew stick men with his finger in the soil. Finally, Dan spoke.

"So what do you think? Think they are beginning to dislike you yet?" asked Dan.

Kane thought for a moment. Smoke rings floated in the air.

"Not all of them. Ty thinks that I'm a father figure and Ben thinks that I'm the best for taking him along. You know, it's funny. No one has mentioned Paul's death. It's like they figured it's one less competitor. Probably a good job I said that Ben was coming back before the whole mission is complete, or, he wouldn't make it back either…poor bastard would be eliminated by his own countrymen. Doesn't make sense. One of them, or someone in the department, is the culprit. Only so many people knew where we were. There's you, me, Kelly, Genna, Ty, Ben, Alex, Giles, Blair, Paul, Buchanan, and the pilots. Common sense tells me that it's not you or I. Kelly, I trust with my life, even if she did go and play some stupid computer game. Then, there's Paul and Blair and they are history…"

"You don't like it when she does things with her own age group, do you, Dad?" Dan didn't look up from creating art.

"That obvious?" asked Kane.

"Yeah…you have nothing to worry about, you know that. Those blokes are just boys in Kelly's eyes."

"Deep down, I know that, but it just worries me. I worry about that girl. Sometimes, well…, never mind. But what really scares me is if the one person that we really trust isn't truly trustworthy after all."

"You think the culprit's Buchanan?" asked Dan.

Kane shrugged his broad shoulders.

Dan continued, "If it is Buchanan, we're really in trouble. He'll send us in and never fetch us out; we'll be on our own. You're right. No one did mention Paul again. Didn't you ask Giles to watch for Genna? Then, tonight, I caught him watching both girls. You notice?" Dan asked with some sensitivity.

"I noticed. I set the trap. The man then sprung at the bait, but he won't let go of the bait. That's what will be his problem down the road. Time we set Alex to work. He's been very quiet so far. But then, Alex always is quiet. Still gets what he wants." The last sentence was spoken with conviction. "On the plane, you and I are going to have a disagreement. I'll accuse you of knowing that Kelly's pregnant and she'll go along with it. She'll be as surprised as you will be only her surprise will be genuine. It will make Giles even angrier toward me for bringing her. He'll even be pissed because she's carrying my kid. Right now, he doesn't think that I'm a fit enough person. Maybe then, he'll turn to Genna. She likes him, and actually, she'd be good for him. I still wish that Kelly wasn't going."

"But she is, Kane, and she'll be just fine."

"Yeah." He scrubbed the earth with his boots and Dan's stick men disappeared.

The two of them joined the rest of the group inside for dinner. The stage was dressed, ready for the performance. It was all just a rehearsal. Buchanan joined them. Ben took three people's share of the roast lamb. Kelly picked at hers, and the others moved the dinner from plate to mouth in silence. Aside from tension, nervousness began to show. Six men and two women were getting ready to embark on the mission of a lifetime. Kane stopped eating from the last supper on Australian turf, and looked around the table. For a moment, he saw empty chairs, and then the specter disappeared. Some of them weren't coming back. And it terrified him.

Kane lay awake on his regimental cot. Sleep wouldn't come. He watched Kelly in the light from the window. He watched her until full light streamed in across her pillow and onto her long, curly hair. Noticing how she had changed from the twenty-one-old that he had first slept with, Kane thought of how he had come to love her more than life itself. *If anything should happen to her…* He pushed the thought from his mind. Slowly he drifted…

Kane swaggered down the aisle of the plane in his flash gray suit. Two high-heeled and short-skirted girls tottered behind him... a couple of high-class hookers. It was obvious to the first-class passengers what he was, and first class was horrified when Kane took the last row of seats in their luxurious compartment. Ben and a shaded Giles sat in the row in front of them. Dan sat a couple of rows away. In the economy class, Alex complained to Ty.

"Gets first class everything, doesn't he? Makes me sick, mate." Alex leaned back in the well-used seat.

Ty stared at Alex. This was the first time that he had spoken about the subject aloud. "I don't mind. Just getting to go, makes it all worthwhile." Ty fiddled with his seat and tried out the table.

"You're just a kid. Wonder what you'd think if you were a vet? One, who had done as many years as I have." Alex peered at Ty over the top of the shades. "Dressed like that, I can see why Kane has ended up being some kind of hero to you. You damn well look like him. Maybe you're his long lost son." Alex laughed. He was joking.

Ty smiled a wry grin, with his blonde hair flopping onto his face.

"Long flight, darling. Want to sleep some? You, too, Genna," inquired Kane.

Kane let the first class grey seat recline. It was almost a bed. Kelly fidgeted. She dozed and then ate. After she and Genna talked, Genna slept. Genna's head fell on Kane…one girl, on either side of him. Kelly became jealous, and Kane noticed the looks that were exchanged between the two girls. Kane whispered in Kelly's ear. She blushed as he slid his hand onto her thigh. Kelly's face flushed red-hot and she giggled softly.

Although the giggle was only soft, Giles had overhead. His resentment grew. Dan sat back in his seat and watched with interest. When Giles hit the bathroom, the look in his eyes spoke volumes. Kane was right about him. Dan made a note to watch out for Giles. Ben played with his computer. He wasn't yet aware of the problems. The plane dipped. Crossing oceans was often turbulent. Kelly excused herself and hurried down the plane to the bathroom. She threw up, and held onto the sink. Kelly washed her face and cleaned herself up best she could.

'*Turbulence,*' she thought. '*Has to be, can't be the baby this fast,*' and she returned along the isle to her seat.

"You okay, darling?" Kane's concern was genuine.

"Fine, Kane. Just the turbulence." Before she could even completely answer him, she began to feel sick again.

"Hope that's all. Not something you want to share with us is there, baby? You know you have a job to do out there." His voice was just loud enough for the row in front to hear.

"Kane…you said…" She looked astonished.

"Not just turbulence, is it? You've gone and got yourself pregnant again, haven't you? Even after what I said?" All his sentences seemed to hold double meanings.

Dan leaned over to Kane… right on cue. "What's up, boss?"

"Think our Kelly didn't listen to me. Think the little lady has gone and got herself pregnant again. Isn't that right, Kel?"

Staring blankly at Kane, she could not believe that she was hearing him correctly. *Why was he embarrassing her so badly?*

"You didn't know, boss?" asked Dan.

"Did you?" retorted Kane.

"Sure," laughed Dan. "Most of us did."

The look of disdain shocked even Dan. Giles leaned over the opulent seat and stared at Kane.

"Man, you can't take her in like that." Giles voice wasn't so quiet either.

"I'm sick from the flight, that's all," whined Kelly, trying hard to get the subject to end and everyone to quit focusing on her.

"That's not what you told me," compounded Dan.

Kelly stared at Dan.

"Damn you, Kelly. Fancy getting yourself pregnant right now." Kane's face was one of indignation.

"Hey, Kane, it takes two. You, of all people, should know that," interrupted Giles.

"You, keep out of this. Who in God's green earth says it's my kid, anyway? This baby could belong to anyone of the johns. And Dan, from now on your loyalty is to me, not to Kelly."

"Boss!" and Dan looked away slightly embarrassed.

Kane was careful not to mention the word wife. He wasn't sure who was listening. The charade had begun in such a dramatic fashion. First class would never be the same again. Passengers and cabin crew alike were stunned by Kane's actions.

Kelly bit the inside of her lip and turned her face away, not wanting anyone see her reaction.

When Kane thought that no one was looking, he slid his hand onto hers and squeezed Kelly's fingers. He didn't turn her way. She returned the gesture, but still felt a little fearful of what he was truly feeling about her. The words stung like a bee, and a tear trickled down her face.

Hours of flying took its toll on all of them. Kane headed for the bathroom. Kelly understood what he was doing, just not the way he was going about it. He was gone for some time, far longer than it took to take a piss. She figured that he was calling Buchanan from his cell phone, which now lived in its usual place in Kane's boot. Genna, Giles, and Ben were all asleep. Dan moved past Genna into Kane's seat.

"Sorry, Kelly. Kane's orders," he whispered. "He'll explain. Just go with the flow."

She smiled, but Dan could see a sadness that she hadn't been confided in, and a hurt in her eyes that wasn't there previously. Dan moved just in time from Kane's seat. Kane returning from the bathroom, sauntered back down between the seats, and sat his well-tailored butt in his chair.

Dan followed up with the conversation. "Boss, want to apologize for holding out on you. Really thought you knew," confessed Dan.

"Yeah, sure you did. Now, get back to your own fuckin' seat," Kane ordered.

As the two crossed paths, Dan had whispered in Kane's ear while cutting his eyes over to Kelly. Kane shifted into his seat. He saw the look in Kelly's eyes. There was nothing he could do to remove it at the moment… there would be time to repair the damages later.

Kelly turned and looked out through the glare of the sundrenched window. They were on the descent…over Lantau, now. In the afternoon sun, she could see a vast expanse of water. She peered more closely.

"That, darling, is Lake Phenomenon," he said loudly. Kane continued in a quieter voice. "So named because of its remarkable shape. And because of the way that the mountains rise up out of it."

Kelly had never seen anything like it. Watching the view caused her to forget the previous few hours. "It's phenomenal. That's what I'll call it. Do we get to go there at some point?" she asked.

"Maybe," came the reply.

Kane hoped she didn't. That's where the prison was located.

As the plane taxied on the runway, Kelly peered out the window. Suddenly she was nervous. She didn't know why. Hong Kong International was not what she expected. From the runway, the place seemed ultramodern.

"We're here, Kel. Remember, you'll survive at any cost," he whispered with meaning, and then Kane was up and moving. Typical Kane. "Get your things, ladies!" he boomed. "We have ourselves a mission. I need money and a few other things. Let's get moving here." Pulling the bags down, he handed them to the girls.

They had traveled 4,500 miles, across land and sea, and all he could do was boss them. Giles had just about had enough of Kane's domineering ways.

"Go drop fucking dead," Giles whispered.

"You say something, Harris?" demanded Kane, looking him square in the eyes.

"Nothing, *Mr.* Branson, sir." Giles easily reached his luggage from the overhead bin.

They shuffled down the plane at a laborious pace. First class or not, everyone filed out the same way, even Kane. Huge doors heralded International customs. False passports issued by the AFP passed through customs without any problem, and outside in the stuffy air a car waited for them. Kane and his little entourage piled inside the car. Kelly accidentally snagged her skirt on the car door. She looked annoyed.

"No problem. You won't be needing that skirt much, anyway!" sniggered Kane.

At that point, Kelly decided Kane was enjoying this little charade a little too much. It was getting dark when the spacious limo pulled up outside of the hotel. Skyscrapers shot into the sky like fingers of destiny pointing upwards. Giles paid the driver. He glanced out of the back window looking for the other car. Alex and Ty followed in a small, stuffy taxi.

"Don't say it, Mr. Powers. It's even getting to me, now." Ty fidgeted in the backseat.

"Really? Was beginning to think that it was just me... it didn't really bother me 'til the plane. Now, it's bothering me even more. Bet we get the smallest room… while, they all live in the penthouse suite. Think the bastard will invite us up for a drink?"

"Kane's a good bloke. Just doing his job, I guess." Doubt began creeping in for Ty.

In the hotel suite, Kane reached under the tables, behind the picture frames, and around the edges of the lamps. It was clean. He didn't really expect anything but clean. No one outside of the department knew that they were there…yet.

Kelly stared around her. "If this is how pimps live, quit your day job," she joked. '*Time I lighten up*,' she thought.

Kelly longed to be on her own with Kane, and to hear his explanations. Nonetheless, she was unable to get her wish, as he moved from room to room. There were two large bedrooms. One contained two beds and a spacious couch, bathroom and shower room, and the other with a king-sized bed, and a double bathroom. The main room housed a large leather couch big enough to seat four.

Sitting down on it, Kane unbuttoned his jacket, and threw it on the back. The jacket flopped there and then he plumped up the cushions.

"Got my bed. Just need a blanket. You girls take the double room." Kane looked at Giles and the other two guys. "You three can have the big room. Make yourselves at home." Kane put his trademark snakeskin boots on the marble table.

"I can sleep out here, sir. You and Kelly can have the room," chimed in Genna.

"It's okay. Kelly knows where I am," replied Kane flippantly.

"How long we gonna stay here? Kind of cramped, even for a penthouse." Giles was still irritated.

"Long as it takes in order to make the right contacts… few days at most. Then we move through the island." Kane pulled the phone toward him. "Anyone up for room service? I'm starved."

"Yeah, you look like you're starving," retorted his wife.

Kelly sat down next to Kane and put her arm through his. Not her usual action. He glanced at her.

"Want me to help you with the luggage?" He needed to talk to her and now seemed a good time a time to do so.

"Please. Order the food first, though." Kelly was unusually quiet.

Ben set his laptop on the table. He looked tired, with lines under his eyes, as did the rest of them. Dan headed for the bedroom. There were indeed three places to sleep. He dropped his bag on one of the multicolored bedspreads. Ben could take the couch, as he was the youngest.

"Dan, what you want to eat?" Kane yelled.

"Anything is fine," came the muffled reply from the bathroom.

Kane dialed the number for room service. He waited. Then he mumbled something that sounded like words down the phone. All Kelly understood was cigarettes. She wasn't aware that Kane could speak such fluent Chinese.

"Okay, that's done. Now, Kel, let's go."

Kane rose from the couch and took Kelly's bag. The rest of the group watched with interest. He smiled a leering gesture at the party as he closed the door behind them. Kane sat down on the enormous bed and leaned back on the luxurious white covers, his boots resting on the end of the bed.

With a slight grin on his face, he said to Kelly, "Go on, say it. You're pissed off with me because I did that on the plane. Had no choice. You know that. And you are pregnant, so what's your problem?" His plan was to try to distance himself from her.

"I'm on your side, Kane. Couldn't you have found another way to tell them and to get Dan? I know what you're doing. I also know why Alex and Ty are in some tiny little room out back. But, to use me…" She yelled, and then she floundered. Kelly sat her tight little butt on the oak table.

Kane stood up from the bed. "Stop right there! I offered you a way out back in Sydney. You wanted no part of it then. I told you, when we got on the plane, I'm your boss. Being your husband has to be second-ary until this gets done. Get that straight, right now. Eat tonight and get some sleep. I'll see you in the morning."

"But I thought…" She stood up in front of him, a bewildered look on her face.

"Then you thought wrong. I'm tired, too." He turned away from her and headed for the door, his hand reaching out for the handle.

"You son-of-a-bitch. I'm your wife. Don't you turn your back on me," she yelled.

He stopped, but never turned back. "And you, Agent Branson, are way out of line." He carried on turning the door handle.

"Sir, yes, sir," she replied sarcastically.

Kane smiled to himself. "Around midnight might be good." Never looking back, he left the room, closing the door behind him. Kane glanced around the room.

"Kelly's just fine… that's just in case some of you are interested," and he sat down once more on the couch.

The observers dropped their heads and busied themselves. Things were going down pretty much as Kane wanted them to go. A few minutes later, Kelly emerged from the bedroom. She glanced around the group. No one looked up at her.

Alex and Ty got the call for dinner and arrived on the scene seconds after Kelly. Ben opened the door, and let then in the suite. They sauntered across the room to where Kane sat on the couch.

"Nice place." Alex fingered the velvet drapes and ran his hand along the back of the soft leather couch. "So which poor soul gets this luxurious couch to sleep on tonight?"

"Kane," replied Giles as he moved to the drinks cabinet.

"Interesting. Did Kelly come to her senses and kick you out of her bed?" Alex asked.

"That's a statement that I would expect from Giles, Alex, not you. Obviously, you've never had sex on a leather couch, Mr. Powers. I would have thought you had. What's your room like?" Kane asked nonchalantly, brushing the dust from his snakeskin boots.

"You fuckin' know what it's like. You made sure that Ty and I had the smallest room in the place. Frightened that we might get us some company for ourselves?" and Alex wheeled around to the front of the couch.

"Made sure that you had no room for that." Kane was positively unpleasant. "And by the way, don't you start. I've gotten enough hassle from Giles, over there."

Alex was about to reply, when a knock at the door heralded room service, interrupting the argument. Buchanan had thought of most things. Traveling money had accompanied the passports. Kane slipped the bell-boy some change, as he wheeled in a trolley full of great-looking foods to the middle of the room. Fresh fruits, pastries, rice, different kinds of meat and sauces, and several kinds of tea and juices, filled the air with all kind of aromas.

Kane hadn't touched base with Buchanan since they arrived. Now, while they were all occupied with the succulent foods, Kane slipped into the bedroom and called 'home-base.' Kelly noticed that he was gone, and appeared not to be the only one who thought he was making a too-long pit stop. Giles watched with interest. Kelly set her half empty plate down on the marble table and went in search of her husband. Closing the bedroom door, she tapped gently on the bathroom door.

"You okay?" Kane's mild heart attack some years ago had always been a concern, although it had been ensued because of some particular incidents in their lives. And the stress right now wasn't helping. Trying the door handle, she found that it wasn't locked. "Kane? I'm coming inside." Kelly pushed open the door open.

Finishing his call, Kane waited with anticipation for Kelly. He was behind the bathroom door. He slipped out from behind the door, and encircled Kelly with his arms. Turning her expertly around, he kissed his wife hard on the mouth, almost taking her breath away.

It was a few minutes before anyone noticed that both Kane and Kelly were missing.

"Where'd they go?" asked Dan.

"Where do you think?" replied Alex. "He really does like to make enemies, doesn't he? You know, Giles, maybe you had a point back in Australia. Maybe, I'll keep to myself just a little more. I could do with a drink, and a woman. 'Specially a woman." Alex glanced at Genna.

Genna cringed.

"Think later that I might just go find myself both," continued Alex.

Genna was well aware that she was the only woman in the room. She'd been watching Giles. But the man worried her. She saw him watch Kelly. But then, all the guys watched Kelly. What normal man wouldn't look at her? And now, Alex was surprisingly angry with Kane and his lust for Kelly. Her thoughts were interrupted as Kelly came back through the room. She had a glow about her and the hooks on her blouse were on the wrong eyes. Kane followed at a leisurely pace. Kelly sat down on the couch, and Kane stood next to her.

"Leave any food for me?" asked Kane.

"Thought you probably already tasted dessert," Alex commented in a low tone.

"Watch your mouth, Alex. I thought that you and I were friends. One more crack like that…"

"And what?" He got right in Kane's face. "You need me. Just like you need every one of us in this room. You got a mission to fulfill and I know you well enough to know that you won't stop till you succeed…or fail."

"I don't fail…not ever." The two men stared at one another.

"No? I'm sure that Giles remembers last year. Maybe, you're a little too overconfident this time. Maybe Kelly is on your mind too much," stated Alex.

"And maybe, you're just too full of shit. In fact, I think that you might just need some of it knocked out of you, like Giles did. Why this sudden aggravation from you?" Kane's voice boomed, and he took a step closer to Alex.

"Maybe, 'cause you have something that we all don't. We used to share everything, remember? And maybe, you would have been better off if you had left your wife behind. She's gonna get us all killed. Oh, not directly, but because your mind seems not quite as focused as it once was. And possibly, I would like to have me a woman...or hadn't that thought crossed your mind? Seeing you constantly screwing Kelly would make some of us just a little jealous, don't you think?"

Fifty-four, Kane maybe. Over the hill, he certainly wasn't. Sensing serious trouble now, Dan stepped in between them, his hands on Kane's chest.

"Boss, this isn't the time or the place. Think about it."

Kane turned his head away. Alex sniggered. Dan still held his hand on his father-in-law's chest. Ben was embarrassed, and Ty watched with amusement. Now, he was playing in the grownup's world.

"Alright. I'll let it go... this time. Still, you bring Kelly and me up again, and you're dead, Powers." Kane turned from the situation and walked away. Grabbing his keys, Kane, left the suite, striding out into the lobby. Kelly grabbed her purse and went after him.

"Does he have her on a chain or what?" asked Giles sarcastically.

"It's called devotion, Giles. You must have had that once in your life," commented Dan.

"You Branson family. You always get the best of everything." Alex turned to go. "Now that they are gone, I'm going...to find what I want. You coming, Ty? Share a drink with me?"

"Nah. I'll just finish the food off and then get me some sleep." He still found it amusing. Ty finished his plate of rich smelling rice. Too much good food to leave it behind.

"Fuck you!" and Alex slammed the suite door behind him.

After Kane hit the elevator button, it was there in seconds. They stepped inside and took it to the second floor.

"Want a drink, Kel? Feel like a hard drink." Kane also had other reasons for stopping at the bar.

"No, you don't. And I can't. You know that," she reminded him.

"Yeah, baby, sorry. Let's just take a walk out in the street. No one gonna see us this late at night. And anyway, a pimp doesn't pay for his tricks," he laughed. At least the tension was sliding away.

Kane took hold of her hand, and they took the stairs to the ground floor.

"Let's hope," she muttered as they went through the main doors.

Only the doormen watched them go. Outside, Kelly stopped and pulled at her shoes.

"What you doing?" Kane asked.

"Damn heels are killing me. I can walk barefoot. Hong Kong streets can't feel much different to Sydney walkways." Something caught her eye. "Look at that fountain over there. It's beautiful. Let's go see it."

She held the shoes and purse in her hands, and her eyes were alight, glowing in a darker world. Without warning, Kane picked her up in his arms and carried her to it. She was light in his grasp. He sat her down on the side on the stonework, and Kelly dangled her hand in the water. Kane dusted off the ledge and sat down next to his wife. Small cherubic stone angels spouted water from their mouths and it flowed back into the ever-decreasing water under her fingers.

"What's wrong, Kane? Everyone is turning against you. But you know that. There's something else. You can trust me. We've been through too much for you not to trust me. Tomorrow is a new day. But there is something else wrong that no one upstairs knows."

He looked her in the eyes. He stroked her hair in the lamplight. Kane loved her very much. How could he tell her that he'd received a letter from a woman in Lantau? How could he tell her that this woman claimed to have a child? How could he tell her that he had to find and kill this child? And how, in God's name, would he tell her that this was his son, and that he was a Chinese agent?

"There's nothing, baby," he lied. "We just have to find out who's passing the info along. Nothing else. Time for you to get some rest… long day ahead. You get to become the leading lady in the next part of this charade. Tomorrow we visit the Club Coco."

"The club what? You're making that up, aren't you? Maybe, I'll get lucky," she teased.

"Oh, you will, baby, with me!"

Kelly threw her arms around her husband's neck, complete with shoes and purse still in her hand. Kane carried her back inside the hotel. In the elevator he set her down, and held her close. His thoughts were still in turmoil from his brain veering towards his other reason for being here. He tried to think clearly, and hit the stop button on the elevator panel. It jolted and stopped, and the pair stepped out, eventually…

"Where the fuck have you been? You've been gone for ages. Something happened after you left," yelled Giles almost hysterically.

Kane looked around the room. Alex was missing. He felt a surge of undeniable disbelief. Kelly felt his hand tighten on hers.

"Not Alex!" Kane exclaimed.

"What do you mean, *not* Alex'?" Giles glanced at the others. "Where have you been anyway?" He smacked his hand on the door, and it slammed closed reacting to the pressure. "Damn stupid question!"

Kane turned and caught Giles by the shoulders. "Tell me it's not true."

"He walked out of the room. Said that he was going to get what you had… a woman, and something else to drink. Ty and Ben went to look for him and Alex had gone already. What the hell did you think that I meant?" Giles clenched his hands on Kane's arms. "You thought he was dead, didn't you? My god, which one of us is next? Which one of us are you going to get killed?"

He looked deeply into Kane's eyes and saw something that he had never seen before. The hunter was becoming the hunted. Kane released his grip, but Giles didn't.

"What the hell do you know that we don't? Don't you think that it's about time that you told us what is going down here? Bet even Kelly, doesn't know the real truth," protested Giles.

Kane looked at Giles' hands. "Get your hands off me… now. And don't ever put them there again!" He was a deadly missile waiting to destroy its target.

Giles removed his hands instantly from Kane. Even he knew where to draw the line.

"You were supposed to keep an eye on him, Ty. Why the hell, do you think that I put the two of you together? Alex likes to drink. Always has. Just a very well-kept secret," yelled Kane.

It was all coming apart in front of his eyes. Kane wanted them at least where he could see them. He needed to regroup, and fast.

"You want me to go look for him again? The bar's still open in the hotel…" offered the young agent.

"No. You messed up once, and we need to stay together. Change of plans. Ben, you go camp out with Ty. I suggest that we all try to get some sleep." Leaning across to Kelly, he whispered in her ear. She scurried away to the bedroom.

Dan lay awake on the hard bed. What was really on Kane's mind? Even he was confused. They were here to find where the information was coming from about the drugs. But there was more. Much more. Staring at the white tiled ceiling, he thought of his daughter…he missed Sage.

He didn't miss Giles' snoring. It was loud and irritating and kept him awake.

In the other room, Genna was asleep. Kelly was waiting, doing what she was told. She could see Genna, innocent and untouched. Kelly slid her hands down her body. She ached inside, wanting Kane. He was her obsession. She got him quicker than she anticipated.

"Police…open the door. Sirs, open the door." The banging was enough to wake the dead, and the neighboring suites.

"What the fuck?" Giles came around very quickly from his slumbers.

Kane jumped off the couch and ran into the girl's room.

"Move over," he yelled.

"What?"

"Kelly, move over and let me get between the two of you." Bare-chested, he climbed into the bed.

Dan knew what to do. He suspected that something was about to happen and checked the room to make sure Kane was ready. Dan walked calmly to the suite door and peered through the peephole. They were police all right. Chinese uniformed branch. Dan opened the door. Dan opened the door. "You want something, officer?" hoping they spoke English.

"You, this your suite? You Mitter Brandon?" a Chinese looking official with the uniforms asked.

"No. *Mitter* Brandon is in the bedroom. Who are you?" replied Dan.

"We go to bedroom." He started forward.

Giles stood in his way, arms folded across his chest and glaring down at the little man. "Maybe, maybe not. You got a warrant?"

"No, sir, have news for Mitter Brandon. Name is Inspector Chow."

They let him by. The little man knocked on the door, not waiting for an invitation. His eyes popped. Kane lay between the two girls, one on each arm. Kelly draped herself across her husband her breasts resting on his chest. Genna was quivering against him.

"Come in, why don't you? This better be good." He pulled Genna closer. "You can see I'm busy." The man might be working with Buchanan, but he was also Chinese.

"Mitter Brandon? I have some bad news. Can you come with me to headquarter? We think we have your man, Alex Powers." Chow hovered.

Both girls felt Kane's muscles tighten.

"You think you have? For god's sake, just ask the man his name. Or is he that drunk? Knowing Alex, he had too much to drink…that it?" laughed Kane.

"No, sir. He's that dead."

CHAPTER 6

"Say that again?" Kane asked, rising up from the pillows.

"Mitter Powers, he dead," Chow said, in his less-than perfect English. "They found him in alley behind our headquarters. Officer thought he drunk, but he dead. Want autopsy. You have to come wit me and check. Make sure who it is. We found passport with his name."

Chow's eyes circled all three people, a menage-a-trois. Was this man really an Australian Federal agent? He'd heard of his reputation. He didn't think it went this far.

Kane wasn't sure of Chow. On the surface he looked okay. But how were they able to find Powers that fast? And how did Chow know where to find Kane? Too many questions and way too few answers.

"So where are we going?" asked Kane.

"Just to headquarter, Mitter Brandon. Car will take and bring you back." Chow hovered.

"You really want to blow my cover, mate? Jesus. Why don't you just announce to the world who I am?" Kane climbed over the girls and out of bed. "You girls wait for me. Stay right here in this room."

Giles and Dan hovered in the doorway like two bluebottles on the wall.

"Get your shirt and jacket on, Giles. You're coming with me," Kane said as he passed by them.

"What's the matter, Kane, don't trust me with the girls?" questioned Giles, staring a hole through Kane.

"Something like that." Kane passed Giles in the doorway. Kane reached in his luggage from beside the couch and found a sweater. He pulled the thick brown wool sweater over his head, and straightened the neck of it. Pushing his gun down inside the back of his Levis, Kane announced, "I'm ready!"

Giles frantically pulled on his clothes in an attempt to keep up with Kane, something he would never achieve.

"Let's get this over with quickly. Dan, stay with the girls. Okay, Mr. Chow, let's go."

Kane pushed past Chow and out the door. Giles hopped across the floor still pulling on his leather shoe. Kane pressed the elevator button. Inside the elevator, Kane was calm; too calm. Leaning against the elevator's glass walls, he stared straight ahead. In contrast, Giles was nervous and showed it by shuffling from one foot to another. Chow studied the two men. He had been filled in, more or less, and now he was making his own assumptions. Kane was dominant, tough and was the leader of the pack. Kane was the hunter.

"Think they'll be gone long, Dan?" Kelly asked, as she emerged from the bedroom pulling a thick, white hotel robe tightly around her.

"Don't know. It sure does make a mess of the plans, though. Better get Ty and Ben back up here. Tell them the good news," he said sarcastically and turned in the direction of the phone.

"Good news?" shrieked Genna climbing out of the bed and stepping through the open doorway. "Good news? Is that what you call it? Alex is dead and you call it good news? And you," she looked at Kelly, "you didn't even flinch. What kind of people are you?"

"Federal police kind of people, professional ones. We're the kind of people who don't show emotions very often. I don't remember you being this freaked out over Paul being murdered. So why Alex? You like him or something?" Dan remarked with a side-wards glance at Genna.

"I don't believe you said that, Dan Lord. In fact, I don't believe any of this. One by one, the team is dying, and no one seems to care!" Genna was indignant, and raised her arms as to gesture the point.

Kelly sat on the edge of the couch and lit up a cigarette, something she didn't do very often. Her robe slipped slightly, allowing the butterfly tattoo to show above the gown. "What would you like us to do? Can't bring him back. And you're wrong, we do care. Kane cares. They were friends for a long time. Just 'cause he don't always show it…well, he cares; cares about everyone. Guess Ben will go with us now for the whole trip. And you and me, babe." Kelly finished the sentence and waited for a reaction.

Genna appeared to be horrified. "All the way in?"

"All the way in," was Dan's reply.

Their conversation was interrupted by a knock on the suite door.

"Yeah…" Dan moved over to the door and carefully opened it.

"Cop in the lobby let us by after we proved that we worked for Mr.

Branson. What's going on up here? Is it Alex? Did he do something other than get really drunk? For some reason, he's not so bright lately. So why the cop out there in the hallway? And where's the boss?" asked the first head around the door.

"Which question would you like answered first, Ty? Alexis dead. Not sure how that happened yet. Boss is on his way to the local headquarters of Hong Kong's finest to identify the body with an Inspector by the name of Chow. Giles is with him. Did I leave out anything?" queried Dan.

"Yeah, you left out the bit about us all going the whole way with in," added Kelly.

Kelly glanced at Ty. Ben stood like a flabby statue. Kelly followed the stare from his eyes, realizing that the robe she had pulled on was reveal-ing too much of her breast, so she pulled it tighter. *So Ben did notice other things aside from computers.* After taking one more puff on the cigarette, she put it out.

Ty sat down on the straight-backed chair. "What? How? When did it happen? I don't believe this. I should have gone when he asked me. I thought that when he wanted to go get a drink, he would just go to the bar downstairs… Are you sure Alex is dead?" His eyes stared ahead of him.

"That's what Kane has gone to determine. Don't think he believes it either. You guys bring your things up here. Be better if we all stayed together tonight. We'll make do in the suite somehow, not that many of us will get sleep tonight. I'll get coffee sent up," stated Dan. He assumed responsibility in Kane's absence.

"That's it; you'll get coffee sent up for us? Haven't we been through this before with Paul?" yelled Ben.

He had come to life. And had mentioned Paul. He was the second of the young agents to do so. The others stared at him. Ben was shaking. Kelly slid off the couch and stood next to him.

"Ben, it's okay. We're not absolutely positive that it is Alex yet." She took his arm and sat him on the couch.

Dan watched her. She was a natural. Then, she had a good teacher. He wondered what his boss was doing right now. All they could do was wait until he returned.

"This going to take long, Inspector Chow?" Kane asked as they walked through the hotel lobby and into the night air.

If Chow had known Kane better, he'd have known the Australian was being sarcastic by using the term Inspector.

"Only have to identify your man, and then you can go back to your women."

The term women, was good. That meant he didn't know Kelly was a Branson. Evidently, Buchanan hadn't told him everything. Chow obviously believed that Kane was undercover working as a pimp. Perfect. Buchanan didn't trust Chow completely. And Kane didn't trust Chow or Buchanan.

They reached the parking lot, escorted by two uniformed cops. The night was dark. Out of the half-light, stepped a lone figure. No one saw him behind the pillar. No one saw their shadow get into another car. No one noticed the headlights follow the Inspector's car downtown to headquarters. Or park on the other side of the parking lot when they arrived there.

Inside the grey, stone building, Chow led the way. With ID tags swinging round the visitor's necks, they followed the Inspector. Giles and Kane hadn't spoken to each other the whole trip. Giles didn't appreciate the casual attitude about death that Kane seemed to be adopting. Chow stopped the procession at the mortuary door.

"It not pretty, Mitter Brandon," and Chow opened the door.

"Death never is," Kane replied, and stepped inside the open door.

However, even Kane wasn't prepared for what greeted his eyes. Someone was dead all right. The body in front of him was beyond recognition. Someone had beaten this person to death. The man had a disfigured face. He had been possibly beaten to death with a baseball bat. There was a distinct smell of alcohol that filled Kane's nostrils.

"You think that Powers?" asked Chow.

Kane felt anger and revenge all in one go. He thought it was Powers. Was he sure? No. If it was Alex, someone was sending Kane a message loud and clear. *Someone was eliminating the suspects for him. Weren't they?* Kane recognized the clothing and the onyx ring Alex always wore. The dead man appeared to be the same height and build as Alex, but was it Alex?

"You find his passport and papers on him?" asked Giles.

"We did. They in plastic bag for Mitter Brandon. I called your embassy in Australia to let them know one of your people was dead."

"Wasn't that jumping the gun there, mate? What if it turns out not to be him?" retorted Kane.

"Tell me your gut reaction though, do you believe it is him?" asked the Inspector.

"Yes," replied Kane, and turned away from the body.

"You sure, Kane? It could be anybody under all that blood," argued Giles.

"I'm sure," he lied. "Go ahead. Do your autopsy. Can't for the life of me see why you want to though… it's pretty damn obvious what caused this man's death."

"Is it, Mitter Brandon? I don't think it that obvious and I suspect neither do you. I think he already dead when he battered like rag doll."

Giles turned away and headed for the door. It gave Kane the opportunity that he needed. Turning his back to the body, he rolled up Alex's sleeve. In the crook of the arm was a pinhole. Alex never injected drugs. If it was Alex, someone OD'd him. If it wasn't him, someone had gone to a whole lot of trouble in order to convince the police and himself that it was Alex. Kane felt sick. His heart began racing. Who hated him enough to kill the whole team? His team. He thought of Kelly and Dan and the others who were relying on him. How could he protect them and still finish the job? He had to have allies. Whom did he trust the most? When he went back to the suite, he would tell two of them everything.

"You still think it Mitter Powers?" whispered the Inspector.

"Yes." But Kane wasn't positive.

"Okay. You go. Car will take you back to hotel. Tomorrow, you do what you have to do." Chow continued whispering to Kane. "Mitter Buchanan told me why you here."

Of that, Kane was sure. Kane didn't want his group harassed anymore than they had been already. Chow led the way to his office, allowing Kane and Giles to enter first. Kane sat down on a very hard chair, which reminded him somewhat of Buchanan's office. Bare walls and no atmosphere. A dim light hung overhead, making Kane feel as if he was in an interrogation room.

"Please sign here that you ID him. Afterwards, you can leave. We will know where you are most times. We can keep track of you." Chow handed Kane a pen.

Kane wasn't at all certain that he liked the idea of someone keeping track of him. He put pen to paper anyway. Standing up, he pushed the chair back under the table and headed for the door. He wanted to get back to Kelly.

Chow and two rather short Chinese policemen escorted the two Australians down to the lobby and then down to the underground garage. Chow shook hands with Kane, a grasp that surprised even Kane.

"Thank you for coming Mitter Brandon. I am sorry one of your people was killed. A man in your position needs his bodyguards."

Chow was good. If anybody had overheard their conversation, they would have been convinced that this was what it seemed.

"Yeah, well make damn sure you catch that son-of-a bitch that killed him. You know where to find me. Next trip you take to the hotel, feel free to stop by and have one on the house." Kane turned and walked away.

In the unmarked car, Kane leaned back. He was tired, tired of playing games. When he thought no one was looking, Kane had taken Alex's ring from his stiff finger.

"You trust the slant eyes?" Giles asked casually.

"No. But then, I don't trust the white eyes either."

It was past two when they arrived back at the hotel. Giles stepped out of the car first. Kane turned and glanced through the back window. He saw a car pull in behind them. It was the same car that had followed them all the way back to the hotel. Kane stepped out of the unmarked police car and placed himself between Giles and the other car's headlights. The lights blazed in the darkened deserted lot. Giles turned around to see why there was such a glare. Kane shielded him.

"Go!" Kane yelled while banging his fist on his own driver's window.

The car pulled sharply away, leaving the pair of Australian's an open target.

"What the fuck…" muttered Giles.

"Stay behind me," Kane ordered.

The car approached slowly. Shadows of three men could just be seen, but the glare made it impossible to determine anything else. The passenger door opened. Two feet dropped to the floor. Dressed from head to toe in black, a thin, muscular man stepped out of the car. He was tall, with Chinese features… yet, he had blonde hair. He stood still, pulled his gun and raised it until the gun was aimed straight at Kane's chest. Kane never flinched.

"The bastard's going to shoot you," yelled Giles, determined to make Kane his shield.

"No, he's not, or he would have done it by now. Stay with me and move into the lobby. The doorman is in view. He can just about see us. He won't kill me. Not yet anyway."

Protected by his walking shield, Giles moved slowly. Kane moved with him. The sight on the gun moved with the two of them. Kane was careful to keep Giles behind him. The men made it inside the lobby without anyone getting their head blown off; and, outside, a door slammed shut. The car and its passengers took off at a high speed.

"Who the hell was that?" asked a shaken Giles. Following Kane to the elevator, he turned back and glanced at the hotel door.

"At a guess, I would say it was my son." Kane pushed the button.

Giles replied as if in slow motion. "Your what?" His expression was one of astonishment.

"Get in the damn elevator. There are people around us and we don't need to cause any more trouble than we already have." Kane ushered Giles inside the open elevator. "You heard what I said. I was going to tell Kelly tonight, now it seems I have to tell you all."

"What the hell are you doing with a fucking slant-eyed son? He was way in his thirties. Wait…" Giles tried to make sense of this jigsaw. "We came over here when you first became a Federal agent. Our first mission together, if I remember correctly. Last year was our second mission here. We came in here and turned around and then left…abruptly." Giles waited for that statement to sink in before he spoke again. "I remember now. There was some girl that you were meeting, and you were supposed to be back at base. You always had the pick of the women. That *was* your son, wasn't it? You're not joking, are you, mate? That's the main reason we're here this time. Who else knows about this? Buchanan? Yeah, guess that's why he sent you. The guy has been picking off our buddies one by one. Does Kelly know? Was that bastard the one back in Alice Springs? No, couldn't be. He must be working with someone over there. And was that really Alex? You have to do some explaining before you get any more of us killed on your behalf…"

Kane thumped his fist on the stop button. The elevator shuddered to a halt between floors. He swung around and his arm pinned Giles up against the panels. Giles could hardly breathe, and on his face was a look of terror.

"Enough! That's all I'm gonna take from you. So fucking drop it right now! I've lost a third of my team. Just made an ID on my friend in the mortuary, had one of my team members was letching after my wife, and now I've got a gun pointing at me in a fucking parking lot. That's it, man! Even I have a breaking point. We came here to find out who is working with whom and how the China white is getting into Sydney. That's what we came for… and to discover why we failed last time out."

"But that's not it, is it? You know who he is, don't you? I saw the car, and the way he was dressed. You came on one more mission, didn't you? You came to kill him! Isn't that right?"

Kane's eyes became slits. Their eyes locked. Still, Giles kept his cool. He was afraid that Kane was going to kill him right there and then. Kane pushed hard on Giles' throat until he was dizzy. He stared at the man in front of him. Suddenly, Kane let go. Giles clutched his throat and gasped for air.

"I'm sorry. I baited you. I thought that the spy might have been you. All I'm saying is you just better leave my damn wife alone." Kane stepped back and leaned on the panels.

"I was your partner, Kane. It was never me! I only went after Kelly 'cuz I wanted to get even with you. She's really hot, Kane, and you are a very lucky man." While coughing, he had blurted the last sentence with a lie in his heart.

Kane pushed the button and restarted the elevator. He had lost his cool. Accident or intent?

"You want time to tell Kelly first?" asked Giles. "It's gonna be a real shock to her and to Dan." Dusting himself down, he attempted to regain his composure.

"May as well tell you all together now. There's not enough time to tell it twice. All your questions will be answered." Kane shivered in the air conditioning. His sweater was not thick enough to keep out the cold chills.

"You okay, mate? Guess it's not every day you find your son pointing a gun at you." Giles wiped the sweat from his head on the arm of his jacket.

"How can you be sure I'm telling you the truth?" asked Kane leaning back on the railing.

"Never seen blonde haired slant-eyes in the flesh before. But you have. Had you seen pictures?" Giles was on a fishing expedition.

"Yeah. I've seen his picture and obviously he has seen mine." Kane looked confused. Everything was not going as he'd planned.

"Are you okay?" Giles asked again. He could quite clearly see the pain Kane was in and it troubled him.

That was a joke. Kane stared at the glass walls. How was Kelly going to take this? He closed his eyes. He'd fathered three children as far as he knew, and one was on the way. Each child was totally different. His and Kelly's baby, Star, a gem of a child. Sage by his first wife, and mother of his grandchild, was old enough to take care of herself. Then, there was this shit of a man, born out of wedlock. On top of everything else, and in spite of how he needed things to go, Kelly was pregnant again. He banged his fists on the doors.

"No, I'm not okay! Would you fucking be okay with all this shit going on in your life? Half of my life just went down the fucking toilet. The other half could possibly be about to blow completely!" Leaning back on the glass, Kane gave the appearance of a man coming apart at the seams. That was only the appearance.

The elevator stopped at the penthouse suite. Giles watched a distraught man broaden his shoulders and turn back into a leader of men. In a matter of minutes, Kane was back…back was the hunter, a complete transformation. Did this man not have a breaking point?

They walked in silence to the suite door. Kane knocked loudly. Dan peered through the peephole and opened the door. Giles and Kane entered the penthouse together. Kelly sat huddled on the couch wrapped in a blanket, waiting for him. Genna was asleep in the chair. The rest of them were hovering around the room like unsettled flies. Kelly dropped the blanket and ran to Kane.

"Where you been? I was worried. I even tried calling your cell. Wasn't on. Was it Alex?" her face was anxious and her voice full of questions.

Kane took hold of her left hand. His hand felt the warmth of her love as he led her back to the waiting couch. Sitting down, he pulled her to him, and held her tightly in his arms. Stroking her face, for a second, he forgot who all was in the room with them…he kissed her lips very gently.

"Kane, you're scaring me. What's wrong?" She pulled slightly back from him.

He felt it. Genna awoke.

"Sit down, all of you. There are some things you have to know." He glanced at Giles. "It was Alex in the mortuary." He dared Giles to contradict him. "He was a mess. Beaten very badly, looks like he was beaten with a baseball bat or something. Chow knows that we are looking for a drug deal. Didn't bother him too much. Knows we are in the prostitution game. He'll go along with letting a group of Australians work the night clubs out here for a few days."

Kelly felt his arm tighten on her. She knew his signals well enough.

"There is, however, one thing more to this mission." Kane paused, his voice low and uncharacteristic of Kane. "There is a Chinese agent that the AFP has been watching for a short space of time. We have to take him out and we need to make no mistake about it. He's believed to be working with the Australian drug rings. Tonight, Giles and I encountered the bastard in the parking lot. His mood was anything but friendly. He knows who I am and he knows that we are here. Why he is playing along with our charade escapes me right now. The fact remains, he is. The guy's name is Sam Cheng. He is related to the infamous Colonel Vau Cheng of the Hong Kong government, the gentleman that Giles and I came to get on the last mission. He is also related," he looked from one face to the other. Kane took a slow deep breath, his voice just above a whisper, "to me."

Kelly's face turned ashen. Kane felt her skin go clammy. Genna dropped the bowl she had picked up, and it broke on the marble table. Ty's chair fell backwards against the wall. The others simply stared. Kane felt Kelly's arms stiffen.

"How can that be?" she whispered, her eyes round and staring.

"As Giles is fully aware, my first assignment with the police was out here. I met a girl in Lantau. Unfortunately, Sam Cheng is my son."

A pin dropped. All eyes focused on Kane, then switched to Kelly.

"Excuse me." Kelly pulled herself from Kane's arms, clasped her hand to her mouth and ran into the bedroom.

Genna rose to go after her. Kane was much quicker.

"I'll go. She needs me to be the one to explain now. Kelly and I have to sort this out, tonight. See if you all can get some rest. We'll continue this in the morning."

"How much of this did you know, Dan?" asked Giles.

"Most of it. I knew there was a Chinese agent, but I didn't know that agent was Sam Cheng. I also did not know it was Kane's son," Dan lied.

Giles fielded questions like, "Is he sure? I mean how does he know?"

"He's sure. Outside in the lot, the man had the same Branson defiance. A Chinaman with blonde hair kinda stands out and Kane says he has documentation. He pointed a gun at Kane, and Kane never flinched."

"How old is he?" interrupted Ty still trying to come to terms with all the new facts.

"Mid-thirties, I guess. Somewhere round there…has to be about right."

"Fucking hell," Ty said without realizing he didn't normally use curse words.

"Yeah, that about sums it up for now anyway. Wonder how he's doing with Kelly?" mussed Giles.

Giles glanced towards the bedroom door. Would this ruin everything between Kane and Kelly? He hoped it would.

"Darling, you okay in the there?" Kane could hear his wife throwing up and he was sympathetic.

She washed her mouth out with fresh cold water and brushed her teeth.

He paused. "I'm coming inside, Kel."

Turning the knob, he discovered that the door wasn't locked.

She stood in front of the mirror staring at her reflection. Was she not about the same age when he first made love to her? It was in his past life. Another world away, but these worlds were about to collide right in front of her eyes. Kane came up behind her and slid his arms around her waist.

"Baby, it was a long time ago. I was young and so was she. I didn't know until very recently that I had a son. I received a letter some months back. His mother knew I was in the AFP, and guess she figured I still was. She wanted to let me know he was a Chinese agent. Sure enough, she was telling the truth. Sam Cheng is who she claimed."

"What is her name?" The words made it from her brain to her mouth quite coherently.

"Lilia."

"Are you going to see her?"

"Should I?"

"Yes, you should. She is the mother of your child and you must have felt something for her." Kelly was acting very mature.

"Yes, I did at the time and it was a special time. She was very special too. I remember her crying on our last day together. Crying unashamedly when we pulled out back to OZ. Now I know why." Kane said quietly.

"Do you want to go on your own?" She watched his expression in the mirror.

"No. I would like you to come with me…if you would."

She closed her eyes at his touch, never would she ever get used to how wonderful his touch felt. Kelly could smell his cologne and smell the cigarette odor that had become a natural part of him.

"It's you I love. I love you more than I would have believed possible. You gave me the will to go on with my life. You, Butterfly… Kelly."

"I know that. I know and I'll always love you. Why do you think I came with you here and took the risk of so much danger? Even if I was skittish, I still couldn't let you out of my sight. There has never been a man like you in my life. You are my friend, my husband, my lover, and my life. Without you, I would be dead or on some pimp's payroll." Kelly laughed. Her body relaxed and she turned in his arms to face him. "I am on some pimp's payroll."

He held her tightly to him. "Thank you for understanding. For being there and… for being you."

Kane let her go for just a second. There had not been enough time to dry all of the water off her chin. It glistened and her eyes shined. He reached behind him and turned the key in the bathroom door. In an urgent need for Kelly, Kane tugged the sweater over his head. Although the room was small, he still managed to slide out of his jeans. Kelly let the robe fall from her. He needed her, and he wanted her to need him. It was important right now. Taking her in his arms, the pair slid down onto the luxurious white rugs that the penthouse bathroom had to offer.

This time, the two loved each other in almost silence. Also no one disturbed them as he kissed the butterfly and then her stomach where his new seed was growing. He tasted the musky fluid of his own personal butterfly, a scent she allowed only him to savor. Her hands clung to the rug as his tongue searched her body. Kelly's eyes closed tightly as tears of pleasure ran down her cheeks. Wanting to scream, still she held quiet as he rose upwards and looked her in the face.

"Kane," she murmured. "Don't ever leave me."

"I have no intention of doing that." His mouth closed over hers. Kane stifled Kelly's moans as his erection entered her body. He pushed harder. She was the only woman that he could remember who caused him to want more of them within seconds… more even more, he needed Kelly. He felt an incredible urgency to let her know how much he loved her. Finally, Kane could feel her orgasm. He could feel her muscles tighten.

"You okay, baby?" he whispered nestling into her hair.

"Yeah…" her voice was hardly audible.

Gradually, she relaxed under his weight and Kelly clung to him. Kane stroked his wife's hair. Slowly, her breathing returned to normal. He held her to him, frightened that any moment he would lose her.

They dozed on the floor. He pulled the thick cotton towels over her and his arm became her pillow. Someone softly tapping on the door awakened him.

"Kane, you awake?" Dan's voice was low and cautious.

Dan was trying not to wake a sleeping Genna lying on the king-sized bed in the room. Kane pulled his jeans on and slowly opened the door.

"Come in, Dan." Kane let him inside the bathroom.

"Sorry, boss. It's almost daylight." He saw Kelly lying nestled in the big fluffy towels. "Thought you may want to talk before the rest of the team starts waking."

"Where are they all?" Kane whispered. He glanced down at Kelly.

"All squashed in the one room. Genna's out there on the bed. Kelly okay?"

"Yeah. Hold the door for me."

Kane bent down and picked his sleeping wife up off the floor. Gently, he carried her to the bed and laid her on the side of it next to Genna. Kelly stirred and he whispered in her ear. She smiled and her flickering eyes closed shut. Pulling the blankets over her, he ushered Dan from the room.

"Let the girls sleep some more. No need to wake them now. I'll be right with you."

Kane went back to the bathroom, picked up his sweater, and followed Dan, closing the bedroom door behind him. Kane buttoned up the top of his jeans and wrenched the cigarettes and lighter from his back pocket. Dan had never quite figured out how Kane got into those skintight black jeans in the first place. He hoped he looked that good at fifty four. In fact, Dan wished he looked that good now. Kane leaned back on the couch, lit up a cigarette and watched the rings float into the artificial world of the air conditioning.

"Better not let Kelly see you doing that," mocked Dan.

"Yeah. She's caught me doing everything else, though." Kane inhaled deeply.

"How did she take all of this?"

Kane didn't even have a chance to reply. The second bedroom door opened.

"Morning. Thought I heard voices." A bleary-eyed Giles came through the door stretching his back muscles. "That damn couch is horrible. Tonight, *sir*, you better find us a new way of living." Giles ran his hands through his hair and smoothed down his clothes.

A knock on the door heralded room service. Giles was quick to pull his gun from the back of his pants, and stood behind the door. Slowly, he opened the door, checked under the cloth and let the waiter push the cart inside that was loaded with a palatial feast of food.

"How much food did you order?" asked Kane and stared at the overload of calories from breads, jams and juices. Eggs and bacon carried on the British tradition.

"Well, Ben eats enough for two and Kelly should be eating for two," replied Dan with a chuckle.

"Yeah, point taken." Kane put the cigarette out in the ashtray.

Over coffee and eggs, the three discussed the situation.

"We can't pretend none of this is happening, but we also have to act as though we are doing what we should be. Tonight, Kelly, Genna... you and I will go to the club Coco. Dan, you and Ty will follow us in a separate cab. I want Ben to stay here as backup. I want to buy into a drug deal. But the best deal. Kelly can start work tonight. She knows what to do. If we can get her and Genna in with the right people, we can take it from there. There's no more time to waste. Cheng is going to know where we are. The man's not going to give us away. He's letting us carry on for one reason only. I believe that he wants us to find out just what is going on here. Maybe he doesn't care about the China white going in and out, but then again, maybe, he does. He, like us, knows there is someone working both sides and he wants to find out who is double crossing us. Colonel Cheng is the guy that we want. The one we want from their side. We are doing Sam Cheng's dirty work for him and he's going to let us. I don't think it's him, that's bumping off the team; it's someone on our side. That's the person we need to catch. I have my suspicions as to who it is, but no proof...yet." He paused and looked at the two men. "Have Genna ready by eight. Dan, get us some nice flashy car. Sam Cheng won't cause us any problems, not during our time here. Now deeper in the island, that's a different story. If Sam were going to hit us now, he wouldn't have shown himself to us. We know exactly where he is and what he looks like. Before, we only had pictures. When Kelly wakes, she and I are going to go visiting."

Kane pulled a letter from his bag and picked up the phone. He dialed the number on the letter. A woman answered, with a voice that he immediately recognized. The number was still good.

"Lilia, its Kane Branson."

Giles almost choked on his coffee.

"Yes, I'm in a hotel near the airport. By the address in your letter, you can't be far from here. I would like to come and see you later today, if that's possible?" He spoke to her all in a big babble of words like he was nervous. "Two? That's fine. My wife will be with me. I can find the way. We will see you then."

He hung up the phone. Lilia had obviously been expecting his call.

"Was that her?" uttered Giles.

"Yeah."

Kane leaned back on the couch. Dan looked at his father-in-law. He was going to meet a woman he hadn't seen for some thirty odd years. The mother of his only son… at least as far as he knew. And he was taking his wife with him, a twenty-four-year-old woman. Then Kane realized why he was taking her. One reason was to show Kelly he had nothing to hide. The other reason he was taking her was that his wife seemed to understand the situation better than anyone else would. At a very young age, she had given birth to Kane's child just the same as Lilia.

"Kane, you are a clever man. I admire you very much," Dan said with some reverence.

"Well, I don't see why, but thank you anyway. It's time to wake the others. Think I should rent a motorcycle for the day?" A shrewd smile spread across his face. "Kidding. I'll go wake Kelly." He stood up with a smirk on his face.

The bedroom door opened. A woman with long sun kissed hair clad only in a light yellow blanket emerged from the room. She shook her head, and her hair sensuously moved in the space around her. At the same time, two young agents fought to get through the other bedroom door. They stood in the entranceway enchanted by the golden image that stood before them.

Kelly had a very special glow about her. Kane thought his wife had never looked so beautiful in all her life as she did at that moment. Another person in the room thought the same.

CHAPTER 7

Kelly looked across to Kane. She smiled at him, and the morning took on a new meaning for more than one of the group.

"Baby, go get showered and dressed. We have a place to go. Lilia is expecting us at two." Kane glanced at his gold Rolex watch. "It's not far. Shouldn't be that hard to find the apartment, and a good cabbie will know how to find it."

"Fine. Any breakfast left? I'm hungry," Kelly asked. She shook her head again and the long curls cascaded down her back.

Kelly sat down on the couch next to Kane and snuggled in beside him. He spooned eggs onto a plate for her and poured her some orange juice. She gobbled the eggs down like a refugee, and Kane was surprised.

"Finished?" Kane asked.

She nodded, and handed him the plate. He studied it. Unusual for Kelly.

"Genna awake?" Kane asked, looking towards the bedroom door.

"Yep," she replied.

"Good. Go get ready. Wear something classy. A black dress would be good. That's if they thought to throw one in the luggage."

In the few years that Dan had known Kelly, he had never heard Kane ask her to wear anything special. This was a first.

"Should I wear my hair up or down?" She piled it on top of her head and turned around so that everyone could see the style.

"Looks good both ways," Ben said. Immediately, he turned crimson.

"Well, Ben. Then you pick. You're more Kelly's age. What's the fashion?" Kane lounged back on the couch, and watched intently.

"I didn't mean to say that, sir. It's up to you, not me." Ben wanted the floor to open up and swallow him.

Kane was amused. Puppy love, but dangerous.

"Come on, boy. Have the courage of your convictions. Up or down?"

Kane stood up, and pulled all Kelly's hair on top of her head. He held it there.

"Down, sir," Ben blurted out.

"I agree," added Kane. "Gives her more of an innocent look." He clipped her on the backside as she scooted away. "Thanks, Ben."

"What did I do?" he said with obvious embarrassment.

"Made her feel good," replied Kane.

Picking up his coffee cup, Kane sipped the contents. He peered at the young man over the rim. Was Ben as innocent as he looked?

In the bedroom, Kelly took time to get ready. She rummaged through the bags, finding a sexy dress in there. The short, back dress enhanced her golden brown legs, and the little capped sleeves and sweetheart neckline made her look demure. Her hair hung down, curls of sunlight dancing in the morning breeze. She slipped on high heels and put back on her wedding band. Kane had made her remove it before the flight, but she missed being Mrs. Branson.

"Where are you going, Kel?" asked Genna. She watched the whole time from her position sitting on the top of the pillows.

"To see the mother of Kane's son," Kelly replied trying to sound casual.

"You're going where?" Genna's eyes popped.

"To see Lilia. You know, the mother of Kane's son."

"Did I hear you right?" she exclaimed, tumbling from the pillows.

"You did. How do I look?" Kelly viewed herself in the mirror, and did a spin around.

"Great. No one would ever know what you were…"

"And still am," laughed Kelly.

"I didn't mean were before. I meant what we are here to do," said her friend.

Kelly smiled. "I know. Okay, I'm going to show Kane what I look like. See if he approves. See you later. Tonight's the night for our debut into the big world. Won't be looking like this later." She looked one last look in the giant mirror. Kelly was satisfied with the demure image that looked back.

"Yeah, see you. Don't leave me alone too long with these guys. They talk about real men stuff and I just hang out on my own. Giles talks to me. Kelly, do you think he…aw, never mind. You go and good luck. This is one time I'm glad I'm not you."

Kelly thought that a strange statement. She opened the door into the main room. Dan happened to be facing the door.

"Wow, look at you," boomed Dan. "All mother-in-laws should look like you." His eyes viewed her from head to foot.

"Thank you," Kelly said, blushing.

"Yeah, darling, you look terrific." Kane looked at the perfect picture she made. He stood up and took her hand. "Let's go do this. I can't say I'm really looking forward to it."

"Do you think your son may just happen to be there?" Giles asked. He spoke to Kane but his eyes stuck like glue to Kelly.

"Good question. Wouldn't think so, but who knows? Think he'll keep out of this right now. He did what he wanted to do, make himself known to us. He's waiting for us to make our move. He could give our identity away just like that and he hasn't. Unless…"

"Unless what?" Giles asked still looking at Kelly.

"Unless he doesn't know exactly who we are. Lilia may never have told him. He knows we're here as a team, but we could be exactly what we're pretending to be: Australians looking for a drug deal. He's a secret agent. He's also a player. Depends how well he's done his homework. I already said I didn't think it was him behind the killings. We may have this figured all wrong. I don't think he knows a damn thing. Last night could have been for a different reason."

"And that would be?" asked his son-in-law.

"Lilia could have told him I was his father and not that I was AFP. Maybe there is a real good reason she wants me to go there. Would you want some Australian turning up thirty odd years later and having to call him daddy? You know that makes more sense. Chow doesn't know Kelly is my wife, so probably Sam doesn't. Only way he could know is by one of our agents telling him, and if my theory is right, that agent hasn't told him yet. Not sure why. Guess they have a reason. We may still be undercover." His hand tightened on Kelly's. He was tense.

"You're serious?" asked Giles, as he poured another cup of steaming hot coffee.

"Very and now is a good time to test the theory. I'll know if Lilia is telling the truth or not. She wasn't good at lying. Wonder why she chose to tell me after all these years? There has to be a good reason." He let go of Kelly's hand. "Come on, baby, let's go. We'll be back." He picked up a pen and paper, scribbled down the address and left it on the table. "If we're not back by five come looking for us. And I mean that." He pulled on a black leather jacket that complemented his tight blue jeans. Down the back of his jeans he stuck his .38. "You want a jacket, Kel?"

"No. I'm fine," Kelly replied.

"Uh huh. Sure are, baby," retorted her husband.

The cab only took fifteen minutes to get to Lilia's apartment block. It was nice, very nice. Kane paid the cab driver, and the couple stood on the well-manicured lawns. Kane raised his shades to get a better view.

"You never said it was like this." Kelly looked up at the skyscraper. It wasn't what she expected.

"I didn't know, baby." He stared up at the building till he reached the top.

Kane glanced at the envelope making sure he had the right address, and then looked back to the apartment block. It was palatial. Either Lilia had married well or her business interests had fared prosperously.

"Sure you want me to go with you, Kane?" She really didn't fit in with this picture.

"You're my wife, Kelly. Nothing is going to change that. Lilia didn't have such a snow white past, either. Anyway, you look terrific. You're young and pretty, and she is in her fifties. She's not going to look like you, that is for sure. Let's go do this."

He took Kelly's hand, and gently, and together they faced his past. Clearing the armed security guard at the front desk of the apartment block, they were allowed to go on through the lobby. Lilia had left word in the entrance that she was expecting special guests. The glass elevator stopped at almost every floor. Kane watched his wife. She was nervous and it amused him. Butterfly Kelly, usually not afraid of anything. The elevator finally settled on the twelfth floor. They stepped out in an elegant lobby. Kane walked down the hallway, piece of paper in hand, looking for the right number. There was a guard at apartment 1203. He was expecting them. A tall, lean white male dressed in black radioed inside the suite. He received the correct reply and Lilia's bodyguard opened the door for the pair. Kane wondered if this was a setup.

The wealth practically smacked them in the face. Persian rugs, marble furniture, and state-of-the-art paintings hung either side of the door-frame. They stepped inside the doorway. A slender, black-haired woman sat cross-legged on an expensive black leather couch. Two exotic-looking vases stood each end of the sofa. When the Branson's entered, the woman rose to greet them, her silk cream dress clinging to her tight shapely body. Kelly felt Kane's hand tighten around hers, and she glanced up at his face. There was a look Kelly had never seen before on her husband's face. This woman was not what either of them had expected, especially not Kane.

"Lilia?" Kane asked almost surprised at the person in front of him.

She extended her hand to him. Long fingernails of crimson red reached out. He never let go of Kelly as he shook the woman's hand.

"Kane, how good of you to come." Her voice was penetrating. Her English was far better than he remembered. *She* was far better than he remembered. Age had only enhanced her beauty.

"It's good to see you again. You look…exceptional." Kane was lost for words, something Kane was not used to being. He looked at her, intently.

Lilia noticed. "And you have a daughter?" She looked directly at Kelly.

'Bitch,' Kelly thought.

"Yes, I do have a daughter in her mid-twenties back in Australia. This is my wife, Kelly." Kane pulled her slightly forward.

"How nice to meet you. Kane always did like pretty young women. And you, my dear, are both." Her tone was sarcastic and condescending.

"Thank you. I'm sure you were, too," conceded Kelly, and she smiled demurely.

"Kelly and I are the proud parents of Star, a three-year old little girl who is just as pretty as my pregnant wife here."

'Nice going, Kane! You told her your whole prolific history in one sentence. See if that takes some of the wind from her sails,' thought Kelly.

"Congratulations, Mrs. Branson." Lilia replied almost curtly and turned her attentions to Kane. "And you also now have a son, Sam Cheng. You must be wondering why I let you know about him and also how much I told him." She sat down and gestured to them to do the same. "I assume your wife knows of our affair?"

"Kelly knows everything. We have no secrets. Marriages are not built on dishonesty. I was married for twenty-five years before I met Kelly. But I assume you know that."

Lilia picked up a solid silver box from the marble table, opened it and offered him a cigarette. Kane declined. Not usual for Kane. Lilia took one of them from the box and closed the lid. Kane pulled out his lighter from the back of his tight, black pants and offered her the light. Lilia cupped her hands round the flickering flame, and lightly touched Kane's fingers. For a moment he saw her over thirty years ago. He blinked, and focused on the cigarettes. Russian, if Kane was correct.

"I make it my business to know. One has to know when one is the consul's wife. My brother-in-law is Colonel Vau Cheng. But then, you knew that didn't you, Kane?"

"Yes. I also know that Sam Cheng is my son. What I don't know is what you have told him and what you will tell him. I assume he does not know about Kelly, nor that I am AFP?" His concentration was back.

She smiled, red lips showing pearly white teeth. "Still as astute as ever. And still as attractive." She had noted the fit of his jeans. Lilia turned her head and looked at Kelly. "I am sure you know how attractive your husband is to women. He obviously has had many," and she gestured them to sit.

"I know, and I know he is faithful to me as he was to his first wife. What he did before that is none of my business."

Kelly crossed her tan legs and Kane rested his hand on her knees. Lilia looked irritated. She put the cigarette back to her glossed red lips and puffed harder, blowing the smoke into the air.

"Something to drink? Tea, coffee, or something stronger? Whiskey wasn't it?" She flashed her mint white teeth at him.

"Coffee is just fine," he replied. "I don't drink."

"No alcohol? Apparently that's the only vice you gave up."

"Apparently. Lilia, stop playing games. Why did you write to me after all those years? And why haven't you given my identity away? You didn't, did you? Otherwise I would be dead by now. Your…our…son would have seen to that. I'm sure you know he visited me in the hotel parking lot. He could have shot me, but he didn't. So what reason do you have for getting me here?" Now, Kane was becoming irritated.

"A very good one. At first I just wanted to tell you that Sam was your son. I felt you had a right to know, but I couldn't do that while my husband was alive. I married him to give the child a name, and because he was aiming for the top. He had drive and determination. A lot like you had. He was older than I was. I think I was looking for a father figure. He knew I didn't love him. My heart always belonged to someone else." She stopped speaking, ashamed at her lack of control. "My husband attained the position of consul in Hong Kong. There was no need to say anything to anyone until recently. As I said, his brother is Colonel Vau Cheng, a name I'm sure the AFP is familiar with. Colonel Cheng has no love for my son, but he has had a love for me. A few months after my husband died, Vau asked me to marry him. I declined the offer. It did not sit well. He has pursued the question many times. Just before I sent you the letter, Sam came here and demanded to know who his father was. He had been talking to the colonel. All he knows is that you are his father. Even though he is a Chinese agent, the way was blocked for him to find anything else out about you. Someone is protecting you, for now."

Kelly stared at her in a complete trance. Even Kane was in shock, but at least the pieces were coming together one by one in this giant jigsaw. Lilia was telling him to be careful on one hand, but had led him there on the other.

"And why does he think I am sitting here right now?" Kane asked suspiciously.

Lilia cleared her throat and continued. "Because… I am dying. I want to clear up the past and let you know who your son is."

Kane was shocked and it showed. "Are you?"

"Yes. Don't be fooled by my appearance. I don't have long to live."

She stood up and crossed the room. Standing by the window in the half-light, Lilia was still the beautiful young Chinese girl Kane had fallen in love with. Or thought he had. When he had returned to Australia, he realized it was more lust than love. Now, he watched her standing there. The only regret he had was that he had left her pregnant, even unknowingly. Lilia turned her face to the window.

Kelly didn't take her eyes off Kane. Not that she doubted his love for her, but she wondered what he was feeling. Kane could sense her eyes on him and turned his anguished face toward her. His hand tightened around her legs and she could feel the strength surge though his fingers. His lips formed, 'I love you', and then he let go. Kelly nodded.

Kane stood up, and moved to the window behind the woman. She turned to him and he took her in his arms. She looked into his eyes, put her head on his shoulder and cried for the first time in thirty-five years.

Clinging to him, she made one more admission. "And I wanted to see you one more time before…" and her voice was lost in emotion.

Kelly stood up. "Er, I need to go outside a moment. You know for some air…" and she let herself out of the door. Outside, Kelly leaned on the doorframe. She smiled at the bodyguard. How Kelly thanked her god that Kane had fallen in love with her. There, but for the grace of... She could only pity the lady inside the room. Kelly knew she would not have been as strong as Lilia had been

"Lilia, thank you," said Kane. "You did the right thing. You have nothing to be ashamed of. It's me who should feel guilty. I left you, and never bothered to find out how you were. I could have at least done that. I really had no idea you were pregnant. I would have been responsible for my actions, and done the right thing by you." His face was full of concern and regret. He had lost a son for thirty-five years.

"But you didn't love me, did you, Kane?" She raised her eyes and looked deeply into his eyes. "Please. Don't answer that. I already know."

"I still would have acknowledged the child as mine. Now, he hates me and I really can't blame him. If he finds out exactly who I am, if he even gets the slightest suspicion, he or his uncle…" His hands stayed put on her back.

"He won't. If the agency were going to give him an answer, they would have done so by now." She interrupted Kane far too abruptly.

"How do you know so much about how the Chinese agency works?"

"My husband was the consul. I told you that," her voice raised a little.

"Yeah, you did. But somehow I don't believe you. He enlisted you, didn't he?" He held her tightly to him. "You're also a Chinese agent. Do you know who is the agent working both sides? Is it you? You would have the ability to block the information getting to *your* son."

She tried to move from Kane's once caring arms, and failed. "All right, I blocked him from finding out who you are. I also know you are the Hunter. And the Hunter comes." Her voice raised another octave.

He released her, startled that she knew who the Hunter was. He backed away. "Why did you protect me?" Kane's voice was none too quiet.

"I love…loved you so much, Kane. I know you didn't know about the child. When I found out I was pregnant, I wanted to die. I married my husband out of spite to you, and became one of their top agents. I was on the other side, so to speak. But I couldn't betray you. When my husband died, I retired, but I still had enough power to block Sam from finding you."

"Are you really dying? Or is that a lie?" Kane stared at her, his mind racing and on overload.

"How can I convince you? I have three months; maybe four. That's it. That's the whole truth. There isn't anything else to know! You have my word," and her voice reached fever pitch.

"Your word! How the fuck can I trust the word of a Chinese agent?" Kane shouted back at her, venomous in his tone.

Kane stood in front of the window. The door opened and Kelly reentered the room. Kane stepped aside as if to go towards his wife, and Lilia moved in behind him trying to hide herself from Kelly's stare. The shades on the windows reflected slats in the sunlight and shone on Lilia's back.

"Kane, you can be heard halfway down the floor. What the hell is going on?" asked Kelly trying to figure things out.

From out of nowhere, there was a loud crack of glass, and the large window shattered into a thousand pieces. Sun blasted eternal heat through the empty frame.

"Kelly, get down!" yelled Kane.

He pulled his gun from the back of his jeans, dropped to the floor and his eyes searched the window. Then he saw Lilia lying on the Persian rug writhing in pain. He slithered across the floor to her. His stretched his free hand to her, and searched her body. He slid his arm under her back and pulled his bloodstained fingers from under her. Kane raised her slightly, and braced her against his knee. The bullet wound was a gaping hole of gushing red blood leaving a huge crimson patch on the rug.

"Oh, my god! No, not you…."

He slid his arm around her and held onto her. He still kept hold of his .38. His eyes scoured the buildings opposite. Kane could see nothing. The guard entered the room. Instantly he could see what had happened. Kelly lay face down on the floor, her body protecting her unborn child.

"Kane, I was telling you the truth," Lilia stammered. "Now you have to believe me. Someone out there wants you dead. That bullet wasn't meant for me, but I have told you too much." She winced in pain. "Go, get out of here before the police arrive. My guard will get you out the back way. Go, Kane. Please," she begged and her breathing became labored.

The guard motioned for them to leave.

"Lilia, I did love you…for a short time I loved you."

"Thank you, Kane…I have always loved you…" Lilia Cheng closed her eyes on a face she loved, and one that had cost her her life.

Kane let her gently slide to the floor. "I will get the son-of-a-bitch that did this to you. On that, you have my word."

"Mr. Branson, let's go!" the guard yelled.

Kane stood up, pushed his gun back in his jeans, and grabbed Kelly by the hand. They took off out of the bloodstained room, scurrying down the lobby behind Lilia's faithful guard. He hurried them along the corridor till they reached the side door. The noise from the gunshot and breaking glass seemed to have attracted people's attention.

"Go down the stairs and out the back door. I will explain what happened. They will never know you were here. Go." He opened the door for them.

"The security downstairs, they knew we were here…." Kane pleaded his case.

"Even they have a price. Now, please go…" he begged.

"Why are you doing this for me?" Kane asked the man in front of him.

"I'm not doing it for you, but for Lilia. I loved her. But you never gave her back her heart."

The mournful look in the man's eyes told Kane all he needed to know. Kane nodded to the other man. A look passed between them, which was all that was needed. Kane pulled Kelly through the door and they took off running down the back stairs. Twelve flights took a few minutes, and Kelly was breathing hard.

"Baby, you okay?" Kane peered into her face. Her hand was clammy in his.

"Yes," she gasped and held her side.

"We have to keep going. If we're caught here it will be the end of the mission. Man, how did all this happen?" Kane was exasperated.

"You have to ask? You're the one with the prolific history, remember?" she murmured.

"Only you could think of that at a time like this. Baby, you are one hell of a woman," and Kane hugged her to him.

"Yeah, I know. That's why you married me." It was said with a double meaning.

The last few steps were easy. They burst through the back door and out onto the parking lot. Kelly made him stop and she leaned against the wall. She was gasping for breath.

It was then Kane noticed the blood on the hand that was wasn't holding Kelly.

"Fucking hell…"

He pushed the bloodied hand into his pocket as they walked across the courtyard. Police sirens got louder as cops surrounded the palatial homes. A few more seconds and Kane knew they would not have made it out of the melee. If Kane was stopped now it was all over. He could see Kelly trembling, but she still had the sense to hail a cab for them.

Once inside the rickety, old vehicle, they sped off in the afternoon sun. Neither of them noticed the scenery. Each had their own thoughts racing through their heads. Kane broke the silence.

"You okay, darling?" Kane asked. "The baby…"

"I'm fine. Was she…" She knew.

"Yes," he whispered.

Kelly leaned back in the seat. "When you told her you loved her, did you mean it?" She hesitated. "Not that it's any of my business."

"It is your business. You're my wife." He paused. "No, I didn't. I wanted her to leave this life with some dignity. I had feelings for her, but not like I had for my first wife, or anything like the ones I have for you. Sometimes you have to say…"

Kelly put her fingers on his lips. "It's okay. You did the right thing. Do you think *he'll* come looking for you now?"

"Depends if she was telling the truth. But he probably will. It won't be in public. He'll bide his time and find the right place to do it. But he'll come. Depends on how corrupt he is. Or who really is paying his salary. But he'll come, sooner or later." Kane closed his eyes, trying to block out what had happened.

That's what Kelly was afraid of. And she knew her husband would be waiting, in or outside of the law. It took twenty minutes going back. Much more traffic than when they arrived at Lilia's. Finally, after crawling though the last few streets, due to heavy traffic, the cab pulled into their hotel lot. Kane was subdued. Kelly paid the driver after he held up enough fingers that amounted to the cab fare. Kane could feel the sticky blood drying on his hand. He tried to wipe his hand on the inside of his pocket. Still some of Lilia's blood clung to his fingers. There was a strange expression on his face.

Keeping his hand in his pocket, they walked across the hallway and into the elevator. Kelly pushed the button for their floor. This time, she broke the silence. "You think it was him who shot her?" she asked tentatively.

"No."

"Well, who do you think it was?" Kelly toyed with her hair, twisting it nervously round her fingers.

"Don't know," Kane said with finality.

The noise from the television could be heard from outside the suite door. "And live from the crime scene…"

Kane tapped on the suite door. He saw an eye through the peephole, and Giles let them in. The couple entered the room closing the door behind them.

"Turn it off," Kane said quietly.

The group huddled around the set and turned to look at the pair.

"What?" asked Dan, glancing up at Kane.

"I said turn it off," replied Kane.

"But it's…" replied Dan.

"Turn the fucking thing off…NOW!" Kane yelled so loud the neighbors could hear him. He went into the bedroom and slammed the door behind him, shaking the frame as he did so.

This time Kelly let him go. He needed some breathing space.

"What's with him? Was that her place on the news?"

Giles whispered. "Aw, man, it was wasn't it? Shit. Is she dead?"

"Yeah, Giles. She's dead. Shot in the back by a sniper. The bullet wasn't meant for her. She stepped in its path. Lilia was telling Kane some story and I had stepped outside. I came back in the room 'cause I could hear them arguing. And then there was this loud crack…" her eyes became moist.

Dan rushed to her side, and sat her down on the leather couch next to a seated Kelly. "You okay?"

She nodded. "I am, but he's not. She died in his arms. She was beautiful. I mean really beautiful. Her husband was the consul…" and Kelly hesitated. How much should she tell. She continued. "Kane was right. Sam doesn't know why we are here or who we are. He just knows that Kane is his father."

"Does Kane think Sam was the sniper?" asked Ty.

"Don't think so," she muttered.

Dan fixed her a stiff drink and handed her a scotch. One wasn't going to hurt. Kelly drank it down in one go. She handed the glass back to Dan.

"Another…"

"Kelly, you think that's wise?" asked her son-in-law.

"I'll sip it…" And Kelly took the fresh drink from him.

"And what do you think?" interrupted Ben.

"If it wasn't him… then who?" Kelly replied. She took another sip of the bitter sweet.

"The same person that is bumping us off one by one," replied Giles.

"So now what? Do we go on?" asked Genna.

"We go on," Kane boldly replied. "We didn't come this far to turn back now."

Kane reentered the room and closed the bedroom door behind him. He had changed into clean clothes. Gone was the blood but not the memory. They all turned to look at him. He was wearing a suit, with an immaculate gray cut cloth and a silk shirt, and looking every inch the rich pimp. With his hair pulled back in a ponytail, and clean-shaven, he looked younger than fifty-four. He stood looking at them all.

"Okay, you two," he said inclining his head toward the girls. "Go change. Giles, you have a suit…use it. Dan, you and Ty are coming with us, too. Slight change of plans. We all go together, except Ben. You stay here and don't open the door to anyone but us. You understand?" Kane was a new man.

"Yes, boss," Ben babbled. He was disappointed, and it showed in his voice.

Kelly felt sorry for Ben. He wasn't going to see action; just the hotel bedroom and a computer. She grabbed Genna's hand and they disappeared from the guys.

Ben sat down on the couch. "Do I have to stay? Couldn't I go just one night?"

"Did I say something you didn't understand?" retorted Kane.

"No, sir. You made yourself very clear." His spectacles steamed up.

Kane turned a ladder-backed chair around and sat on it. "Okay, so now the girls are gone, I can speak freely. I don't want to scare them too much."

He looked first at Dan, his son-in-law; then to Giles, a veteran AFP agent; then at the two rookies. Round and jovial Ben had more than computers on his mind and Ty he hadn't quite figured out yet.

"All of us here know must have their suspicions who that person is. I'm going to let you think about it. See if you can figure out who the double agent is. One of you in this suite knows exactly who it is. We are gonna see some serious things happen now, if today is anything to go by. I want you all to be cautious, and watch out more for the two girls. We have to take them with us, and it's dangerous." Kane paused, more for effect than anything else. "Giles, be ready in ten minutes. Dan, did you get a nice flashy car like I mentioned earlier today?"

"Yeah. Man, you'll like this one. Better than the Mercedes you have," he chuckled.

"I'd rather be riding on my motorcycle down some beach than stuck here in this heat," replied Kane flippantly.

"It's not that hot." Dan commented.

"Didn't necessarily mean the temperature, Dan."

The bedroom door opened, and the girls stepped out. Kelly wore a skirt that covered little more than the imagination. Her legs led to a promise that she could keep. Her button-up T-shirt showed the butterfly, and a choker hung round her neck. Her hair was pulled tightly up on her head. There was enough makeup for both girls on her face, but somehow the look enhanced her.

Genna, in her tight leather jeans and strapless top, hair hanging loosely, saw them all look at Kelly first. Was this Genna in the bright red lipstick and deep blue eye shadow? Giles decided it was an improvement, and Kane saw the way he looked from Kelly to Genna.

"Hey, lady," quipped Dan, looking at Kelly. "How much do you charge?"

"More than you make, and wouldn't it be considered incestuous?" Kelly joked.

"Yeah, but it would be worth my badge, and possibly my marriage." He joked.

Ben looked at Kelly's black stockings that led up to the skirt. He raised his eyes to the T-shirt and he was crimson. Kane saw him.

"Take a good look, Ben. One day, you'll be able to afford that!" Kane was just a little irritated.

Giles came bustling through the bedroom door, straightening his suit and said, "Not a bad suit for a bodyguard. Maybe I'll keep the job. It may have some perks yet."

Giles looked at Genna. He thought she was blushing under that makeup. Giles looked good in black. Genna thought so anyway. He was beginning to grow on her. He wasn't her first choice, but he was nearing a fast second. And then Giles looked at Kelly, and looked again…

"Okay, Kane interrupted the staring competitions, "you all know what to do. Kelly, you have any problems, you get me. We now have a shorter space of time to do this. We have to make that connection as soon as possible. Any deal that looks good, we take. Any! You all understand?" Kane glanced around the room. "I'll find us the right crowd, Kelly finds the main man. Genna, you back her. Giles will be with you both all the way. Let's do it."

He checked his gun was loaded, and then Kane hid his piece in the back of his suit pants. The other men did the same.

"Remember, Ben. No one comes through the door except us." Kane's last words to him were falling on deaf ears.

Ben nodded, but his mind was elsewhere. They left the room together. Kane stuck his head back round the door.

"Remember, Ben. Only one of our team. No one else comes through this door," he reminded him. Kane ushered them to the elevator and stood back on the glass, his eyes never leaving Kelly. Ben stood in the room. His head was full of Kelly. There was a knock at the door. Ben was startled.

"You guys forget something?"

"It's room service."

"Didn't order anything," Ben replied.

He peeped through the spy-hole.

"Mr. Branson ordered for you before he left. Thought you might be hungry." The voice was muffled.

Ben opened the door. It was room service, but Mr. Branson hadn't ordered it. Someone else had. And Ben's eyes were as round as silver dollars.

CHAPTER 8

Dan stopped the big silver Jaguar with the tinted windows outside the Club Coco. Ty jumped out first, rushed around and opened the door, beating the club's valet to the job. Then Giles stepped out into the evening shade. He brushed his suit down and turned back to the car for Genna's hand. She climbed out behind him, and the two stood there, wanting to be noticed. They were successful.

Kelly waited a second then swung her high-heeled, black stocking legs out of the car and onto the curb. The short skirt followed revealing more of the legs. The line of people waiting at the entrance of the club took notice, especially the men. Kelly stood on the pavement waiting for her man. Kane leaned out of the car, and emerged with the desired effect. The gray suit sat perfectly on him and the silver silk shirt reflected in the lamplight. The line watched intently as Kane took a girl on each arm. A blonde-haired white man in this part of the world was a novelty. One with two young white girls on his arm was an obvious situation. Giles slipped the doorman a couple of twenties to let them in. No one argued. Giles held the door for his boss and the woman while Dan tossed the keys to the valet. Then, he and Ty joined the group. Both the young guys dressed in black to complement their pimp and his bodyguard.

Kane sauntered through the club entrance. His obvious power and money did not go unnoticed, and it got the group the best table. They were viewed with blatant curiosity, especially by one table in particular who watched a good ten minutes as the operation went down. Kane leaned back in the plush red seating and pulled Genna close to him. She felt like her heart missed a beat.

"Not my turn tonight then, boss?" asked Kelly, snuggling up to Kane.

"Decided on this sheila instead. You go and make me some money," replied her husband.

"Sneak," muttered Kelly pulling a face. "You offer him something I didn't?"

Genna laughed nervously back in her face.

"Don't think I can get myself a john for the night do you, missy? Well just you watch and learn," Kelly sneered at Genna.

Kelly stood up, wiggled her backside, and took off in the direction of the bar. She stopped by the dance floor and caught onto a single guy. She slid her arms around him, moved in close and they danced in time to the beat. Kelly moved away from him, and seductively swayed with the heavy, pounding music. Kane watched. Her backside never missed a beat.

Genna watched Kane's face with interest.

"She'll be fine, Kane. She can take care of herself," whispered Genna in Kane's ear.

"Yeah, I know that. It's just that…never mind. I know she can," and Kane unbuttoned his jacket and attempted to relax.

"So, boss. What are you drinking?" asked Giles. He was standing behind Kane's seat awaiting his orders.

"Think I'll have…"

"Allow me," responded a voice from Kane's side.

A short, olive-skinned man sat down at the table. He had an air about him that said, '*Don't mess with me*'. Behind him stood his bodyguard complete with very obvious .44 sticking out from under jacket.

"And you would be?" asked Kane, turning his head to look at the man next to him.

"Interested in the girl that just left you. The name is Koenig. I am a respected businessman around these parts. And you are?" His English was more than good.

"An Australian businessman over here on my kind of business," Kane answered.

"The prostitution business…or something else?" Koenig replied.

"A little of one… and more of the other. You want the girl?" Kane asked tentatively, hoping deep down he said no.

"I want," Koenig replied, "otherwise, why would I be at this kind of club, and why would you be here also?"

"Two thousand Hong Kong dollars," stated Kane looking into the man's face.

"Done," and Koenig clicked his fingers to his bodyguard who patiently waited. "I'll bring her back here tomorrow." His eyes wondered back over to Kelly.

The bodyguard handed the money to Giles. Giles took it but didn't count it.

"You'll bring her back at midnight tonight. Otherwise she'll cost you another thousand." Kane was pushing. And he shifted position in the seat.

Genna felt Kane's arm tighten on her shoulders. She swallowed hard.

"Okay," the Oriental nodded. "Does she need anything to get going on? Any fix she might want?"

Koenig didn't hesitate to ask the questions. Either he trusted his first instincts of the party, or Kane had put on a good show as a pimp. Kane hoped it was the latter. It just all seemed a little quick. But he figured these guys didn't have time to waste. As Koenig pointed out, that's why they were all there.

"No, she doesn't need anything. She's good with or without," said Kane knowing that was true. "But you may want to ask her. She may like something." Kane didn't believe his own words.

Koenig whispered to his man. The bodyguard disappeared across the floor and returned holding Kelly's arm. Her eyes were round and full, like a puppy separated from the rest of the litter. Giles could see the look on Kane's face and he hoped that the Chinaman could not.

"Boss, you want that drink now?" Giles asked.

Kane came back to reality. "Yeah, double whiskey. Get Mr. Koenig one also." He was trying to detain them.

"Not for me. When I decide on a girl, then I go." He turned to Kelly. "And I have decided. What is your name, child?"

"Star." It was the first thing that came to her mind. She stood by the table almost nervously.

"Then, shining Star, we will go and have some fun. Just you… and me. My car is outside. My driver will take us to the apartment and will bring you back here by midnight." Koenig ran his fingers down her arm, and Kelly tried not to squirm under his clammy touch.

"Sounds good to me." She looked directly at Kane. "You'll be here, boss?" her eyes piercing Kane's.

"I'll be here." His arm tightened even more on Genna's shoulder. "One of my guys goes with her," and Kane looked at the Chinaman.

"Don't you trust her with me?" asked Koenig, his eyes becoming even more slanted.

"I don't trust you with her. How do I know you'll return her? She earns me a lot of money. And she has more work to do for me tonight. You might decide she's good, and want to keep her. Ty goes."

Ty stepped forward, slightly shaken but not stirred.

"Okay. So let's go, then. We bid you farewell till midnight. Your man can stay *outside* the bedroom door."

Kane nodded his approval, and he watched the small party disappear out of the club doors. Kane downed the whisky in one go. It was up to Kelly now. She knew her job well enough and that was to find the name of a drug dealer. This club had come highly recommended by Chow as the central point of distribution. The next few hours were crucial for the mission.

Kane looked at his watch; almost nine. The next three hours would be the longest in his life.

The chauffeur opened the limo door, and let his boss in first. Kelly followed next and Ty got in last. The car was luxurious by any standards. Lavish seating, Crystal decanters of whiskey. Koenig talked in quick excited rhythm while Kelly listened. He rested his pudgy little hands on her knees, running his fingers along her leg. Kelly never flinched.

"You are very pretty Australian girl." His hand wandered a little higher.

Ty cringed. How was Kelly going to deal with this man, and why the hell had the boss let her do this?

"See. I told your pimp not that far to my home." Koenig gestured to the surrounding apartment blocks.

The limo pulled into the parking garage, and the automatic door closed behind them.

Koenig led the way, and they climbed a flight of plush carpeted stairs. Koenig opened the door, and ushered Kelly and Ty into the palatial apartment. It was a typical rich Hong Kong businessman's place. Rich tapestry's hung on the walls, and Ming vases seemed to be tossed in every direction Kelly looked. Koenig wasted no time in telling Kelly what to do.

"Bedroom right through there." He waved his fingers towards the door. "You go and I will follow. You want some cocaine to give you a nice buzz?" Koenig asked her, his eyes looking at every curve on her shapely body.

"Sure, why not? Better be a good class of drug though. It's the only kind I do." Kelly looked at her fingernails as she spoke and dropped her eyes down.

"Only the best for a girl like you. I'll bring some wine. Want to see you dance on wine and cocaine, and then see how high you can get when we do it."

Ty looked astonished. He wanted to get them both out now before this went any further. Kelly saw his look.

"Mr. Koenig," asked Kelly. "How about my friend here joins us? He is… well, I'm sure a man of your habits knows what a pretty man can do?"

Koenig laughed and touched Ty's blond hair. Ty cringed beneath his touch.

"A bonus. You are talented people. Let's go. I will get the wine. On the bedside table you will find glasses and stuff to make your own joints." He scurried away delighted he had both wishes in one night.

Kelly almost pushed Ty into the waiting bedroom, and shut the door behind her.

"What the hell are you doing, Kelly? Neither of us is going to do any-thing with that guy. Have you gone crazy? Man, you must have already been at the drugs."

Kelly emptied some things from her purse on the overly large bed, and showed Ty the small file of talcum powder. "Switch the cocaine with this powder. Koenig can do his own. Just put a little on each slip of paper and shake it so it looks right. When you smoke the joint, make sure you don't inhale any of it. Not sure what would happen if you did. You'd probably choke. Leave the rest to me. Give me one of those when you've done." Kelly paused. "Oh, and get your clothes off."

"What?" Ty looked at her like she had gone completely insane.

"Get your shirt and pants off. You've been to bed with a girl haven't you? For God sake's, Ty. Go through with this or we'll never get out alive. This may be our best chance tonight to find out who the local supplier is, and where the supply comes from."

Ty shook his head, but did as he was asked. He dropped his clothes over the chair back. He wore tight black briefs underneath and Kelly couldn't help but notice his shape.

"Not bad for a *youngster*. You'll make a great guy when you're older," she laughed, and tossed her head back. Kelly took her skirt and top off. Underneath she wore a black bra and a G-string. Garters held up her black stockings. She was devastatingly seductive. She pulled the pins from her hair and curls cascaded down her back. Ty was suddenly very aware of Kelly, and extremely jealous of Kane.

At that very moment, Koenig came through the door and viewed his catch. "Very nice, Miss Star." His eyes feasted on Kelly. "You and your friend are very nice. Here, let's toast your health and then do the drug." He looked at the bedside table. "Oh, you found it? I have my own brand right here. You want to try mine?" The wine bottle and glasses shook in his hands. He sat them down.

Kelly was backed into a corner. "Only if you try mine first. But why not try without the drugs? Here, let me help you with those clothes."

Ty watched in amazement as she seductively maneuvered the China-man out of his expensive suit. She slid the clothes from him with such experience. His shirt departed down his chest and she sat him down on the bed. Kelly licked her lips in a provocative manner.

"How do I know your stuff is pure? Where do you get it from?" Kelly asked.

As she spoke she rubbed her hands down his back and massaged his neck. She stood in front of him with her breasts near his face. Ty could hear him breathing hard, and Koenig struggled with his words. His hands rested on her garters and his fingers caressed them. Ty felt sick.

"It come from Lantau Island. Only good stuff from Lantau," stammered Koenig.

"What if my boss wants some for us? Can we get it? Can we get China white if we want that also?"

The Chinaman hesitated. Kelly sensed it.

"Ty, undo the hooks of my bra for me, would you?" and Kelly moved back towards him.

Koenig looked on with popped eyes. This was worth his money.

She could feel Ty's hands shaking on her back, but he did it and was careful not to let the black lace object fall.

"Coco Club has a contact. Your boss can buy anything from him." Koenig's lips drooled.

"This contact have a name?" She lowered the bra.

Again Koenig hesitated.

Kelly took the man's hands and laid them on the cheeks of her back-side. Koenig was salivating at his mouth.

"His name is Cheng. Now we have sex?"

"Oh, yeah. Now we have sex. But first, we smoke, and maybe take some uppers. After you, Mr. Koenig." She opened her purse and handed him something from it. "Special for you, Mr. Koenig. A gift from me," and she handed him the pills. Pouring out a glass of wine, Kelly handed it to him.

"You too. Try some of my present for you." Koenig handed her the joint he had brought in with the drinks.

She had no choice. She took the real joint from him. Kelly took one drag on it.

"More, more. You smoke more, Miss Star. Want to see what you do. See I take what you gave me," and he swallowed the pills down without question. What he thought were uppers were really very strong knockout pills.

Kelly inhaled deeply and a stream of smoke came through her nose.

Koenig's eyes swirled around in his head, and he was out in seconds. He fell back on the giant, fluffy pillows. Kelly popped her smoke back on the bedside table ash tray.

"What the hell did you give him?" whispered Ty.

"You don't want to know, but you do want to get me back to Kane. It's a long time since I smoked, and I don't know how I will react. Hook my bra back up, would you?"

Hesitantly, he did as he was asked. Kelly pulled on her skirt on her tight round butt and her top back on fast, and then helped Ty lay the little man back comfortably on the bed. They pushed the pillows around his sleeping head, and then covered him with a blanket.

"He'll sleep, that's all." Kelly looked down at the little man. "Mr. Koenig, when you wake you will have had the best sex ever…" She patted his face and stood by the door ready to go. "Come on. I want out of this creep's place. Reminds me too much of the old days." She already had a buzz.

The bodyguard looked suspiciously at the pair as they opened the door and stepped out into the hallway. He peered back through the door and saw his boss sleeping. On his face he wore a smile. The bodyguard quietly closed the door, and escorted the duo down to the waiting car.

Kelly felt a little wobbly on her feet and she clung to Ty's arm. She climbed in the car, almost banging her head as she stepped inside the vehicle. Driving back to Club Coco, Kelly felt more than a little sick. She closed her eyes and tried hard to think of more pleasant things. They eluded her right then.

The car came to an abrupt stop. A valet opened the door for the pair. Ty stepped out first and Kelly followed in a rather clumsy fashion, her heel catching on the seat. The doorman found time to take another look at Kelly's great shape.

Kane went through a packet of cigarettes in the time Kelly was gone. He used the restroom. He ordered drinks, and was generally irritated with everyone around him. He'd pulled the band from his hair, letting it hang down. He removed his tie, and opened the top buttons of the silk shirt. His jacket hung on the back of the chair. Kane stood. His watch ticked by but not fast enough for his liking.

"For god's sake, Kane, sit down. You're attracting attention. Here have another whiskey." Dan handed him a glass.

Kane downed it in one go. No amount would make him drunk. Then he saw his wife come through the door. He knew immediately what she had done by the unsteady way she was walking towards him. She was holding tightly onto Ty's arm.

When she reached him, she looked up into Kane's eyes. He cupped her face in his hands and he looked at her eyes. Kelly's pupils were dilated.

"Fucking hell, Kelly. What did you do?" Kane looked at Ty, a deep anger inside him. "Why did you let her do it, Ty?"

"He didn't have a choice." Kelly's voice was slurred and her eyes glazed. "I'm gonna throw up…" She exclaimed, her hands flying up to her mouth.

"Take deep breaths." Kane sat her down in the plush seats, and she fell back against the cushions. Kane focused back on Ty. "Did he touch her?"

Ty thought if he gave the wrong answer, Kane would kill him where he stood.

"No, sir. She gave him something that put him out. Something I assume you supplied." Attack seemed the best course of defense.

In the club lighting Kane peered at Ty. "How come your T-shirt is inside out?"

Kelly intervened. "That would be my fault. I made him take his clothes off. He's kind of got a cute butt for a young guy," and she giggled as she remembered, and wrinkled her nose at her husband.

"What did you smoke?" Kane was not in a good mood.

"Don't blame Ty. I had this plan and it kind of got turned around. Guy only got a flash of my boobs. Hell, Kane, plenty men have seen those. You saw those the first day we met, and much more. No need to get upset, baby," she was rambling at Kane.

"Let's get her out of here. Dan, go get the car." Kane's stony face looked upon them.

"Don't want to go, Kane. Want to dance. Dance with me, Kane?" Kelly pulled on his arm. "Have something to tell you. Will make you want to stay."

She stood up best she could and wrapped her arms around him, seducing Kane in front of his people. The rest of the group watched in amazement at her antics. Kane was right. Kelly was good…with or without drugs.

She led Kane onto the floor. Not so much led, as moved with him. The strobe lights flashed around them. Kelly raised her hands and ran them through her hair. Her body moved in time to the pounding music. Kane was aware people were watching, especially his own group. She closed in on him and clasped her arms around his neck. Her body was as close as she could get it to him. His hands rested on her backside. He moved with her and she stood on tiptoe, whispering in his ear.

Kane rose up from her cheek and looked out across the dance floor. The beat of the music embraced his mind and her words echoed in her ear.

Giles couldn't take his eyes off them. He stared at Kelly. Was this what drugs did? He'd done pot but that was all. Then Giles saw where Kane was looking. Kane had sighted his target coming through the door. His vision was as tunneled as it would ever get. His eyes narrowed as Sam Cheng and his entourage entered the club. Kane kept on dancing, mainly due to Kelly forcing him to.

Sam stepped into the light and through the semi-crowded dance floor he saw his father. And he saw the girl with him. His father… the Australian pimp. Cheng could feel his heart racing, and his blood on fire. Their eyes locked. Sam glanced around with the feeling a man like Kane Branson wouldn't be alone. He wanted to kill the man that sullied his mother. Time stood still, but the music didn't. It stopped and so did the dancing.

Kane knew now who the local dealer was. Kelly had told him it was Cheng. Sam Cheng, his only son and Chinese Agent, was one of the guys distributing drugs, and Kane knew that his uncle was in full control. In Kane's mind, he'd convinced himself who was in league with Cheng. Only one other man had known of Sam's existence. Or so he thought.

"Darling, let's get the hell out of here." Kane whispered in her ear. "You did your job. I'll take it from here. Genna and you are out of here. It's too dangerous. These guys are playing for keeps."

She raised her head. "Where you go, I go…"

The world began to spin around her and Kelly fainted. Kane caught her in his arms. Her head flopped backward, and Kane carried her from the dance floor.

Cheng never moved, nor did he take his eyes from the pair. The dancers cleared a path to let Kane through, and he carried her back to the seat in the booth.

"She okay?" Genna asked, as she knelt down beside her friend.

"Ask your good buddy Ty. He's the one who let her smoke dope," retorted Kane.

Giles stepped in on Ty's behalf. "Come on, Kane. He's just a kid."

"A kid? Then what the fuck is he doing here?" Kane's eyes were wild.

"Same as us all, Kane. Following you," came Giles cynical reply.

The music started again, loud and pulsating. This time the floor was crowded, and Kane turned to see that Cheng was gone. His eyes scanned the room. There was no sign of him or his group. Kane picked up his jacket and slung it over his shoulder.

"Get the car. We're out of here. Dan, call Ben at the hotel. Tell him we're on our way."

Kane helped Kelly out of the seat, and moved her bodily towards the club entrance, her legs struggling to find the ground. Non-the-less, they made it to the door.

Outside in the fresh air Kelly came around. "What happened?" Her pupils were still dilated. Kelly looked round her trying to figure out why the world was spinning.

"You fainted. You'll be fine. No lasting effects." Her husband tried to convince her. "We're going back to the hotel. Where the hell is that car?"

"The valet should be back any…"

Dan never finished the sentence. From the parking lot an explosion shook the ground and a ball of fire rocked the night into life. It sprang up and billowed on past the entrance. The blast was intense and sent the group back into the doorway. Kane shielded Kelly from the heat with his body, throwing himself across her. Giles grabbed Genna and pulled her back into the club. The force of the explosion sent the customers running for their lives, as flames engulfed the parking lot.

As Kane cradled Kelly in his arms he felt something hammer him on the arm, but paid it no attention. "Kelly. You okay, baby? Answer me." He patted her face gently.

She had slumped down in the doorway. She, Dan and Kane were closest to the explosion.

"Kelly!" Kane shook her violently fearing the worst.

She sputtered then burst into life. "I'm okay. Where's Dan?" she whispered. She wiped the dust from her eyes, and peered though the mayhem.

Kane looked around. As the smoke cleared Kane saw Dan lying face down on the hard concrete.

"Oh, God. No! Don't move, Kelly. Stay right where you are!" And he planted her firmly there. Kane sprinted across the driveway to his man. There was no movement from Dan, but there was a fair amount of blood on the ground. Gently, Kane turned his son-in-law over and felt his pulse. It was slow, but it was solid. Dan was still breathing, but a huge gash on the front of his head was causing blood to gush down Dan's face. Kelly followed Kane and sat down on the ground beside them both.

"I thought I told you to stay put, Kelly?" But Kane's thoughts turned back to Dan as he saw his fingers moving. "Dan, open your eyes. Damn it, open them!" yelled Kane.

His son-in-law's eyelids flickered and he came to, briefly.

"My god, don't ever do that again. How would I tell my daughter? Where else do you hurt aside from your head?" Kane was angry and relieved all in one go.

"Everywhere. I feel like a punching bag. Everyone else okay?" Dan murmured. He blinked his eyes. Everything was cloudy, but he did try to move and it really hurt.

"Yeah. Fine. Lie still. God's sake, where are the police in this hellhole?" he yelled. Kane saw Ty coming toward them. "Where the fuck have you been?"

"Checking on the others. How bad is he?" asked the young man, kneeling down beside Dan, blonde hair flopping in his eyes.

"Bad. How are they?" Kane was supporting Dan's head against his body. "For god's sake where are these people? Ty, what did you say?" his concentration focused on his son-in-law.

"Giles and Genna went back inside the club," said Ty. He coughed on the smoke that still swirled around the lot, and looked across at the burning car.

'*Really?*' thought Kane.

"My god, that could have been me in that car," Dan muttered.

"Or me,"Ty replied trembling at the thought.

"Yeah or you," said Kane, and an ugly thought passed through his brain. Wasn't any fucking accident. It was hit number three. It should have been one of them in that car.

After what seemed like an eternity the local police arrived. Inspector Chow arrived seconds after. Chow jumped from his car, and hurried over to the scene of the crime.

"Mitter Brandon, we meet again. How you come to be mixed up in this?" the chubby little man asked.

"Valet was driving my car. Listen we need a hospital. Can you get an ambulance for my bloke here? He's hurt pretty badly."

"Looks like you need the hospital also, Mitter Brandon. Your arm."

In the confusion Kane hadn't noticed his shirtsleeve was hanging off and blood was seeping down his shirt. "Just a scratch. Nothing to it."

"No? Then why blood streaming down your arm? Mitter Brandon, think bomb was in car."

"No shit!" Kane replied. "And my arm is fine."

"Not look like that to me. Blood is everywhere."

Chow ripped the sleeve from Kane's shirt, and pulled away the piece of cloth. He saw a scrap of metal from the car sticking out of Kane's muscle.

"Hold still and I will…" He had a handkerchief and was trying to make a tourniquet.

"Look, Chow. This bloke lying here needs more attention than me. If it makes you happy…" Kane put his fingers on the metal and slowly pulled it from the muscle without flinching. "Now you can bandage it or whatever."

"Mitter Buchanan was right. You are brave." Chow looked up to the fiery Australian.

"Or stupid. And what else did Mr. Buchanan have to impart?"

"That you are stubborn and reckless to get where you want to go," retorted Chow.

Chow continued making his tourniquet, and tried hard to stem the flow of blood. He was doing what he could. A feeling of respect was growing between the two most unlikely men.

Kane looked across the lot. The ambulance had arrived and the paramedics were making great haste to where Dan lay. They made a determination of Dan's condition, and then lifted him gently on to the stretcher.

"You go easy with him. He's precious cargo, you hear?" Kane said to them.

"Now you go to hospital with your man and take this girl here with you. She look like she need you velly much, Mitter Brandon. She much more than one of your group to you. I watch. I see. The rest of your group come wit me. I have to question them. I have to question anyone here tonight. I see you later. Police car bring you back to headquarters. You and the girl." Inspector Chow had spoken and right now Inspector Chow was the bloke in charge.

Giles emerged from the club with Genna firmly attached to his hand. Kane shot him a look and inclined his head toward himself. Kane wanted Giles near him. After a few minutes of confirming he was with Branson's party, the officer outside the door let Giles through the now-cordoned off area. Police were everywhere.

"Kane, that was a bomb, wasn't it? What the hell happened to your arm? And I saw Dan on the stretcher. Is he okay?" Giles was edgy. He looked down at Kelly who still sat on the ground.

Kane stood holding his arm. "He'll survive. Kelly and I are going to the hospital with him. You guys go with Chow and, for god's sake, and be careful. We're all split up now. Just what they wanted to happen. Take Ty with you. Remember, keep your friends close to you, but keep your enemies even closer," and he reached down for Kelly's hand.

Kelly stood up beside him. Her stockings were torn and her T-shirt ragged. Kane put his arms around her and the two walked towards the ambulance.

In the ER Dan slipped in and out of consciousness. This incident tonight was another blow to the mission. One more down; only six left.

Several stitches and an expertly bandaged arm later, Kane sat on a bench near Dan's room. He stared at the ceiling. This may be his hundredth mission, but it sure felt like his first. Everything that could possibly go wrong had. And where the hell was Kelly? She had been gone too long. All they had to do was to check her out.

Kane's jacket lay across his lap and he toyed with the lapel. From his boot he retrieved his cell phone. He tried Ben. There was still no reply. Kane was concerned. Out the corner of his eye, he saw Kelly walking down the lobby. She was crying. Kane jumped up from the seat and rushed to her. He encircled her with his arms, concern written all over his face.

"Baby, you okay? What did they do to you? You've been gone so long. Kelly?"

Kane sat her down on the bench. This time she let go and tears streamed down her face. "The cocaine," she stammered, "or maybe the blast from the car…but I'm bleeding Kane. I may lose the baby."

Kane stared at her like she had just told him she was dying. Kane pulled her closer to him and held her. He rocked her in his arms, and his chin rested on her head. This was too much of a price to pay. She was going back to Australia along with Dan, whether she liked it or not.

"Mitter Branson?" A voice interrupted.

"Not now, doc. My wife needs me," rebuked Kane.

"Dan Lord need you also. Could you come wit me?" The doctor asked. "Mr. Lord need more attention than we thought. His vision, it blurred. You sign papers for him to stay here a few days," and he tried to usher Kane away from the bench.

"Whatever," replied Kane, and collected his wife and their belongings.

The doctor continued talking as he led them down to Dan's room. When Kane stepped inside the door, he knew immediately the doctor was right.

Dan turned at the sound of the door opening. "Kane, is that you? I can't see you too well. Everything is blurred. They want me to take some tests. 'Tis you, right?" asked his son-in-law. Dan reached out across the sheet towards Kane, as if in search for a guiding light.

"Yeah, it's me and Kelly. You're gonna be just fine." Doctor said he would be, but not just yet. "You have to stay here for a few days. Get yourself straight and then you and Kelly will go back to Sydney."

Kane reached for Dan's hand trying to give comfort. Dan clung to him. This was not the Dan that Kane knew. This was someone scared. Kane stood close to the bed, holding Kelly in his other arm.

"But I want to see this through," muttered Dan, his fingers clutching at the Kane's.

"Well you can't. Neither you… nor Kelly. You're going back together." Kane had spoken.

"The hell I am," interrupted Kelly. "I'm going on. If I'm gonna lose this baby, it's not gonna be in vain," and she pulled away from Kane.

"You're what?" asked Dan, still trying to focus on them.

"They said I might lose the baby, but I won't. I know my body and me.

I can take it. I'll stop bleeding. And I'm not leaving you, Kane, till death do us part, remember?" She looked at his face.

"Whose death, Kel? Don't I get a say in my child's life? You're young. How many more chances do I get to father a son legitimately?" His tone was selfish. He hadn't meant that.

"I'll be careful, I promise. If this doesn't stop, I'll go back." She gazed up into his eyes, and as usual, he couldn't resist her.

Kane cleared his throat. "Ok, for now," he muttered. "We have to go to headquarters. Chow wants our statements. He'll want one from you also, Dan. You know what to say." He held onto Dan's hand, and shook it. "Good luck, son." Kane paused. He realized it was the first time he had ever called Dan son. He continued in a more professional manner. "Buchanan will have you out of here. Take care of yourself. It's up to the six of us now. By the way, did you ever get hold of Ben?"

"No," he replied slightly shaken by the word 'son', and as the medication took over, he continued, "Did you?" Dan's speech became slurred, and he began to drift into a sleep.

"No," was the only word Kane uttered.

When they reached headquarters the rest of the group was waiting. Kane's bandaged arm could clearly be seen.

"Hurt much?" asked Giles. He hoped it did. Giles looked at the expression on Kelly's face. Something was very wrong.

"Only when I laugh, and I don't see that there is going to be a whole lot of laughing around here. Dan is out. Kelly's still in." Kane glanced at her. "For now. You all talked out with Chow?"

"Yeah. He's just waiting on you two. Bomb was timed to go off after a couple of blocks. If the car had been out front... well we wouldn't be sitting here discussing it now."

"Hell. That valet was just a kid. We must be getting too close for their liking. Some Australian more than likely set us up. They sent us in and they don't care what happens to us. It's up to us to get ourselves out of here. The only one who is safe is Dan. Only cause he can't see properly. Anyone reach Ben yet?"

No one had.

Kane figured someone had already got to him. What he wasn't sure of was who.

CHAPTER 9

Tired and despondent, the five members of the group were driven back to the hotel. Kane's arm was painful where the metal had hit the muscle, but that was the least of his worries. He had his other arm around Kelly and she leaned against him, her face pinched and tearstained. She needed to rest, and rest was not part of the agenda. He should have insisted that she stay in Australia. Now, it was too late.

They trailed across the lobby of the hotel. Kelly held the strap of her purse and it dragged behind her. It made a kind of clinking noise as it hit the floor. One by one they climbed into the elevator. It stopped on the penthouse floor. Kane and Kelly were first to the suite door. It was ajar. Kane pushed Kelly behind him. She leaned against the wall offering no resistance to him. Kane drew his gun. He held it straight out in front of him, and kicked the door slightly with his foot.

"Ben," he yelled.

There was no reply. He called again. Giles immediately stepped to the other side of the doorframe and held his gun ready. Kane looked at Giles.

"One, two…"

They burst through the door together, guns frozen in their hands. The two women stayed outside, while Ty stepped carefully inside. Giles stood firm while Kane searched each room.

"All clear in the bedrooms," Kane yelled, and he surfaced back to the main room. "Nothing. He's gone."

"This doesn't make sense. Not even a clue," stated Giles wandering room the room..

"No? Look at this."

Kane picked up something from the floor. It was a piece of cream silk material the same kind that Lilia had been wearing on her body. He held the material to the light. Possibly whoever had killed Lilia had Ben.

Kane reached for the phone, and laid his gun down on the table next to the couch. He dialed the Inspector's number.

"Hello, Inspector Chow?" said Kane. Confirming it was, he continued. Kane dropped his voice to a whisper. "Keep someone on Lord's door day and night until you get him safely onto that plane to Sydney. Another one of my people has gone." He paused and raised his voice so everyone could hear. "Yeah, I think possibly same people that killed Lilia. We're out of here at first light. I think I know who the double agent is. Who else knows? Only that person. It's not me and it's not you. That's all I'm gonna say. I'll be in touch." He hung up the line.

Kane picked up his weapon and put it next to him on the arm of the couch.

"Kel, please go get some rest. I'm not asking you, I'm telling you as your commander. Take the master bedroom, and I'll join you in a little while. Please, Kel?" Kane ushered her to the door and closed it behind her. He returned to the couch and sat fingering the now retrieved gun.

"She upset over Dan?" asked Genna.

"Yeah, she's upset over that situation and another." Was now a good time to tell them? He looked around the room. "She may also be miscarrying."

"She's what?" Giles practically choked on his own words.

"You suddenly have a hearing problem, Giles. Either the cocaine or the bomb blast caused her to start bleeding. My guess it was the blast. But she's tough. And before anyone asks, she won't go back. She wants to go on. I could order her back…"

"Then why the fuck don't you?" Giles voice was raised.

Kane remained calm. "If it was your wife, would you? I want that child, but I want Kelly more. I also respect her wishes. She stood by me with Lilia, now I have to stand by what she wants."

This was a side of Kane that no one had seen. A side he never showed to the outside world.

Giles sat down on the floor and stretched his long legs in front of him. To Giles, she should go back but Kane Branson had a point, and Giles didn't really want Kelly to go back.

"You mentioned to the person on the phone that you know who the double agent is. I assume you called Buchanan?" Giles paused.

Kane said nothing.

"Do you? You think it's me?" asked Giles very matter-of-factly.

Kane shrugged his shoulders.

"Or me?" added Genna.

"I said I know. Didn't say I was going to announce the person's name. I suggest we get some sleep. We leave here at daybreak. All of you be ready. We are only five. If Ben is still alive, they will contact us. If he isn't… I do suggest that Genna, you sleep in the same room as Giles…Ty take the couch. I'll leave the bedroom door unlocked. If you hear anything out here, come get me." Kane's face looked like forty miles of bad road. He had no control over the way things were going and that was not his style. "I'm gonna go see my wife. If Chow calls…wake me. All of you know what to do. You're not children." Kane stood up, took his weapon with him, and walked to the door. He checked the deadbolt on the main door and followed that with fastening the chain. "Goodnight." Kane left them still staring at their leader.

Kane took off his suit and boots. He laid his .38 and his cell right next to his pillow. From his bag, he pulled out a pair of gray sweatpants and slid into them. He sat down on the bed next to Kelly.

"You asleep, Kelly?" Kane whispered and rested his hand on her hips.

"No," she murmured, her head turned away from him.

"You will not lose my child. You hear?" He gently took her by the arms and pulled her up to him. He cradled her there.

Without warning her emotions got the better of her and Kelly cried huge racking sobs that tore at Kane's heartstrings. "I promised you I wouldn't and I won't," she uttered, the words barely reaching her mouth.

"Kelly, Kel. I want this baby as much as you do but not at the expense of your life. Always remember that I love you, no matter what happens. I love you more than I have ever loved anyone in my life, baby or no baby." He laid her back down on the pillows and pulled the covers over them both. Kelly clung to him, vulnerable and right now unsure of herself. She was his chink.

"You don't have to say that. I came along way after Sage Jay. You were married to her for so many years. I know you love me," she sobbed.

"I meant what I said. I love you more than I've loved anyone. You give me the incentive to go on. Something no one else ever has. Tonight, when I saw you crumpled down in that doorway, I was scared. Scared that I was going to lose you. And while you were gone with that john, I thought I would go insane. That will never happen again, never!" Kane reassured her.

He raised his voice and Kelly knew he meant just what he said.

"It's okay, Kane. Really, it was okay. He didn't touch me."

And Kelly realized she was the one jeopardizing the mission. Kane was paying far too much attention to her and not enough to his squad. He was right she should not have come. She clung to him and could feel his strength. Like Samson, she was his Delilah. Kane lay back on the pillows and comforted her. He kissed her forehead, and stroked her hair. Then he thought of his son, a man he would have to kill: a man who probably was up to his eyes in the filth and slime of Hong Kong's crime. He knew exactly whom Sam Cheng was working for and whom he was working with. The whole thing frightened him. They needed to get out of that hotel and on into Lantau. Dan was safe. Ben, maybe, or Ben could already be dead. At last, Kane dozed. Sheer fatigue overcame him.

Kelly hadn't fallen asleep. She let Kane think that. She watched how he tossed and turned, that he was fighting with his conscience. She saw him lie on his arm and cry out as the injured muscle ached under his weight. Kelly also had her suspicions who the double agent was. If Kane's theory was correct, they were all in serious trouble. Making sure he was asleep, she went into the bathroom and climbed into the shower.

"Thank god," she murmured. For now, she had quit bleeding. Showering, she pulled on clean underwear and prepared for the day ahead.

"Here, catch." Giles tossed Genna her backpack. "Got in it all the things you'll need. Ty, here's yours."

"Morning," said Kane. "You people ready? Figured we'd go down the back stairs and grab a cab to the docks. Boat would be a good way to get round the coast. Should be able to rent a powerboat, then we can dock it in the harbor in case we need to exit quickly. I've been looking at some maps. From the harbor we can cut across country…"

"Sir, how's your wife?" Ty interrupted.

He was the only one who asked.

Kane put his hand on the boy's shoulder. "She's just fine. Just fine." And Kane had just made Ty a marked man. Ty was on Kane's side.

Kelly appeared dressed in a gray sweat suit, the same as Kane's, and her backpack already hung from her shoulder. She'd packed what Kane had told her to. The rest of their stuff was left behind.

"Let's go, troops. We can eat later." Kane was last out of the door and closed it behind him without even a glance back.

As they hustled out of the penthouse suite and down the landing, Kane caught up to Kelly.

"You sure you're okay?" he whispered.

"Sure. I'll tell you if I'm not. Stop letting me cloud your judgment. That's just what the traitor wants," and Kelly moved ahead of him and out of earshot.

Opening the side door, the five scooted down the back stairs, a thing Kelly was getting used to. Giles was out front first and hailed a cab. The five-person team climbed in. Kelly stayed a little distant, staring out of the window through most of the ride to the docks. Kane gave the Chinese cab driver instructions to the harbor. In the morning light, the harbor looked enchanting encompassed by a delusion of the corruption shrouded round it.

Kane's first mission in Hong Kong was coming in useful. His use of the Chinese language, their ways, even down to helping him procure a small powerful fishing boat named the Nighteagle. Kelly thought it an appropriate name. Kane slowly steered it out of the harbor. The crystal waters swirled around the boat, and the engine roared with tempestuous glee. Kane handled it easily.

"Where the heck did you learn to steer a boat like that? No, don't tell me. Don't think I want to know. Last time I asked a question like that you were flying choppers and rescuing me from my pa's compound," Kelly commented, and she moved away from him, and sat down in the back of the boat.

Giles moved over and stood next to Kane at the helm. Through the sunshine of the early morning came winds from the water, and the ocean became just a little choppy. "You call Buchanan before we left the hotel?" Giles yelled at Kane.

"Course. Someone had to take care of the bill. Know now where to pick up the explosives and the guns. Some bloke has them in store for us. Hopefully, we'll be one step ahead of the Chinese. That's probably the last thing Buchanan will do for us."

"What'd you say, Kane?" yelled Giles. "Didn't hear you?" the wind blew in his face.

Kane's voice was lost as the boat powered into faster action, and the Nighteagle took out to sea. The current was for them and steering was easy. They had gone only a mile when Genna noticed a small boat behind them.

"Someone's tracking us," she screamed against the wind, her fingers pointing to the stern.

Giles turned to look. "She's right. You want me to give them all their guns, Kane?"

"Good a time as any…in my backpack…give all three of them out."

Kane picked up speed sending the passengers to the side of the boat. "Hold on! And load your weapons."

Giles frantically handed out ammunition.

Kane powered on through the sea. The small boat behind them was gaining. Built especially for speed, its engine capacity was greater then the Nighteagle.

"Someone really doesn't want us to go anywhere. Man, the drugs must be flowing out of this shitty island. We have to be heading towards the right place," yelled Giles.

"Yeah, Giles. It's either the prison or the fort. Figured they're running the drugs from there. If those bastards behind get any closer…shoot the buggers."

"You serious?" screamed the girl, her eyes wide.

"You want to die right here, Genna?" yelled Kane.

He hit the gas as hard as the boat would go. How did they find them so soon? One more piece of the jigsaw. The big blue Nighteagle bounced through the choppy water. Kane was skillful, and he twisted and turned the Nighteagle to throw the pursuer's aim off guard. But they were catching up fast, only a few hundred feet between them now. Giles could see the automatic in the man's hand. A man dressed from head to toe in black.

"Kane…they're gonna fire!" screamed Giles.

"Then take them out before they get us! Fucking hell, you know what to do! Ty, get over here and take this fucking wheel. When I tell you, stop the boat dead in the water."

Kane climbed over the backpacks and braced himself between the girls and Giles. The small boat let off a round of ammunition. It fell just short of the Nighteagle's bow. The spray of water flew into Kane's face. He spat out the salty water.

"Hold your fire!" Kane crouched down by his comrades.

"Ty, now! Cut the engine!"

The Nighteagle came to an abrupt halt with the wake rising on each side.

"Fire over their heads!" screamed Kane.

Three of them fired one shot each. It didn't work. The small boat came even closer. The gunman raised his automatic to fire again. Kane glanced at Kelly. She was there, gun aimed high and smoking, ready to kill at his command. Kane stood up, aimed, opened fire before he gave another order, and the gunman in black was dead before he hit the deck. Kane turned slightly, altered his aim, fired again, and hit the gas tank square on. The force of the explosion ripped through the boat. It was gone in seconds and along with it all thought of pursuit. It caused a swell and rocked the Nighteagle roughly in its path.

Kane leaned back in the boat, reloaded his gun, and put it back in his pants. His injury had not impaired his aim. He rested his hand on Kelly's and lowered her gun. Once again she was there for him.

"What the hell are you two staring at?" remarked Kane. "Genna, you may be a beginner, but you should be used to death by now. And Giles, did you even fire? If Kelly can shoot at her own father, I'm sure you two can take out a couple of Chinese clowns…" He stopped dead. His anger had caused him to say what he was thinking.

Genna was the first to reply. "You did what? Your own father?"

"Shocked, Genna? Yeah, I shot at my own pa to save Kane. My father shot me! And then I watched pa die. He deserved it. He was operating a drug ring out near Brisbane. Kane busted it. He was also holding Kane's daughter… by one means or another. When she tried to run away with some bloke, my father openly slaughtered the man in front of us." She paused. "He also fed me with China White…" She sat down on the floor of the boat, her legs stretched out in front of her and a strange look on her face, like firing that gun had brought back horrors of yesteryear.

"Kelly! Don't say anymore," interrupted Kane. "I wasn't thinking when I said…" He bent down beside her.

"But I was when I pointed that gun. It is okay, Kane. Really it is. It's time to talk about it and put it behind me." She turned to her audience. "My pa and his friends took away my virginity and turned me into a prostitute. That's how I met Kane. I picked him up on a plane." She smiled as she remembered and turned her eyes to him. "And he changed my whole life. If it hadn't been for Kane, I don't know where I would be now." She looked at Kane. "You saw me fire, didn't you, Kane? I would have done killed that bloke."

"I know you would, baby, I know. That's why I fired first." He sat down next to her, pulled her to him, and Kelly leaned back against the man she loved more than her own life. The boat rocked as he moved.

"So you did set up Walker? You kill him too? We always wondered. Buchanan…" Giles didn't get to finish.

"Buchanan what? His name crops up at every turn around," snapped Kane, a look of anger in his eyes.

"He swore you killed him on purpose. That the car fire was no accident, that he couldn't prove it. He covered for you, but it cost him a promotion. He never did get over it…so they say, anyway." Giles' tone was almost accusatory.

"He was in line for that executive job then? I wondered why he didn't get it. But he did make commander though?" asked Kane.

"He made that, but he wanted more and you stopped him. You'll get the job he wanted, and you know you will."

"Don't want it on those terms. I like missions, not paperwork," Kane lied and stood up.

Ty was staring at Kelly as though she was on the 'hundred most wanted' list. Kane saw the look on the kid's face.

"You got a problem, Ty?" asked Kane.

"No, sir. Just surprised, that's all. We all saw this girl as your wife and a dead pushover in training class. Turns out she's tougher than all of us put together. You have my respect, Mrs. Branson."

Kelly smiled and stretched her hand out to Ty. He pulled her up from the deck of the boat.

"Okay, mutual admiration society meeting over. Let's get moving before they realize their little scouting party is not coming back. We'll find an inlet somewhere and dump this thing."

Kane took the helm, restarted the engine, and bounced the Nighteagle through the waters until he saw an inlet suitable to pull into. Carefully, Kane maneuvered the boat between the craggy rocks. The Nighteagle extended its bow under Kane's command. He'd found a nice little incline on the west side of the island. He stopped short of land.

"Okay, everyone out. Keep your guns dry, and your feet on the ground, even though it might be wet. Take a corner of the boat and follow me," Kane paused. "You all understand?"

They all understood. The group donned their backpacks, bailed out into the ocean, splashed through the waves and dragged the boat in behind them. They dragged it onto the beach, their wet clothes sticking to them, especially the girls, who were lower to the water. They reached land, dropped backpacks and waited. Kane pulled off his sweatshirt, and wrung out the salt water. He hung it from his belt. From his pack, he pulled a black bandana. He twisted it in a rope and tied it round his head. From his neck hung the silver K. He stood in front of his group.

"Don't all just stand there. Change your clothes and get comfortable at least. Everything we need is in the center of the island. I used the boat as a decoy to make a diversion. It worked better than I had intended. We need to pick up the explosives and the guns. Ty, stay with the girls. Don't let either of them out of your sight. Not for any reason."

"No, sir," he replied. Ty was stacking backpacks together.

"Giles, you and I are gonna go sink a boat. I thought about keeping it, but if it's found, they have our location." He dropped his gear down by a seated Kelly, and handed her his .38. Pulling of his boots, he set them down in the sand, and stood waiting for Giles, which to Kane was an eternity. Giles was shedding clothes and taking his time doing it.

On Kane's command, he and Giles pushed the Nighteagle back out from the shoreline. Kane took the wheel, and they powered out a fair way. It stopped on its own, out of fuel.

"Hell! Wanted to take it out farther, but this will have to do." He looked exasperated.

Kane picked up a crowbar and hit the deck boards. Water spewed though the open holes and touched Kane's feet. It began to seep along the boards and within minutes was a good six inches deep in water.

"Okay, Giles, start swimming. I'll catch up to you."

Giles gave him a parting look, and then dived into the water and made for the shore. He looked back. The boat was disappearing fast and Kane was nowhere in sight. Giles trod water and turned to look for Kane. Where the hell was he? From nowhere Kane surfaced, water spewing from his mouth.

"Thought I'd left you? You hoped? Let's get the fuck back to land and get this mission going," and Kane laughed as he dunked his head back under the water.

Kane raced ahead of Giles. Kane was first on shore. Kane was always first, and that was the problem. He stepped onto the shore, soaking wet, his sweat pants sticking to him. He winked at Kelly, and she smiled back. It didn't go unnoticed. The sand was hot under his feet which reminded him to put his boots back on.

"All of you put on your fatigues. Black is good in this kind of terrain. Keep one set of civilian clothes in your backpack, and make sure you have your weapons and ammunition. That's all you'll need."

Genna hesitated.

"That includes you, Genna. Just get your damn clothes off and get changed. You don't have anything that no one hasn't seen before: especially one of us." Kane had hoped by putting her in Giles room that…

"Sir, I didn't spend the night with Giles and I don't intend to," grumbled Genna.

"That's obvious," Kane muttered.

"You say something, sir?"

"Maybe that's what you need, Genna?" Kane was getting very irritated with her. "To get laid…"

"Kane!" cut in Kelly amazed that he would actually say what he was thinking.

He checked himself. "Just get changed, Goddamn it. Ty, when you're all done, go dig a hole and bury the rest of this stuff. Okay, listen up. Before we leave, there's something I want to say."

Kane finished straightening the black bandana round his head. He had been watching them all while they changed. Giles, with his military background, and until now had been a damn good federal agent. Even his clothing was all strictly regulation. Long black pants and vest and both pieces of clothing hung baggy. Kelly, always ready, willing, and able in more ways than one. She even looked sexy in her skin-tight fatigues. He secured his concentration. Genna, little Miss Popularity, was still stiff and starchy. He felt sorry for Giles. And Ty young but very dedicated, looking kind of like himself, Kane thought. Kane realized they were all staring at him in expectancy.

"As I was saying. I came to a decision today. If anything happens to me," he hesitated aware he would now be making the rift Grand-Canyon-sized, "my wife takes over the mission."

"Don't be ridiculous, Kane. I'm Kelly Walker remember? And I won't know what to do." Kelly was horrified.

"You're Federal Agent Kelly Branson, my wife and quite capable," Kane yelled. "Giles will help you. Anything you don't know he'll show you. And when you answer me from now on, it's sir."

"Yes, sir. But I…"

"Which part didn't you understand, Agent Branson?" Kane yelled back at her.

Anger showed on Giles' face. Kane may just as well have hit him on the jaw. Backing up a kid, and Kane's wife to boot?

"Sir, may I say something?" Kelly asked tentatively.

"No! Let's go." Kane pulled the compass from his backpack and checked the desired direction. This was the only way he could block out Kelly being his wife.

Kelly thought back. That's why she had been sent with Kane. Not because he may not come back, but because she was the only one the AFP could trust.

The going was tough. Long grasses and a steep mountainous range lay before them. Kane led the way. They had landed near Tai O fishing village, but they couldn't risk going there. Five white people would attract more attention than they wanted. One by one, they filed through the land. Giles brought up the rear.

The afternoon sun was hot, but Kane wanted to put some distance between them and the glittering gold beach. Even though no one except him had communication to base, he wasn't happy with the situation. This time no one knew where the group had landed. Not Buchanan, not anyone. And only Kane knew where to pick up the ammo, he and Buchanan.

Time was not the Australian's friend. Kane brushed aside the undergrowth with his hands, clearing a path for them to go through. Banana plants in abundance surrounded them. If nothing else there was a tremendous supply of fresh fruits. The warm sun dropped behind the peaks of the snow-capped mountains, and darkness came quickly bringing with it the coolness of the night. Dense masses of trees made shelter easy pickings.

At Kane's command, they dropped their backpacks under the biggest and most inviting-looking tree. Tired and hot, Kelly sat down on the hard ground. Not eating all day had made her feel sickly. Ty offered her a piece of his gum from his backpack. She un-wrapped it took one glance at it and dropped it on the ground.

"'Scuse me," and Kelly rushed behind the next biggest tree.

'And this is the woman that's going to lead us on,' thought Giles.

Kelly returned after a few minutes, complete with fruit for the feast that they were about to eat. Giles and Genna collected more, and Kane pulled out bags of nuts and raisons he had *borrowed* from the hotel.

"Lightening diet," muttered Kelly. "Get slim fast." But she did manage to get through a banana and some strange looking berries they found.

The others devoured the contents of the bags and the fruits. The whole time they ate, Kane was on the alert, his eyes darting from place to place. They sat in a circle watching out for each other.

"Suggest when you have finished this exotic feast, you get some sleep. Lie by each other for warmth and protection. Genna, get by Giles. Ty, next to Kelly. I'll take first watch. Ty, you take second and Giles the last two hours. It is gonna be a long day tomorrow. Anyone drops asleep on their watch and we may not have a day to wake up to."

Kane paused by Kelly and kissed her goodnight, a brief and meaningful gesture to her. He pulled his sweatshirt from his backpack and wrapped it around her.

Scouting the area, Kane found a good boulder to perch on. He started to light a cigarette and changed his mind. He chewed on the tobacco instead. By his side was his .38 AFP pistol. In his backpack he had hidden his cell. Now it was back in its right place of his boot. How the damn thing reached as far as it did, he never knew. But then nothing he carried was standard issue.

Lantau was exceptionally beautiful at night. All of Hong Kong was. Kane looked up at the sky. A zillion stars beamed down, and noises he only remembered from years ago echoed in his ears. The night air was alive with a thousand kinds of bug noises. He thought of Kelly. Good job she was sleeping. Kelly didn't like bug noises. Nor had Lilia… The sounds brought back memories he thought he had forgotten. He could have chosen a different kind of life. He'd chosen to go back to Australia on the right side of the law. Kane tried to figure out what his son would be thinking. Why had he gone into the Hong Kong force? Was it his idea? Or was it Lilia's? How much influence had Colonel Cheng had over him? What if Sam had known he had an Australian father many years before? Would Sam have changed? There was no way to find out now. And Buchanan? What had gone wrong there? Was it possible Cheng was holding Kane's son over Buchanan's head? Kane didn't believe Buchanan would betray him just over the promotion. They'd been through too much together. There had to be something else lurking that he couldn't see. His mind was full of questions. With no answers.

Kane glanced at his watch. Way past his shift end. Kane stepped down from the viewpoint. He'd wake Ty, show him where to sit, curl up next to Kelly and get a few hours' sleep. Kane moved stealthily across the ground. It was covered with dry branches fallen from the trees overhead. Trying not to alert Kelly to the bug noises, Kane reached down carefully and touched Ty on the arm. There was no movement. The blonde hair lay still. He touched him again afraid of the sudden fear that was going through his mind.

"Kane, that you?" murmured Kelly.

"Yeah, baby. Go back to sleep," he whispered.

He tried not to panic as he turned Ty over and two eyes stared at him. He'd seen someone poisoned before. He turned Ty back onto his stomach. Kane moved across the clearing to where Giles lay. He leaned down and securing his hand over his mouth, he whispered in his ear.

"Wake up, gently. Come with me. Make no noise."

He released Giles. They stepped carefully back across the camp. Kane leaned down and turned Ty over.

"My god, he's…" exclaimed Giles.

"Yeah, he's stone cold dead."

The enemy was within.

CHAPTER 10

"Let the girls sleep, Giles. Help me lift Ty up," whispered Kane as he slid his arms under Ty's shoulders.

Giles lifted his feet, and carried the young man away from the camp laying him beside the boulder he was to have kept watch on.

"What do you think killed him?" whispered Giles.

"Well, it wasn't a banana. Sorry." He knew that was in bad taste. But the field was narrowing rapidly, and so was Kane's patience. "By the looks of him I'd say he was poisoned. Did he eat anything we didn't?" Kane looked at Ty's staring eyes, and then with his fingers gently closed them.

"We all had the same food…except he had some gum in his bag. Remember, he offered Kelly a piece?"

"What kind of gum was it?" Kane questioned. "I saw him offer it, I didn't take much notice."

"Just regular stuff. You think it was in there? He had it the whole trip. Anyone could have messed with it. Even someone back in Oz."

All roads led back to Buchanan.

"We have to assume, for now, it was in the gum. Otherwise it's one of us who killed him. And I don't want to think that right now." Kane paused. "Giles, you have to get close to Genna any way you can. I can't do it. I know what she said about sleeping with you, but goddamn it, mate… try something. You've been around as much as anyone. You have to get her to confide in you. We have to be sure it's not her."

"Easier said than done. Man, I've tried twice. She's like the original ice maiden. I thought she liked me. Maybe you should try?" he replied casually not even looking at Kane's face.

"Are you crazy?" He raised his voice slightly, and glanced around to see if anyone stirred. "First, I have no inclination to, and second Kelly would kill her and me. Especially right now." Kane paused. A plan sprang into his mind. "Unless, I scare Genna so badly that she will run to you for comfort." His statements were a riddle.

"Are you maybe suggesting what I think you are?" Giles' eyebrows creased in disgust for the man near him.

"Maybe. Just watch out in case I go for it. You'll know. You know my moves after all these years. Now, more important things. Ty deserves a burial. We'll bury him behind those trees and tell the girls he's gone on ahead. Tell them I sent him. That way, if it is Genna, it won't tip our hand. I'll do it. I was his commander."

Giles sat for an hour while Kane was gone. Neither girl stirred. He thought about the situation. Four of them left, possibly five. Would Kane go though with his plan? Knowing Kane he would, and that could cause a problem.

Kane picked Ty up easily, and carried the young man's body over his shoulder to a dense clump of trees. He laid him on the ground and Kane dug a shallow grave with his bare hands. Asian soil piled up behind him, and he wiped sweat from his face causing dirt to stain his cheeks.

Kane stood in silence then by the mound of dirt. From the makeshift wooden cross of small tree branches, he hung Ty's black bandana. As Kane turned away, the bandana blew gently in the night breeze. He needed no spoken words, but Kane's thoughts ran wild. If only Ty had been his son…

Kane tapped Giles on the shoulder. "Done. Let's get back to them. The sun will be up soon and I need Kelly." He glanced up to the sky.

Giles jumped. "You son-of-a-bitch. You half scared me to death. We all need a Kelly," muttered Giles.

"Say something?" asked Kane turning slightly.

"Kane, don't you ever show emotion over someone dying? You just buried one of your group and you want sex? Are you not human?" Giles raised his hands in exasperation.

"You stupid bastard!" Kane hissed. "That's not why I need her. I just need to hold her. She's the only one who understands me. And probably the only one who ever will." Kane walked away, his mind lying back with the boy he had just buried.

Kane heard Giles mutter as he strode away. He sat on the ground next to Kelly, and settled down beside his wife. "You're all warm, baby." She was in stark contrast to the boy he'd just buried.

Kelly wrapped her arms around him and pulled the sweatshirt over them both. "Ty's dead, isn't he?" she whispered.

"How…" Kane pulled back slightly from her.

"When you turned him over his hand touched me. He was stone cold." She shivered.

"Darling, I'm sorry. I left you lying by him. Why didn't you say something?" He pulled strands of her hair from her face.

"'Cause I wasn't sure who was with you and who killed him. But you know, don't you?"

He looked her straight in the eyes their faces almost touching. "Yes, I think so. And I was the one who once told him he'd wished he'd stayed at home. Dear god, I wished he had."

She nestled into him.

"He was poisoned. And I'm pretty sure I know who did it. You know why I put you in charge?" He pulled her so close that she could feel his breath on her face, and see her face in the starlight.

"Yes," she whispered. "I am the only one you trust. You and the AFP"

"Good girl. You do know me."

"Very well. I know every move you make is for a reason. And," she paused, "I know every inch of your body and your mind."

"Sure?" he questioned.

"Positive. I love you, Kane, and whatever you have to do, I'm right behind you."

"Even if it involves another woman?" He felt her tense against him.

"Yes. 'Cause I know there's a reason. It's Genna, isn't it? You have to do something that you think will make me unhappy. Just do your job, sir. Job first, me second…"

His mouth covered hers. "You're always first, darling."

The desire for her was strong, but this time he did not follow through. He wanted her to have this child, and he was not going to be any more responsible for the undoing of this baby than he already had been.

Giles sat in the cutting and watched. He couldn't lose the feeling of jealousy he felt whenever he saw them together. His sight altered to take in Genna, the ice maiden. Of course Kane would have a chance with her. Every woman was fair game to him. That was the problem now and always had been. He pulled his jacket around him and sat ready for his watch.

At six, Genna woke. She smelled something cooking on an open fire. She glanced in Kelly's direction. She was still asleep. There was no sign of Giles or Ty. Kane sat hunched over the fire cooking something that had been moving not an hour before. Genna shivered in the morning air as she crept round Kane's sleeping wife. The sun rose in purple shades above the ranges of Lantau.

"Morning, Genna. Sleep well? You look cold. Want my sweatshirt? "

"Please," she replied.

She sat down next to him on his choice of log. He slid the sweatshirt from round his shoulders and wrapped it slowly and with purpose around her. Kane didn't look directly into her face. Instead he continued turning the meaty part of the lizard on the spit.

"Want a taste?" Kane asked her in a low tone. He tore a piece of the meat from the spit, blew on it to cool it, and handed it to her.

Genna wasn't sure if he meant the meat or something else. She could see his muscles glisten in the light, his hair hanging down his back, his pants tight. She stopped there. He wasn't hers for the taking. But she had the feeling he was making a pass at her. Why? He already had Kelly. But right now Kelly may be unavailable, and Kane always needed a woman. He could have anyone woman, but right now she was the only available female in sight.

"How do you stand this cold after the heat of the day? Cold kept me awake a little."

"Really?" Kane flinched. What had Genna seen?

"Yes. The ground is hard and cold. No Ty this morning?" she asked innocently.

"No. Ty and Giles are just scouting around. Thought they may have wakened you. Ty probably has gone on farther. Told him he could if he wanted. Giles should be back soon, and Kelly's still asleep. She was sick early this morning. Beginning to wish she wasn't pregnant. Too much for her and me…well never mind." He held up another piece of the meat to her. "Here. Try another bit. I'm a good cook. I'm good at most things I do, especially when I put my mind to it."

Kelly heard what he said. He was coming on to Genna. Kelly lay there awhile and listened. The smell of the meat made her feel queasy, but now would not be the time to throw up.

"Yeah, I'd like to," answered Genna.

She took the piece of meat and Kane touched her fingers with his. His touch electrified her, and Genna saw him in a whole different light. Kane knew it.

"You two saved any for me?" asked Kelly pretending to wake.

"Sure, baby. Think you can handle it?" asked Kane.

"I can handle anything you put my way," remarked Kelly. She moved closer to the fire, and sat down on the ground next to Kane. She watched the lizard on the spit and felt her stomach churn over, as the succulent juices dripped down to the ground.

Genna had no doubt that Kelly's statement was true. Kane's pass at her made her uneasy, but very aware of him.

Kane turned his head toward Kelly and winked. His wife was a smart, streetwise woman. She understood, Kane hoped.

Giles appeared from the brush. "Can see the smoke from across the cutting. Think it's wise, *sir*?"

"Probably not. But we're done. Want some? And did you send Ty on like I told you to?" He narrowed his eyes at Giles.

"Yeah." He sat down on the ground and slid some meat from the make-shift rotisserie. "God damn! This place is full of bugs," and Giles swatted ants that were creeping on his pants leg.

"Yeah, well…takes one creeping thing to know another one," smiled Kane.

That didn't sit well with Giles, but made the girls giggle.

Genna ate some of the food. "You are a good cook, sir. You're right." 'As usual,' she thought.

"Okay, let's break camp. Ten minutes sharp. We need to get some miles under our belt before it gets too hot. Genna behind me, Kelly, and then Giles at the back."

Seven a.m. saw them on their way. Kane glanced back once over his shoulder. Kelly saw it. Kane had two choices for drug operation head-quarters: the very obvious Shek Pick Prison or far less obvious because of its location, Fan Lau Fort. He'd been led to believe it was the prison. By Buchanan. Some gut instinct told him to head for the fort. The route was almost parallel to the prison and it was also difficult to get to. Kane could see the girls were tiring. It was written all over their faces. Tired-ness and the terrain made it difficult for men, let alone women, especially one who was trying to hold on to her baby. But still Kelly would not give in. They battled on. The elevation became steeper, the dark, green foliage denser, and the sun hotter. He glanced over his shoulder from time to time, and could plainly see their plight.

"Let's take a break. Five minutes. Drink lots of water, especially you, Kelly." Kane drank water from his canteen, replaced it, and then pulled the compass from his fatigue's pocket. "Dead on course." He also pulled out his cigarettes and lit one up.

"Course for where, sir?" Genna asked adjusting her backpack, and moving far closer to him than was necessary.

Kane rested against a tree. "For Fan Lau Fort." He watched the expression on her face with interest.

"But I thought we were headed for the prison?" She was genuinely surprised.

Kane leaned back on the tree one foot propped against the bark, and blew the smoke through his nostrils. "What made you think that? Someone tell you?"

"I heard you all talking. Seemed an obvious choice. Giles mentioned it, too."

"Did he? So what does Giles know?" He finished his smoke, made sure it was well and truly out, and turned to his wife. He waited for Genna's answer. There wasn't one. "Kelly, want to walk with me a while?"

She had found a good place to rest but if Kane needed her... "Sure," she replied, sensing something was wrong.

They walked ten maybe fifteen yards, and he handed her his canteen. Kelly gulped some more water down, like she was dying from lack of it. Kane leaned against the trees, while Kelly filled her hand with water and splashed it on her face. It was refreshingly cool. Ants crept on her too. Giles was right; the place was full of bugs. They disgusted her.

"I don't trust either of them, Kel. Something's going on. Tonight I'm gonna do what I never thought I'd never stoop to." Kane kicked at the dirt. Not his usual demeanor.

"You're gonna make a play for Genna. I heard you talking and I'm not blind, Kane." She continued wiping her wet fingers on her face.

"I want her to run straight to Giles. I can't think of any other way. She won't go of her own free will. What the fuck else can I do?" Kane shrugged his shoulders irritated that he couldn't think of another scheme.

"What you have to," Kelly replied. "She'll go to him. Bet you on that. Then again she may like it. She may think you're hot. Ever thought of that?" She laughed. "I did!"

"Kelly! Keep your voice down and stop making a joke of this."

"What joke? Have you seen you, Kane? Sometimes I don't think you know how attractive you are to women. I know you've had a few, and Lilia told you the same thing, but sometimes you underestimate yourself. You should have been in your own training class. It was interesting listening."

"Well, thanks. Something to think on in my old age…"

"Don't think too hard…I'm still here," she joked.

"Yeah, and that's where you come in. She gets too close you come charging in like a bull."

"Oh, sir, you can bank on that!"

He smiled. That's exactly what he hoped. He starred ahead of him and pretended to be explaining tactics to Kelly. Kane knew they were being watched.

Returning to the group, Kane let them rest a little longer. Kelly sat down next to Genna, and in her mind she held contempt for her. Kane's eyes scoured the horizon. He figured they could cross the next hill before sunset. Right now that hill looked a long way off. Once more they set off in single file.

They marched on for a mile or so. The escarpment rose sharply, and became covered in loose rocks and shale. Kane pulled Kelly up behind him, the uneven ground giving way once or twice from under their feet. She was struggling and Kane knew it. This exercise was hardly good for a woman let alone one who may or may not be losing his child. He left Kelly half way up the side of the hill and went back for Genna. She clung to Kane's hand and could feel his strength. No wonder Kelly was drawn to this man. Genna couldn't see the web Kane was spinning.

They plodded on through knee-deep grasses, and over the small natural eroding rocks. Now the tight, black fatigues tucked into their boots made a lot of sense. There were enough other kinds of insect life to fill an army full of boots, and all were glad that Kane had been so strict with their attire. Kane pointed to a village on the horizon, and gave a guided tour of the small temples left from centuries ago.

"Fucking know-all," muttered Giles.

The compass still pointed in the right direction. Kane was happy with that. The prison was north of their destination, and the group still had to pass Lake Phenomenon. That would please Kelly. He remembered her comments on the plane. As they reached the top of the farthest hill, Kane looked over first. The sun was setting and below them nestled in the valley was Kelly's Lake Phenomenal.

"Baby," Kane yelled to her. "Come look."

She scrambled up behind him, her eyes devouring the view below. Birds of spectacular color flew around the tree line. Villagers carried the last vessels of water for the day. And horse- drawn carts rumbled through the valley. The sun slid down behind the horizon. It was a feast-of-lights and orange color, something from an oil painting. Kane slipped his arm around Kelly, and he heard her sigh.

"I wanted you out of this mess by now. Fucking hell, you aren't supposed to be here, Kel," and Kane raised his eyes to the sky as if looking for some sort of answer.

"Its okay, Kane," she whispered, and looked back at the slowly descending night, a night she dreaded, and one where she would look the other way. She hoped she could do that.

Kane looked again at her. He didn't want to do this. But Genna had to get close to Giles. She just had to. Kane had to find out what was going on in his group's mind.

"A moment longer, darling. A moment longer," Kane whispered.

Above them an eagle soared, its shriek blasting though the sky. It had found its prey. Kane watched it swoop and dive. Like himself, the bird was still the hunter. He adjusted his bandana, tightening it round his head.

They descended much easier going down the hill. Kane could see people in front of him. Not just in front, but camped right where they needed to cross a small narrow bridge. Underneath flowed an estuary of water that fed into Lake Phenomenal.

Sitting around a campfire were two men: one old gentleman with long gray hair and the younger man listening to his elder's yarns. They were right in the group's way.

"Leave the talking to me," Kane announced to his party. They approached with caution.

Kelly was no longer amazed as Chinese flowed from Kane's tongue. Giles stepped forward and backed him up. It was the first time that Kelly had heard Giles speak Chinese since they had arrived, and Kelly had no clue what was being said. The older gentleman pointed his finger south of the lake and Kelly figured Kane had asked them if they were going the right way for the fort.

Kelly waited till they had finished the discussion.

"So what they say?" asked an inquisitive Kelly.

"They said we are welcome to camp with them tonight. They have coffee and rice we can share. And also that there is a nice temple we should see as foreigners to the land. Set your things over there by the fire. I'm gonna go look at that temple down near the water. Anyone want to come?" asked Kane, hoping he got the right answer.

Giles sat down and lay back on the earth, his backpack behind his head, and his extra pounds of weight catching up. "Nah, mate. Go ahead." He could suddenly see time alone with Kane's wife.

"Kelly?" asked Kane.

"I'm tired, too. Genna, you go. You're the temple type. Not really my thing." She bit her tongue, but it gave Kane a clear shot. She dumped her things on the ground and made a big display of lying back and resting her eyes.

"Wanna take a walk, Gen?" Kane pulled his shirt up and over his head. He wiped the day's sweat on it and dropped it by his wife. He stood barechested, hands on hips, openly making a play for Genna.

She hesitated.

'Oh God,' thought Kane. 'Guess she doesn't think I'm hot after all…'

"Okay," Genna mumbled.

Kane reached for her hand. She took his, and he led her away from the bridge and down the slippery slope toward the temple. Slippery was good. It gave Kane as excuse to hold on to her. Kelly watched them become small dots.

"You trust them together? You know what Kane's like. You of all people should know."

"Something bothering you, Giles? I trust them. Him anyway." She squirmed around in her resting place. "Not sure about her. You?"

"Not sure about either of them," retorted a disgruntled Giles.

Once inside the temple, Kane watched his companion walk around. As she stood admiring the wooden carvings Kane made his move. He stepped up behind Genna and rested his arm on her shoulder. Genna flinched slightly at his touch, but she made no attempt to pull away from him.

"Great carvings. Look at the shape."

She nodded. Kane knew he was getting to her. His hand slid down her arm and he went for the kill. Taking hold of her by the waist he turned her to him, bent his head, and kissed her. Her lips were cold and tense. Pictures of Kelly flashed through his brain.

He continued to pursue. Pushing her back against the cold marble wall of the temple he pinned her body against his. He kissed her again much harder than the first time. For a second Genna responded then she tried to pull away. But Kane was too strong. He held her in his grasp, his powerful arms encircling her. She looked up into his face. He slid his hand down inside her pants and reached down as far as he could. Immediately, he felt the moisture flow from her. He had her.

"What the hell are you doing?" she screamed, her eyes glaring at him..

"Come on, darling. We both know it's what you want. You've wanted this for days. Don't struggle. It will all be over quickly if you don't struggle. I just want to…" Kane was in total control.

"I know what you want to do, but I don't want to!" she yelled, trying to pull away.

"Sure you do. Just relax." His voice was low and sexy.

Kane pushed her in every way he knew how. Genna was tough and any minute he thought she would hit him. He was right. She brought her hand up and slapped his face. It stung.

"Now that wasn't very friendly, was it? Let's try again," he said with meaning and brought his mouth down on hers.

This time she panicked. Kane wasn't playing. "I'll tell Kelly," she screamed.

"Go ahead. Who do you think she'll believe? You or me?" and he laughed long and loud in her face.

"Then I'll tell Giles," she yelled, tears streaming down her face.

"Tell him what?" asked Kane calmly.

"That you tried to…" Genna was flustered and had lost her self-control.

"Tried to rape you?" Kane laughed in her face. "You, the original ice maiden? That's what you are. Then again, Giles may be gentler with you. Don't you like to play rough, Genna? And do really think a man like me has to rape a woman to get laid?"

She screamed at him. "Let go of me now or I'll report you! Whether you're my boss or not, you'll be in trouble. Giles will help me. He hates you!" and she struggled against him.

He'd succeeded in finding out just what he wanted to know.

"Really? You know that for a fact, darling?" He found that interesting. Slowly he released his grip on her. "Get the fuck out of here, you frigid little bitch. You're too cold for me, and I have Kelly's warm body to take whenever I want." Then his voice was menacing. "But you ever tell on me and I'll kill you. You understand?"

Tears continued streaming down her face. "I won't tell anyone. Not even your precious Kelly." In Genna's mind, she was thinking she would now stick to Giles like glue. At least he hadn't forced himself on her.

"You wouldn't know how to keep a man like me happy anyway. Go running back to Giles. See if the fuck I care." And Kane remembered Giles saying he had tried twice with Genna.

He leaned back on the pillars, pulled the cigarettes from his fatigues and lit one up. He could see Genna scurrying across the temple stumbling over vases as she went. They rolled away from her feet, and he could hear her crying echoing round the walls. Behind him Kane heard movement. Kane felt instinctively for his gun. It was with Kelly. He turned and breathed a sigh of relief.

"Nice work, Mr. Branson, sir. Couldn't have done it any better myself." A shadow stepped into the light.

"Yeah. Real proud of myself. You made it hard enough to find you. What the hell did you code the message for on my cell? This isn't Vietnam. And you weren't in Nam anyway. Think she bought it?" He puffed harder on the weed.

"Bought it? You deserve an Oscar. The girl will run back to Giles. Maybe now we'll find out the truth. Which one of them is it? But you pretty much know already don't you? You want to share?"

"No." Kane took a drag from the smoke. "You heard any word of my son's whereabouts?" asked Kane.

"Nothing of late. That piece of news was priceless." The shadow moved slightly.

"What, that I had a Chinese son who is an agent?" asked Kane.

"Yeah. Didn't bank on that," came the reply.

"Neither did I, and where is your counterpart? He with you or did the opposition get to him before you?"

"Nope, he's here. Safe and sound. He was surprised, though, when room service arrived. He's back in the trees watching your wife and Giles. Probably having as much fun as I just did. So, we'll meet you at the fort. If you need anything before, let me know. You'll find the explosives have been moved to a more convenient location. No one other than you and I now know where they are. I could take them on for you but that would make the rest of the group very suspicious. Here's the address."

Kane took the piece of paper offered. "And how do I explain that one? The ammo was north of here last time the rest of the group knew," Kane said.

"Just tell them you called Buchanan and he had them moved for you. You'll come up with something; you always do. Don't forget, we set you up with a contact. I just have a codename for him. It's all Chow gave me. It's on the piece of paper with the address. You like the two farmers' right there by the bridge? My idea. I knew you'd need something to divert you and let you know where I was. I'd better go. You have my mobile number if you need me. By the way, we were both sorry about Ty. We couldn't stop that one from happening. Oh, nearly forgot this. It's why I came. Special Weapons asked me to give it to you, and Inspector Chow sends you his regards, *Mitter* Brandon, sir. Oh, and what touch of genius finding the piece of cloth from Lilia's dress. Made it all look so real. Like there really was another enemy out there."

"I thought so. Okay, Genna's had long enough to get back up there." Kane put out his hand and the other man shook it. "Oh, and I believe this belongs to you."

From his pocket Kane pulled a piece of jewelry and handed it over.

"Thank you, sir." He slid it back on his finger. "See you in a couple of days," the visitor said, and was gone. He left Kane with his new toy.

Kane finished his smoke, examined the new gadget, memorized the address, and then made his way out of the temple.

It was pitch dark when Genna arrived back in camp. She didn't even look at Kelly, just sat down by Giles and stared at the fire. She could smell the coffee brewing. It smelled comforting in the night air.

"Where's the *boss*?" Giles asked.

"He'll be up in a minute." She was still shaking.

"You crying? Did he do something to you…?"

"I fell coming up the path. He told me to be careful and I wasn't. That's all. Can I sleep by you tonight? It's cold here," asked Genna, her tone low and very shaky.

"Course you can. You can sleep by me anytime." He didn't see anything else except that she needed him.

From out of the dark loomed Kane's figure. He strode into the camp, and could see the frightened look on Genna's face. And, he saw the look that Giles gave him. A ten-out-of-ten plan. Their Chinese companions busied themselves in their chores.

Kane sat next to Kelly. She looked into his face and could see his pain. He poured himself some coffee and sipped it, then threw the rest on the fire.

"Kane, I need to pee. Come with me? Don't like it too much out here in the dark. All those temples and things. Kind of scary," she whispered.

"Sure, darling." 'Kelly scared of the dark? That would be a first!' thought Kane.

They made it to the shelter of the rocks and as Kelly stepped forward Kane grabbed her. His kisses were so desperate it scared her. She held him to her as he pushed her down on the hard ground. Then, he stopped.

"What's wrong?" she murmured, holding him close to her.

He sat up. "Am I some animal that takes what he wants, when he wants it? Do I do that, Kelly? The girl thinks I tried to rape her. She hates me. Let alone what you think."

Kelly swallowed hard.

"Better for her to hate you than us to be dead. You and I know the truth, and that's all that matters. What's that in your belt?" she asked.

"New toy."

"Where'd you get it?"

"Backpack."

She knew he was lying. Someone else was with them. Someone on their side? Someone else was watching. *They* sat in the shadows ready for trouble, looking out for their boss. The one shadow moved and the other shadow's little slim line box let out a whirring noise, and a little voice said, "You've got mail."

CHAPTER 11

The soft morning light brought tensions that ran extremely high. Genna never left Giles' side. Her tone was polite towards Kane, but it was hard for her to look in his direction. Kane knew he had hurt her deeply, let alone the damage to his own reputation, if Genna decided to make a case of the situation when he got home…if they made it back home.

Kane thanked their Chinese companions for the night's shelter, and the mounds of rice that the four Australian's seemed to have consumed by daybreak.

Then the AFP moved out in pairs. Another day and a half and they'd reach the fort. In between they'd pick up the ammo. Journeying down the side of Lake Phenomenal, Kane thought it fared badly against the sunrise over Sydney harbor. Many times he'd ridden his motorcycle across that bridge, looked down at the Opera House, and watched the morning burst into life. Now, he cast his eyes across the lake. Even with all the splendor of Lantau, he wished he were back in his native land with Kelly and his daughters. He wished for anything right now but this.

Kelly picked up on his thoughts. She missed Star terribly. Every time she thought of the new baby and how close she was to losing it, she was reminded of Star. She slipped her small hand into Kane's powerful hand and squeezed his fingers.

"We're not alone out here, are we?" Kelly whispered.

He was going to lie, but he'd done that once in the last few hours. "No. Don't ask who. Just trust me."

"I always trust you and I wasn't going to ask. You miss Star?" Kelly wrapped her other arm around his waist. She was tiny next to Kane.

"Hell, yes. You know I do. You know everything about me. Have from day one. Stay close to me, Kel. At all times, stay close."

She took his words seriously and they passed on by the lake. Kelly took a long look at her Lake Phenomenal. It shimmered in the sun's rays. Clear and temping for a person to bathe in. Their clothes clung to them in the heat, bodies sticky and grimy. But Kelly knew she couldn't dawdle.

Kane knew that Giles was tolerating him. He knew how far he had gone with Genna but Giles did not, and Kane could see the annoyance on Giles' face. But the plan had worked and Genna had done exactly what Kane wanted her to do.

Kane checked the compass. Still on track. Then a thought occurred to Kane and he couldn't figure out why he hadn't thought of it sooner. There were only four of them now. Why not travel as civilians? They all had civvies with them, al least one set. Kane dropped his backpack where he stood.

"Stop! Get changed back into civilian clothes. We're on vacation. What better way to travel? We can take a bus…"

"We can take a what? Carrying guns? Have you lost your mind?" yelled Giles. He slid his backpack to the ground and rested against a tree. "Sun got to you?" he asked sarcastically.

"No. Just found it. My mind that is. Buses run to the major tourist attractions. We can take a bus. Two blokes and two girls aren't going to cause as much attention dressed in vacation clothes. So come on, get your clothes off." Kane laughed. He saw the funny side of the situation. "Get your clothes off…" He stopped. 'Last time I said that, Ty…' and his thought process stopped, and started again abruptly. Genna had never mentioned Ty again.

"Thank God. I'm so tired of all this walking," muttered Kelly. "You never mentioned I'd be infested with bugs." Kelly pulled some crawling thing from her vest, and one from her hair.

"They only like sweet things, darling."

Genna wanted to throw up, when she heard this statement. Kane was hovering round Kelly to the point of obsession.

Kelly sat straight down on the ground and pulled her boots off. She tossed them onto the earth. The pants came next.

"Thank God." She rubbed her aching feet.

"Kel, you still need the boots. What else you gonna walk in?" asked Kane with some amusement.

She stared at him. "Yeah, right. Stupid boots. I hate them. Must have been a man that designed these things."

Kelly sat there in her AFP vest and pants. She leaned across for her backpack and pulled out her shorts and camisole top. Making sure her back was to everyone except Kane she pulled the vest over her head and slipped the camisole on.

Giles couldn't miss the marks on her back where the sun had tanned her body and the vest had left her skin white. She stood up and stepped into the shorts. At least she was cooler now. Genna did pretty much the same. But both men kept their eyes on Kelly.

The two guys had grey sweats with them, and black, cotton vests. From the bottom of his backpack, Kane produced a long strip of black material, and he stuffed the fatigues back in the bag.

"Where did ya get that, Kane?" asked Kelly. It looked familiar to her. She had a dress just like it back…"That's off the dress I was wearing the day you came home from the States. You ripped a piece off that dress that I wore when you came home…" Now she knew why he had it. It was a symbol of returning. She smiled.

Kane wrapped his new bandana around his head. Ahead of them, according to Kane's calculations, and the tourist guide he'd kept in his backpack, lay Wang Po, a tiny village that bus number 2 stopped at twice daily. If they hurried maybe they could still catch a bus out today. Kane pulled out the maps and the new guide.

"How long you had that?" asked Giles.

"Since I hired the boat. Bloke at the harbor gave it me.

Why?" lied Kane.

"Just wondered," came Giles' reply.

"We need to make up some time. If you three are ready, we will continue."

They made Wang Po by four, in time to see the extremely antiquated bus leaving from the other end of the village, filled to the brim and over-flowing with people.

"Fucking hell," fumed Kane. "Now we have to stay the night here."

Across the street the two-story houses rose up into the hillside. White painted exteriors, doors open showing pink insides scrubbed to perfection. Neat little gardens grew in the rubble of life. A wizened old lady sat on the doorstep of the last house on the left. Kane approached her, mumbled his now distinctive Chinese dialogue, and pulled Chinese bills out of his back-pack, and thrust them into her waiting hands. The woman was delighted with her money and darted into the house to make ready for her guests.

"We have lodgings for the night, and the good lady is gonna cook super."

"What you do, Kane? Offer to sleep with her?" Giles muttered under his breath and he turned away from the others.

Kelly ran across the street to inspect the house. Her hair bounced in the air and her dog tags beat on her chest, and she tucked them back into her camisole top. No one noticed except one. And the same person noticed, too, the man with the long blonde hair who stood and watched her, then followed her into the house.

This man sat in the shadows sipping cold tea. It was by chance that Sam Cheng was there: pure coincidence. He was on his way to confront his uncle. Discovering the character of ones father was one thing. Finding him in the wilds of Wang Po was another, and with the girls in tow. Perhaps this was his chance to find out about the real Kane Branson. His mother had said that two more people knew Sam was a Branson, and it was obvious even to Sam that Kane didn't know till recently. Why? What was so important that Kane couldn't be told? Would Kane have come back for his son? Sam watched his father. Kane was watching Kelly disappearing into the little white house. Sam Cheng had begun to put two and two together. If Kane was a pimp why was he watching the girl with such affection on his face? His daughter? Maybe. His mistress? Probably, and much more likely. But there was a definite connection and he had begun to realize Kane Branson was not a pimp. He knew his mother and what she had become. Suspicion crept in. He'd tried repeatedly to find out through regular channels about his father, and now suddenly the way was clear for him. Was it coincidence that Kane had turned up now when operations were going so well in Australia? Too many coincidences. That was one of the reasons Sam Cheng was on his way to Fan Lau Fort. He watched them all enter the tiny house.

"Nice clean little dwelling. Couple of decent-sized beds. Kelly and I can manage with the smaller one." He grinned at Giles. "Lady is cooking food for us. I can smell it already."

Delicious aromas of meats with herbs and spices filled the house. Coffee brewed continually on the hearth. Kane put his arm around Kelly.

"Phew.........You stink, Kel," and he nuzzled down into her hair. "There's a bathhouse out back."

"Gee, thanks a lot. Obviously I need it. You don't smell so great yourself, Mr. Branson," replied Kelly.

"You want to get a bath, Kel? Ladies first. I'll be out front."

Kane walked out and sat on the front steps where Giles joined him.

Kane was smoking his cigarettes. "Been expecting you. Took you longer than I thought, but you made it. What did Genna tell you?" He finished the cigarette and squashed the butt under his boot.

"Nothing really. How far did you take it? She was crying." Giles hesitated not really wanting to know. "You didn't succeed, did you?" he really didn't know if Kane had or not.

Kane arrogantly tossed his head back and laughed. "She ran to you though, didn't she? That's all you need to know. It's what we both wanted." Kane pulled out that familiar brand of cigarettes and lit up another. "Want one?"

"I'll leave the vices up to you. You're better at them than me." sneered Giles. He figured Kane was anxious for some reason.

'*Touché*,' thought Kane. He stared out beyond the cigarette smoke and along the street. He could see a tiny café similar to the ones in the big city. He laughed to himself. Life in the fast lane… or out of it. Then he looked harder. There were three men sitting on the patio. Three men dressed in black, and one had blonde hair. Kane stared in disbelief. What the hell were the chances of him being here at the same time?

"Excuse me," Kane said, with some urgency, and jumped up from his sitting place. The cigarette fell to the floor as Kane hurried into the building.

He ran into the house, past Genna and into the bedroom. He grabbed his backpack and reached for his cell. He had three new messages on it, and he listened carefully to them. Kane sported a strange look on his face.

"What's wrong?" Kelly emerged from the bathhouse clean and fresh, and wrapped in the biggest bath towel ever. She was drying her long hair on another big fluffy, white towel.

"Nothing, baby. Just something Giles and I need to take care of. You and Genna okay?"

"Well, she only talks when she has to, and then is not polite…" She realized he wasn't listening. "And it's snowing outside…"

"Good, that's great. We'll be gone a little while. Stay with Genna, lock the door and wait for us to come back." He pushed his .38 down the back of his sweats. He picked up her gun also and tucked that in beside the other gun.

"You gonna take a walk or go to a gunfight? You didn't hear a word I said."

Kane gave her a disparaging look.

"Sir, yes, sir. I'll lock the door, and Kane, please be careful."

"Agent Branson…I love you." Kane held her face in his hands, kissed her on her lips and was gone back out of the house to where Giles sat.

Kane pulled Giles up by the arm. "Let's go!"

"Where we going? Kane." Giles tried to match Kane's stride. "Slow down. The world's not on fire." Giles could not keep pace with Kane.

"Isn't it?" Kane replied.

Only the four of them and 'the watchers' knew they were here. And 'the watchers' were on Kane's side. Now was the time to find out where everyone stood. On which side did Sam Cheng really stand? Was he working with the double agent? Kane knew he was distributing drugs at Club Coco. Why, if he wasn't part of the big scheme? Or was he being used by Vau Cheng and Buchanan? Or was he the user? Time to die.

It seemed like an eternity walking down the dusty street. Reaching the brick patio, Kane stepped up onto it. He positioned himself so that Sam could clearly see him.

"Excuse me, *Mr. Cheng*. I think its time you and I talked." Kane stood hands on his hips and used the term Mr. Cheng loosely.

Sam Cheng raised his head slowly, and looked across the table over the stone cold tea. He saw Kane standing there, long blonde hair reminding him of his parentage. He glanced towards Giles. Then Sam Cheng stood up and opened his mouth.

"So, we meet in person: the man who was so much in love with my mother. If that was the case, why did you leave her? And why did you never tell this man that he had a son?"

Kane was speechless. Sam Cheng wasn't talking to him, but to Giles. Sam's foreboding companions stood also, their guns strategically conspicuous on their hips.

"This gentleman," Sam turned slightly to his friends, "is my father, Kane Branson. A man who used, then left, my mother. But this is the man she described to me would come with his friend. She said at some point you would come for me." He turned and looked straight in Giles direction. "I don't know your name and I don't particularly want to. Mr. Branson did not know Lilia was pregnant. But you did, and you kept it from him all these years. Or did you find out at a later date? Did you love her that much? Or do you hate *him* more? If it had not been for my father's bravery that night in the parking lot…you would be dead. I would have shot you right there and then."

Kane was having a hard time taking this in. He had been right. It was Giles that Sam had been aiming at in the parking lot, but for all the wrong reasons. He looked from one to the other. He turned on his heel, grabbed Giles by the shoulders and pushed him against the white stonewall.

"Giles, you knew the whole fucking time that I had a son? It doesn't make sense. That charade outside in the lot and then in the elevator, it was all a farce. And you knew I went to Lilia's. You had the address." Kane held on tightly to Giles hardly giving him enough space to defend himself. "Did you have her killed because she was telling too much? Did you, you fucking son-of-a-bitch? Or was that bullet meant for me? That's it, isn't it? It was meant for me. Lilia got in the way."

Kane's arms were strong and he held his captive without mercy. He didn't even notice the pain that penetrated down his muscles.

"I didn't kill her. Why the hell would I kill someone I was in love with?" Giles yelled. "I wasn't sure until I saw the file on Buchanan's desk," Giles lied. "It was you she wanted. She didn't even notice me, clumsy old tag-along Giles. Why the hell would she notice me when she could have you? That's how it always was and still is. Look at your wife…" and he stopped mainly because Kane hit him in the stomach, and then Kane's fist connected to Giles' face.

Kane didn't know which person he was angrier with. Giles or his son.

"The girl is your wife? The young one with the long curly hair that shines in the sun? You have good taste. She is then my stepmother. I would like to meet her." Sam whispered to his men and they departed.

"What did you say to them?" Kane demanded not losing his grip on Giles.

"I asked them to go fetch your wife and the other girl," his son replied.

"You leave them alone unless you want to deal with me right now!" boomed Kane in his usual tactful manner.

"I have no wish to hurt them, especially your wife. You can let your *'friend'* go. It was not him who killed my mother. The bullet had your name on it. The order came from someone else." He had put two and two together. "I think you know who. And before you ask, yes, I was distributing drugs at the club. I had to. It was the only way to obtain cover. I believe I know who you are aside from being my father. You're AFP. And a pretty high-ranking agent at that. My mother was the block and now she's dead, and suddenly there is no block. The way was clear immediately as though someone opened the door for me to find out. In fact…"

"In fact, what?" demanded Kane.

"Doesn't matter for now," replied Sam Cheng.

Kane let go of Giles. He slid halfway down the wall.

Giles' eyes were closed and he held onto his stomach. He was out cold.

"If you do your homework you'll know who I am." Kane said.

"Perhaps I already do," replied Sam. "Are you the Hunter?" Sam whispered.

Kane Branson's eyes became slits as he stared at his son. How did he know about the Hunter project? The only way was if he was a double agent working for the Australian side. But why would he have been?

"You are wondering how I know about the project? Think about it. I am not what I seem. And, nor it transpires, are you. Lilia taught me a lot. She also gave me the finest education that her husband could buy." Sam saw his men returning empty-handed.

"They would not come with you?" he asked them.

"The women were not there, Mr. Cheng. The girls are gone."

Kelly was dozing on the bed in the back room waiting for Kane to return. She heard two men's muffled voices in the other room. They didn't belong to Kane's or Giles'.

"Genna. Through the window, now!"

"What?"

"Get moving, Genna. The voices in the next room don't belong to our guys. Go," and she grabbed Genna's .38, swung her boots over her shoulder, and stuffed some cash in her shorts pocket.

The window opened easily and Kelly climbed through first. She climbed onto the grassy hill behind the house and scurried up the bank. Genna followed and with her longer legs managed to get to the top much quicker than Kelly. An old brick road sat at the top of the bank, and across it dense trees offered a solid hiding place. They lay down in the grasses.

"What do you think happened down there? Why didn't Kane and Giles come back for us?"

"If I knew that, we wouldn't be hiding in these bug infested bushes," replied Kelly.

Kane had told her if anything like this happened to get the hell away and don't look back. If only the two visitors had identified themselves when they entered the house, instead of rushing straight in. But they hadn't, and Kelly did what instinct, and Kane, told her to do. Kelly looked back. She was frightened, but she was in charge: in charge of herself and a girl who wanted to hate her.

"We'll wait awhile, and see if anyone comes looking for us." Kelly leaned back in the bushes and looked at her body. "Pointless taking that bath," she muttered under her breath. "Kane never got to find out how good I smell with all these oriental oils."

"Their backpacks are still here. Grab them. They went out that open window. We have to find them before Cheng's men do. If we can't, we'll go and get the ammo and wait for Kane. I hope to god he listened to all four messages." The man checked the cell lying on the bed with the newest message still unopened. "Fuck! I'll leave a note in his backpack. He has to come back for it." The watchers departed. The light was fading fast.

"What do you mean they're not there? 'Course they are. That's where we left them. I'm going back to the house. You, I'll deal with after…" As he spoke, Kane pointed a finger at Sam.

"I'm coming with you. Your *friend* can stay here. I have to talk with you," Sam muttered and gave out commands to his Chinese allies.

"Do I have a choice?" asked Kane turning on his heel.

"Yes. You know you could take me out with one blow, and probably the two men with me. You know it, and so do I. But you won't, because you know one of your party is a traitor, to you and to the government," replied Sam.

"Government? Which particular 'government' are we talking about? Yours or mine?" Kane walked at a fast pace noting that unlike Giles, Sam kept right with him.

Sam reached out and lightly touched Kane's shoulder.

"Before we reach the house I have to tell you. Your friend is not a good man."

Kane looked at his shoulder. "No shit! And I suppose you are?"

The hand dropped from his shoulder.

"You were saying? I kind of already figured that out about Giles." Kane looked at Sam. It gave him a strange feeling inside. This was his son.

Sam caught Kane by the arm. Kane flinched just very slightly. Sam saw it.

"The explosion. You were hurt?"

"You should know. You set the thing off…didn't you?" Kane asked. Did Sam know everything?

"You know I didn't. Commander Buchanan must be your boss. Mr. Buchanan. The same Buchanan that you think so highly of. If you are the Hunter, rumor has it he set the Hunter project up to destroy itself. He has no intentions of saving it. Figured that everyone would take care of their own skeletons, including you, and it would save the government some money. You're on your own."

"How the fuck do you know all this? Two days back you only knew me as an Australian pimp who was your father." Then it occurred to him. Sam knew too much not to be in the deal somewhere. "Are you by any remote chance working with Chow? Are you my Chinese contact?" It even seemed far fetched to him to think that.

Sam nodded. For once Kane was thrown. All he had was a codeword.

"Buchanan doesn't know, does he? My blokes said they had set it up with Chow. Chow hasn't told Buchanan everything and vice versa. All I knew was I had a contact. Even I didn't know it was…" Kane hesitated. "But why are you here? The address said Pheng Nom. The ONC's there, right? And where did you say you were headed before we conveniently ran into each other?" Kane was still distrustful.

"I was on my way to kill my uncle. It was him who put the bullet put through the window. It was meant for you, her former lover and my father. My mother did a good job of blocking him from finding out about you. Killing Lilia was his mistake. I was going to take him back to stand trial on Chinese soil. Now he is yours to do with as you see fit. He has been feeding China white into Australia and Europe for years. A very upright government official. My mother suspected, but if she had pushed too far, things would have got too complicated. So she let it go…till now. I offered to go undercover for the Chinese until I found out they couldn't care less. They were happy with their extra payrolls that Cheng handed them. So, I switched sides. Buchanan thinks I'm a double agent. But someone else knows the truth. And…now you. Buchanan couldn't tell you because he didn't know. Only Chow knows."

"If you're telling the truth, you know the password. Only three people knew it. The Hunter, Buchanan, and Chow. Tell me the password and I'll believe you."

Without any hesitation Sam turned to his father and confirmed his story. "Kane's Hundred."

"And my contact makes four," replied Kane.

When father and son reached the house, it was deserted. Two backpacks lay on the smaller bed. One was ransacked and a note was pinned to his cell. Kane read it and destroyed it with a match.

"Fucking hell! The girls fled from my own blokes. We have to try and find them." Kane hesitated. He had no choice than to trust Sam. Kane looked into the other man's eyes. "My wife is pregnant."

"Oh." Sam Cheng pushed his blonde hair from his toned face. "Then we have to find her before Vau Cheng does."

Giles came to. He rubbed his jaw where Kane had hit him. Kane was still good. Giles shuffled from one foot to another, and his lack of self-confidence was obvious to Sam's friends. He wanted Kane in earshot, not three streets away where he couldn't hear a damn thing. He had to know what was going on. It was crucial. And where were the girls? Nothing could happen to either of them for very different reasons. He saw Kane and Sam coming back down the street clutching bags.

Kane tossed him a backpack. "Believe this is yours. Sam is going to help us find the girls."

"You trust him?" asked Giles in front of Sam.

"As much as I trust you, maybe more." Kane pulled his backpack straps tighter and moved out into the fast becoming pitch-black night to find his wife.

"I'm scared, Kelly. All we have is one gun and the clip in it. We have a few dollars and that's it. We can't get far on that. Do you know where they were supposed to get the ammo? And who do you think was in the house?" Genna was giving an Oscar-winning performance of being afraid, and finding out the facts as she went. She shuddered as she spoke.

"Genna, a half-hour ago you weren't talking to me. Now it's twenty questions. I know as much as you. And cut the '*little girl afraid*' crap. That's not you. They will find us and if they don't we'll head on to the fort. I pretty much know what to do. And how come you're the one that's scared all of a sudden? Thought you were the real tough one of the bunch. Saw you crying the other day, too." Kelly brushed unwanted leaves from her newly cleaned legs.

"Told you I fell. Kane told me to be careful…" She didn't want to lie anymore. "He tried to r…"

"He tried to rape you?" Kelly finished the sentence for her.

It was all she could do not to laugh. Why had Genna suddenly told her? She knew what Kane had said. Something was wrong. Kane had told her never to tell anyone and Genna had, without much persuasion. Was Kane right not to trust either Giles or Genna?

"You want me to be angry or what? Why did you tell me, Genna?"

Genna shrugged her shoulders. "Thought you should know that's all…" her voice trailed off, and she pushed back the hair from her lying eyes.

"Let's go wait by the roadside. Someone might pass by. We'll stay in the ditch," was all Kelly could think to say. To say anything else would have given the game away, and she was close to laughing out loud.

From close by voices whispered, "It's too damn dark to find Kelly. Kane will have our badges for this. We'll move on to Pheng Nom. Let's hope he has better luck," murmured the watcher.

The man who accompanied him nodded in agreement, and his backpack made another whirring sound.

In the morning light, the girl's tracks were plain to follow. There were signs of a truck, one heading straight for Fan Lau Fort, and two sets of footprints stopping abruptly. Kane realized how close they had been to his wife the whole time. He was angry with himself for not continuing last night. Sam had persuaded him to stop.

Kane could see the indentations in the brush where the girls had nestled down. No backpacks and no food would take its toll. His cell rang. This time he retrieved it from its rightful place in his boot.

"Do I really want to talk to you?" Kane whispered into the phone, turning his head away from Sam. "Why didn't you just say who you were when you went through the doorway? Not scare the living shit right out of them? If anything happens to Kelly, I don't ever want to see your faces again. Do you understand me?" he hissed. "Wait for me at Pheng Nom. We have transportation, and don't be shocked when you see our traveling companions." Kane hung up the line, and pushed the phone back into his boot.

"You always keep it in there?" asked Sam looking down at Kane's foot.

"Yeah, you have a problem with that?"

"No problem; just seems a strange….never mind." Sam was beginning to realize there was nothing normal about Kane Branson.

The truck was old and rickety, but it was getting the women where they needed to go.

In comparison, Kane was traveling in better conditions. Sam's car was luxurious, especially by Lantau standards. Buses and motorcycles were the main means of transportation in this part of Lantau. Kane lay back on the black, leather upholstery. All he could think of was Kelly and this from the man who had declared more than once that a woman would never cloud his judgment. Sam rode in the back with him and a very uptight Giles. There was an uneasy truce between the three men and Kane considered the possibility that there may be more involved in this than he first thought. Kane closed his eyes for a second and thought again of Kelly.

The road was bumpy and Kelly was sick.

"You okay?" commented Genna very half-heartedly.

"Do I look it?" Kelly sat on a bundle of straw in the back of the truck.

Genna found bananas to eat, and handed her one.

"Damn kid's gonna come out lookin' like a banana." She rubbed her side where she'd been cramping all morning. "Kane was right when he said I shouldn't be here. All I've done is get us really split up. I can't figure out why he couldn't find us. Did we wander that far away from the houses? And who the hell were those guys?"

Suddenly in the back of her mind she recognized the man's voice. If only the light in her brain had gone on sooner. It was a voice she knew only too well from training school and someone who, like herself, should never have been involved in Kane's Hundred.

CHAPTER 12

The road was winding. Kelly and the truckers had several hours start on Sam Cheng's vehicle, and Kane had yet to stop at Pheng Nom. He was restless in the car, where as Giles showed no emotion. Cheng covered for Kane. He may not like his father, but he did have a newfound respect for him. Sam eyed Giles suspiciously. He neither respected nor trusted him. Something in his mind kept rearing its ugly head. Something Lilia had told him, something about her lover's friend. He glanced towards Giles.

"So, you have known my father for many years. Back in Nam maybe?" Sam figured they were both old enough for that piece of history, just.

"I knew him right after Nam. What's it to you?" Giles replied curtly.

"Something my mother told me. Nothing important. War never is."

"To some of us it is," interrupted Kane. He still found it hard to talk about Nam. "What did she tell you?" His look was quizzical.

"I remember talking to her one night and how my father, you, was blamed for someone's death, then had been found not guilty. You were young at the time and when you returned had immediately joined some kind of law enforcement. I did not know it was the AFP...until now."

It provoked the thought in Kane's mind. Giles Harris' older brother had been the officer that finally took the rightful blame. Kane could hear Sam talking. But in Kane's mind's eye he could see Vietnam, and the day Simon Harris had let him take the fall. Choppers in the sky, burning flesh on the ground. Men screaming, men dying... vivid pictures in his mind. Sam's voice droned on.

"And the discharged officer went to Europe in disgrace."

Sam, like his father, never did anything without a reason. And this was for a reason. He could see Kane tense. Sam saw Kane turn and look at Giles and then back at him.

"Genna, I don't feel so great." Kelly held her stomach.

"Not surprised. All that fruit you ate." She paused. "Not that kind of feeling, is it? You think you're losing the baby? God, Kel, don't lose that baby. Want to get off this truck? I'll make him stop. Hey, you," she yelled though the dirty window into the truck cabin. "Stop. I said stop, please. My friend isn't well." And then very quietly Genna whispered something to the driver that Kelly couldn't quite hear.

Instead the truck sped up.

Kelly turned to Genna. "How'd they know who we are? How, Genna? They're taking us to Fan Lau Fort. There isn't any stopping. We're going straight through the gates of hell! Someone gave us up."

"Who do you think would do such a dreadful thing?" an evil smile on her face.

Kelly stared at that smug look of Genna's face and promptly fainted.

The expression on Kane's face changed. "Something's wrong with Kelly."

"How the hell do you know that?" asked Giles. He was fed up with all the double-talk that was flying in this car.

"In a way that you would never understand, Giles. Can't this fucking car go faster? The girls are in serious danger. That truck picked them up on purpose. Someone let them know where we were," and Kane stared at Giles.

"You don't know that. You said it was just an old truck that was passing…" added Giles.

"No, it wasn't. Stop the car right now!" Kane glanced across the road. "There's a bloke over there has a motorcycle. I can go straight to the Fort. Giles, you and Sam go for the explosives. Bring them on to me." Kane scribbled down the address and handed it purposely to Sam.

"Kane, you can't do that? It's safer together…" Giles protested.

"Safer for whom, Giles?" Kane put his hand on the door handle and opened the car door. "Stop the thing, man, or I'll fucking jump!"

"Okay, okay! Pull over," agreed Sam.

Sam's car screeched to a halt and pulled over to where the old man was about to board his motorcycle. Kane jumped out of the car, sprinted across the road, pulled a wad of Hong Kong dollars from his pocket and handed them to the man. The little Chinaman was delirious with his stash of money and handed over his machine to this blonde, impatient foreigner. Kane swung his long legs over it, revved the bike hard, turned around, and then stopped by the car.

"You get the stuff for me. I'll meet you in Fan Lau Fort. Give me my backpack. **Give, NOW.**" Patience had never been one of Kane's virtues.

Sam handed it out of the open door to his father. Kane swung it up around him.

"And that," Kane gestured at the automatic rifle in the car. He'd eyed it most of the way there and had promised himself to liberate it at some point. "Anymore ammunition in there?" Kane swung the rifle up and over his head. "Bring everything you find. Giles, stay with Sam. I'll see you there."

Kane sped down the alien road like it was his favorite racetrack; zero to sixty, that fast. A couple of miles down the road he screeched to a halt, the bike shaking under his body, and activated his cell phone.

"You there? Where the fuck have you been? Didn't you follow Kelly and Genna? Some truck has them. I figure it's heading for Fan Lau Fort. Cheng and Giles are heading for Pheng Nom. Not under any circumstances are you to go there. You understand? Giles and Cheng must not see you both now. They will bring the stuff on." Kane paused and waited for a reply. "Yes, my son, Sam Cheng. Who the hell did you… Oh, I see. You thought I meant the other Cheng. Kelly is in severe danger. I think Genna wants to kill her." He paused again. It wasn't the best connection in the world. "You know why. Just get to Fan Lau and meet me on the south side. You need to be there before the others. If I miss you, split up. One of you try to get inside the place, one way or another and the other stays outside. Out."

Kane closed the cell, deposited it back in his boot, and took off at high speed down the dusty dirt road.

"Kelly, Kel, wake up."

Genna smacked Kelly gently on the face, then a little harder. But she didn't wake up. Genna smiled. Now it would be easy. Two could be poisoned as easily as one. Genna pulled the packet of gum from her pocket. Leaning back in the truck, she settled down for the ride and uttered something to the driver that only they understood. The truck turned and took a different route to Fan Lau Fort.

The bike powered as fast as it would go for a small engine. At the crossroads he slammed to a halt. Kane saw the tire marks from the truck turn the other way and pulled his cell out of his boot.

"Yeah, that's right. Me again. They turned. Where the hell are you now?" Pause. "You don't know? Well you have a fucking map. Check. I'm at Chuck No. That's what the signpost says." He waited. "Two miles from me? I'll wait for you."

Kane rode the bike headed to a clump of trees, and sat back in the saddle. Three could do more than one. He had told his watchers to go on and then split up. Why hadn't they? He knew why. They were not alone. From the cutting of trees, he could see the car arrive. The two men got out. His men. In the back seat of the car were two more.

"Fuck!" and Kane slammed his fist down on the bike handles.

If they had his men, chances were they knew the Hunter was coming. Somewhere between the last phone call and now his blokes had been apprehended. Quite how, Kane didn't know.

Kane was on his own… again. He shook the motorcycle side to side under him. He listened. Not much gasoline in the tank. Not much further to go either. Maybe ten miles. Yet again, Cheng had his men. Cheng was one step ahead of Kane.

Sam and Giles found the explosives right where Kane said they were, stashed waiting to be liberated in a house on the outskirts of the town.

Sam had left his friends in Pheng Nom. Now it was just himself and Giles.

"I say we just take the ONC with us," Giles remarked.

"Why? You expecting just one big bang? I think Kane wants extra guns and ammunition," replied a confused Sam.

"What the hell for? There are only three of us, mate," Giles replied, a little too hastily.

"Firstly, I am not your mate, and secondly, if my father says he wants them, then he wants them." Sam loaded a couple of automatic rifles into the car and sat the spare ammunition onto the back seats.

"How come suddenly Kane is your father? You didn't know him a few days ago. Now it's all 'my father'."

"Whether I like it or not, that is the situation. And, he asked us to do this. He thought at least he could trust one of us." Sam never looked at Giles the whole time he spoke. Then finishing the loading, he slammed the car door shut.

"What's this 'one of us' crap?" asked Giles, his face glowing with anger.

"It does not matter. We will do as he asked. Can we go now?" Sam was blunt and irritating. He was also as tall as Giles, and as blonde and arrogant as Kane.

As darkness fell, Sam Cheng and Giles Harris pulled into the Fan Lau Fort area. Sam could see another car waiting at the gate. He waited patiently as the men got out, and glanced at Giles. Giles leaned forward in his seat and stared in horror through the glass.

"Oh, my god!" shrieked Giles. "That can't be. They're both dead!"

"Apparently not," and Sam laughed.

To Giles, it was the same kind of sardonic laugh that Kane had.

"You knew didn't you? You knew they weren't dead? How long have you known about them? How long have you known about this mission?" Giles asked frantically.

"That, Mr. Harris, is something you will never know. I told Kane my mother told me something else. She told me what a liar and son-of-a-bitch you really are. That you would have stabbed Kane in the back to get her. She knew you loved her, and she confided in you about the baby. You told her that Kane knew; that you had told him. But you and I know you never did. Everything you have told Kane is lies. I should have let my father kill you in Wang Po. But I want to do that myself. You betrayed my mother and my father. I may not particularly like Kane, but he has more guts than you will ever have. He's gone after the woman he loves. You let the one down you loved. You were supposed to be his friend."

"Was I? We'll see about that. You knew we were both in some kind of police force. Pity you didn't look further to see what force we were both in. Oh, I forgot, Lilia never told you that, and she had the way blocked so well that you couldn't find out anything about either of us. Convenient. She couldn't give one away without the other."

Giles turned in his seat. He brought his fist round unexpectedly, and hit Sam so hard in the face that Sam slumped backwards on the upholstery.

"Kane should have killed me when he had the chance. Now, he's on his own, just like he left my brother behind back in Nam. Let's see how he likes it." Giles laughed. "And a bonus to boot with the other blokes getting caught. Should be dead, but captive is okay...for now. I have my own score to settle with Kane Branson. I didn't wait all these years for nothing. My brother, the girl I loved, and the one I do. He has it all. Always has, always will. Yeah, he'll come for her, and your uncle and I'll be waiting." He patted Sam's face.

Giles turned to grab the wheel and for that split second he left himself unguarded. Sam Cheng lunged sideways and caught Giles by the throat and hung on.

A second vehicle pulled through the east gate of the fort and along the dirt track inside. The arrogant and self-made Colonel Cheng couldn't believe his luck. Two male prisoners and now two female: and all Australian. He stepped up to the back of the rickety vehicle and peered inside. A young woman lay motionless on the truck floor.

"How much did you give her?" asked the Oxford educated Colonel. He didn't want her dead.

"Just a tiny bit inside the banana. I would like to have given her more, but you're the boss. Just pay me what you owe me and let me go. There's a man out there who thinks he's falling for me. He's my ticket to freedom." Genna paused to get her breath. "Your nephew here yet? Or should I say step-nephew? I hear he takes after his father." Genna jumped down from the truck and stood in front of Cheng, and in her eyes that's wasn't bad that Sam took after Kane.

One of Cheng's men stepped inside and handed down the unconscious Kelly to another man. Cheng's soldier held the limp young woman in his arms and stood waiting for orders.

"And where is his father? You were supposed to take care of him. Was he too much for you to handle, or didn't we train you well enough in the year you spent here?" The Colonel paced up and down beside Genna, his eyes fixed on her.

"I took care of the team members in Australia for you," Genna pouted. "Got myself on this mission. And somehow the others got themselves out of this mission. Almost got raped by Kane Branson, but Giles will settle that one for me. He confided in me the other night that he hates Kane. Stupid fool thought I would help him. I'm only here to help myself," replied Genna.

"That's what worries me," replied Colonel Cheng. "I cannot let you leave here. You will remain in Lantau till everything cools down."

"But that wasn't the deal. You said…" Genna looked at the colonel with a confused expression.

"I changed my mind, and if you want to get out alive keep your mouth shut. You can go when the job is done and not before. You did well Miss Ingram, but not well enough. Not yet. Your father will be proud of you, though." He turned to go.

"My father? I don't know who my father is. Do you?" She grabbed his arm.

"Your father is a man by the name of Harris."

"What? The only man I know by that name is Giles…"

"He has an older brother, Simon," interrupted Cheng. "He lives in Europe. He went back to Australia a couple of times after Kane Branson testified against him. Simon Harris was dismissed from the military after Vietnam. That's where your mother came into the picture. A brief fling. Didn't you ever wonder where daddy was? I met him on one of his and my trips to England. Simon Harris is your father." He flaunted the knowledge in her face.

At that moment Genna felt totally and utterly alone. Her mother told her that her father was dead. Genna never questioned the fact. She stared at Cheng. He laughed.

"Does Giles know?" asked Genna not quite able to take this story in.

"No. I don't think even a man like that would want to sleep with his own niece. Simon said he never told him. He used his own brother to get to Kane. It was easy. Giles hated him for many different reasons. Giles was in love with Lilia. Come, let me explain as I escort you to your cell." Cheng extended his arm to Genna.

"My cell?" She looked astonished and started to back away, only to find two burly armed guards behind her.

"We can hardly have Mrs. Branson waking up without you, can we?" asked the Colonel.

"How did you know she was his wife?" gasped Genna.

"I have my sources. Someone in the AFP. Giles had been blackmailing Buchanan for some time. He threatened to tell Mr. Branson about his son. Mr. Branson would have been on the first plane out here, and we didn't want that. We wanted it at the right time, which is now, and not the last time that Mr. Branson came visiting Lantau. Simon and Giles wanted Kane, and I wanted Lilia for myself. A great pity she got in the way of the bullet. She died defending the only man she ever loved. And now, I have some friends to show you, along with some very precious cargo. Have you ever done China white, Miss Ingram?"

"No, and I don't intend to. You just kept supplying the stuff into Australia. I wondered how you managed to get it in so easily. But with such high-ranking agents on your side, it must have been a piece of cake. So Buchanan was being blackmailed, and he covered your tracks all for his precious agent. My god, Kane must have meant a lot to him to put his career on the line. But Buchanan must know that Kane will figure it out. Kane is one smart guy and one very attractive man." She realized what she was saying, but it didn't matter now. "I don't want to go with Kelly. I hate her." Genna backed away and glanced towards the gates.

"Don't even think about an escape plan. Why do you hate Mrs. Branson so much? Because she is all you are not? Or because she has Kane Branson?" Cheng questioned.

"Both."

There was no hesitation in her mind. On the day Kane touched her body he had also touched her heart. A complicated twist, and one that even she hadn't banked on. She followed Colonel Cheng down the stairs, beaten by her own greed for money and for Kane.

"Does Buchanan know about me?" she asked.

"No, he, like Kane, thinks its all Giles. Come, there are some people I want you to meet," and he led the way down the steps.

In the underground cells, Kelly awoke. Genna was sitting watching her. Kelly debated whether to throw up, or get up and choke Genna there and then.

Kelly had feigned her fainting turn with expertise. She hadn't swallowed the poisoned piece of banana. But she had squashed it under the bales of straw in the truck. When Genna had turned to talk to the driver, Kelly had dispensed with it.

And Kelly had heard everything. Dealing with the situation was something else. Like Genna, she couldn't wait to see whom the people were they were to meet. Kelly moaned suitably and sat up on the bed clutching her stomach.

"You okay? You gave us a nasty scare." There was concern on Genna's face.

"Oh, it's nothing…" replied Kelly, her conversation interrupted by a noise.

The door to the cells opened. Fan Lau Fort had been an internment camp many years before. It was a very good hiding place surrounded to the north and west by hills, and way off the beaten track.

Through the doors came two men Kelly had not expected to see again. Genna gasped as Alex and Ben stepped into the light. Grubby Ben, minus spectacles: mighty Ben the intrepid warrior. His computer his faithful shield. And Alex who looked like he had seen hell. Beaten and bloody, but not dead.

"You know these men?" asked Cheng.

"Never seen them before in my life," replied Kelly. She maintained the charade of the drug, shading her eyes with her hand, and peering through the rusty bars.

"Funny, because they know you. One of them has a computer and the other, after some negotiating, was found to have a cell phone issued by the AFP. So he was calling someone wasn't he? Seems they were sent in to help clear this mess up with someone dropping China white into Australia. So, you must know them, Agent Branson," commented Cheng, satisfaction written all over his face.

Kelly kept her cool. Genna had told the colonel everything right from the start. But how had she kept in touch with him? She had to be wired. A light came on in Kelly's mind. That's why Genna couldn't let Kane go any further that night in the temple. It wasn't because she didn't want him to; it was because he'd find the tracer bug. They'd been set up from the word go and Kane was walking straight into a trap, and Kelly had no way to warn him.

"Who told you my status? I know it wasn't the guys." She turned to Genna. "So it has to be you!"

She flung herself at Genna and landed full force on her body. Genna's fist was ready and she hit Kelly hard in the stomach. It winded her, but spurred her on. Grabbing hold of Genna's hair she brought her head down hard on the concrete floor. Kelly punched Genna in the face. Her nose cracked. Genna may have been the brains, but Kelly was certainly the brawn. She banged Genna's head on the floor before the cell door opened and two of Cheng's men pulled her off. Through split lips and handcuffed wrists Alex cheered her on.

"Enough, Agent Branson. You put on a good show. I've heard of Kane Branson's reputation, but not his wife's. Maybe we should have hired you instead of Miss Ingram."

Cheng ordered his men to keep the two women apart.

Kelly struggled, but she was no match for two big burly men. They held her tightly, and she pulled against them. Her hair hung across her face. She blew it away as she spoke.

"Maybe you should have, instead of Giles Harris' niece!" She looked at the girl lying on the floor bleeding and barely conscious.

"You heard everything then? Seems Miss Ingram is not as good as she thinks. Would you care to tell us where your husband is?" asked Cheng as he stepped inside the cell.

She viewed him, and the situation. "How the hell should I know? Last time I saw him he was going to confront your nephew. His son! That must get to you, Colonel. Must really eat on your soul, if you have one. The woman you loved has a son by Kane Branson." She was firing on all cylinders. "And what a waste of your time and money Genna was." Kelly looked straight at Genna. "You think Kane would really want to make love to you? You are joking. Look at me and look at you. You were right when you said that. You never stood a chance. Pity he didn't rape you. Would have served you right. At least you'd have known what it's like to be with a real man. But what makes this so funny is that you've been double crossed, too. Giles is your uncle. And the good colonel is going to kill you. You don't really think he's going to let you live knowing all this? And to answer your question, Colonel Cheng. Hell didn't freeze over yet, did it?"

Cheng crossed the cell and hit Kelly across the face. Blood spurted from her lips, and she spat in his face. It was too much for the arrogant Cheng. He hit her again much harder. Kelly never flinched and stared him straight in the face.

"Let Agent Branson go. Let her and Agent Ingram finish this." Cheng stepped back.

Kelly pulled herself free and stood tall, looking down at Genna. As Kelly prepared to fight, she felt a pain inside that she hoped she would never feel. Kelly cried out and slid down to the floor, and lay there.

"That's real big and brave, Cheng. Why not pick on someone your own size," yelled Alex trying to distract them all.

"Maybe I will, Agent Powers. But later. For now, you all go in this cell. Pick Miss. Ingram up from the floor and bring her upstairs. Agent Branson and these two can stay here and rot, or at least till hell comes to me."

"Oh, he will, Colonel Cheng, be sure of that!" yelled Alex and as the guards let him go, he rushed to Kelly's side.

Fan Lau Fort was lined with cannons from a zillion battles ago. Kane sat well back behind the walls. The motorcycle had given out a half-hour ago. He picked out his gun from the backpack, swallowed water, and stuck his new deadly toy in his belt: a blade that carried more than death with it.

He'd ditched the bike, changed back into fatigues, and carried on on foot till he reached his destination. Now, he wiped dirt deliberately down his face, his fingers streaking ominous warnings of war on his face. Slowly and surely he'd retied the black piece of his lover's dress tightly around his head. Once again, Vietnam battle cries ricocheted in his head. He touched the chain round his neck and raised the K to his mouth. He kissed it, dropped the K back onto his chest, and sat waiting for the dawn's light.

The night had not been kind to Kelly. She dozed on Alex's legs, and he had tried to make her comfortable. He'd wrapped his shirt around her young shoulders, and held her tightly. It was then Kelly felt a warm trickle inside her underpants. She knew. Kane's child was dying.

"You sure, Kel?"

"I'm sure, Alex. The pain was so bad," and again she felt that warm sensation. "Kane will be devastated. If only my anger had not gotten in the way. I felt it when Genna hit me. One blow too many…" her words became a mixture of sobs and disbelief.

"It's okay to cry, Kelly. It's okay," and Alex cradled her in his arms.

"Don't tell anyone, Alex. Let me tell Kane myself," she murmured.

Ben sat hunched in a corner disbelieving the situation. They'd taken his beloved computer. But only he had the password. They would never figure it out. His last e-mail out was to the Hunter. Ben couldn't figure out why the messages had stopped the last few weeks. In fact since they had started the mission. He hoped help was on the way. Alex had suggested Ben send out an SOS to Inspector Chow. Ben did so, and then stripped the hard drive down. Ben looked around him. The cell was filthy. Grime clung to the bars and excrement caked itself to the urinal in the corner. Flies hovered around the bowl. Flea-infested mattresses sat on the wooden frame that passed for a bed. Right now, Ben would have given anything for even his old bed back in Sydney. He glanced at Kelly.

"She sleeping?" Ben asked quietly.

"No, I'm not," replied Kelly. Sitting upright she stared through the tiny space the Chinese called a window. "They're gonna lure Kane in and then kill us all, aren't they? Don't even try lying to me, Alex."

"Yes."

Her head flopped forward. "So we just gonna sit here and watch it happen?" Her mouth still hurt from Cheng's hand and she touched her lips. The pain inside her body was unbearable. Kane's and her baby was dead.

"No. One of us has to get out of here. We have to be in two groups. As I am the most experienced, I'll go." Alex said forcefully.

"That's a reason? I should go. I have a better chance with Cheng. After all, it is my husband he wants. And I'm female…"

"We noticed. Even Ben noticed that. And now is not your time, Kelly Branson. You have suffered enough."

"I have nothing to lose, Alex. If they get Kane…"

"They won't…and you have your life. Kane isn't going to be too happy with me anyway. If you and Genna had not taken flight, we wouldn't be here now. I didn't think… and Kane would have." Alex paused long enough to collect his thoughts. "I'll be the distraction. I'll make up some story." Alex knew exactly what he had to do.

"Alex, the dead guy back in…" asked Kelly.

"You don't want to know, Kelly. Tell Kane…tell him I'm sorry. I did my best and my best wasn't good enough. Lie back down." Alex turned away from her. "Hey, you," he yelled at the guard. "I need to speak to Cheng. The girl isn't feeling well. I need some things for her. You wouldn't want her to get sick in here, would you? She's the main reason the AFP's top agent is coming in here. For her…"

Kelly flinched. 'Clouding his judgment,' she thought.

The guard slung his machine gun over his shoulder and pulled out his radio. He mumbled something in Chinese and moved toward the bars. He motioned Alex to stand back. Turning the key in the lock he pointed the gun at Alex. Alex stepped out of the grimy cell and the guard relocked the door. Alex turned to look at Ben and Kelly.

"Look after her Ben, for Kane," and he strode out across the floor, up the stairs and into the morning sunlight for the last time.

"Alex, no!" and Kelly's cries went unheeded, as she rushed to the bars.

"What's going on, Kel? Where's Alex going?" asked Ben. He stood up and clung to the cell bars also, staring at them trying to make them disappear. "Where, Kelly?" he screamed.

"To die." And Kelly buried her bloody face in Alex's shirt.

The statement was both profound and correct.

From behind the barbed wire fence and the lofty cannon towers, Kane chewed viciously on a piece of wood, gun in his hand, and debated his next move. His fatigues were soiled from crawling in the undergrowth and the bandana around his head kept his long hair in check. His moustache and now long beard had grown long giving him a particularly menacing look. Above him an ageing eagle soared.

"Hello, old friend. Come to cheer me on? Bring me luck?"

The bird screeched in the warm morning air.

"Maybe this time I need it," Kane laughed.

He knew the Chinese had his friends, and he was certain they had the girls.

Alex managed to get to Cheng. The Colonel sat behind a huge wooden desk. Samples of white lay on the table, also Alex's cell phone. Armed guards stood at every corner of the brightly lit room. Alex's eyes adjusted from the dingy cell light to now.

"This your kind of thing, Agent Powers? Probably not. You aren't old enough to have been in Nam and you're too much of the good guy. I'm told you have some problem downstairs? But you are right. The girl needs taking care of, for now. All I want is the man they call the Hunter. Then I can dispose of you all in any way I please. Your Mr. Buchanan isn't going to help. He's too scared he's going to lose his pension. And you, Mr. Powers? What can you do to save the world?" He leaned his head back and laughed. "You can't even save yourself."

"That's not my intention." Alex's face gave nothing away. He wasn't frightened of death.

Cheng sat upright. "You on a suicide mission?" He creased his eyes, not sure what Powers would do next.

"If I have to be."

Alex had to warn Kane somehow. He turned slightly, and kicked at the guard three feet away. The man went down with the one blow and Alex reached for the knife on Cheng's desk. He held it ominously in front of Cheng. The other guard backed off.

"Go on. Go for your gun. I'll slit your fucking throat first!" screamed the mighty Alex. Alex grabbed the cell, flipped it open, and pushed the buttons for Kane's direct number. He tried again. There was no connection. The cell was dead. As Alex glanced down for one moment he lost concentration. Cheng raised the gun he was holding under the desk.

"I disabled it. Do you think I am stupid enough to leave it where you could get it?" Cheng raised the gun higher.

Alex dropped the phone and it echoed as it bounced across the stone floor. He looked straight at Cheng, his eyes piercing Cheng's.

"Doesn't matter. Hell is coming. Oh yes, hell is coming!" Alex screamed.

One clean and well-executed shot from the colonel's gun pierced Alex's skull. He slumped down to the floor with a surprised look in his eyes, blood spurting down his face.

The noise of the gun echoed round the chambers and reached Kelly's ears. She screamed loud and long.

"Noooooooo," and Kelly clutched Alex's shirt to her chest, and cradled it there. She slumped down on the bunk.

"Is he?" Ben was shaking uncontrollably.

"Say it, Ben! Alex is dead. He risked his life to warn Kane. This time there is no mistake. If I ever meet Genna Ingram again, no one better get in my way. No one, not even Kane," and Kelly cried tears of anger.

The cell doors opened and Cheng stepped through. Behind him two men dragged a body between them. Kelly forced herself to look into Alex's open eyes. Kelly smiled.

"Something amusing you, Agent Branson? The man is dead. You find that funny?" remarked the ever-confident Cheng.

"No. I find the fact that he died staring you in the face particularly brave. It was a smile of courage. Much as mine is now."

Cheng stepped through the door of the cell and grabbed hold of Kelly's now matted hair. He pulled her head back. Kelly wriggled under his grip. Her camisole top slipped a couple of inches down and he saw the butterfly. Immediately, he let go of her and turned to Ben.

"That's it, isn't it? The password is Butterfly. Now we will find out what you have in that computer." The colonel was overjoyed at his own brilliance.

"You're wrong," Ben yelled, more out of fear than bravery. "You will never open it. Never!"

Cheng reached for Kelly's throat and held on tightly. "No? If you don't talk my hands will tighten around her neck. Then there will be no more Agent Branson for anyone to rescue. I need to know who your contacts are. Obviously, someone other than Buchanan in Australia. And there is someone else out here. You couldn't pull this off without inside help. You're not just here to find out where the China white is coming from, but to close us down…permanently, just like last time. Some Chinese inspector helping you maybe?"

"I don't know who the contact is. I swear I don't. Kane never told anyone, not even Kelly. I don't know who it is," Ben pleaded, his face flushed and panicky.

Kelly was choking. She tried kicking back but she was too weak. And the pain inside her womb was too strong. There was no way that Ben could tell them the password and Cheng was close to finding the truth. One day back at the hotel she was playing with Ben's computer and had put her name in to log on: Butterfly Kelly. Ben had heard Kane call her that once or twice. She tried to release the grip Cheng had on her. He pulled tighter on her throat. Her scream rasped out in a dull noise. She was blacking out. She stared at Ben warning him not to say anything. But Ben was weak and Kelly was the cloud on his judgment.

"Alright! Let her go. I'll tell you," and his chubby little fingers grabbed at Cheng's arm trying to force his hands from Kelly's throat.

"The code first. Then she can go free." Cheng pushed tighter on her neck.

"Butterfly Kelly. It's Butterfly Kelly! Let her go, please," Ben begged.

Cheng released her and Kelly slid down onto the cot. She held her neck and gasped for air. Each breath was agony. Ben sat down beside her and put his arms around her. She leaned against chubby, geeky old Ben who had just tried to save her life.

"Thank you, Agent Gray. That's all I needed. Kelly, I'm sure, that your husband cannot be far behind you. All that's left is to find out who the contact is and get the son-of-a-bitch in Australia that's causing all the problems. Miss Ingram wishes to be remembered to you. I have a feeling you cannot wait to see her again. Now we wait. Anything you would like?"

"To see you in hell, and have the receipt in my hand."

He laughed and walked out of the door. But Colonel Cheng's laugh was not so confident as it should have been.

CHAPTER 13

On the scorched hill, Kane Branson waited for his chance. He heard the sound of the bullet as it echoed around the chambers, and Kane dropped his head. Whoever it was, they had not died in vain.

Kane crouched in the grass, watching. Where were Giles and Sam? Why hadn't the car surfaced? They had the ammo to blow the place to kingdom come. The sun was red hot in the sky, and Kane Branson wiped the beads of sweat from his face. He was alone, yet again.

Behind him the branches cracked and Branson turned with more precision than the eagle and his rifle more deadly than the eagle's claws. He aimed straight at the intruder, finger at the ready. He squeezed the trigger slowly and just as slowly released it. Kane was totally surrounded by Chinese with guns. Once again, he had been betrayed. A veteran AFP agent could not be taken alive. He reached for his pistol and from behind a boot clipped away his piece cracking bones in his fingers. The last thing he remembered was a tirade of boots and guns hitting his body.

"You think Kane's out there?" asked Ben.

"Course. Where else would he be?" Kelly said, trying desperately to sound confident.

Then Kelly heard the doors banging above her. Loud clanging noises heralded a pit with solid steel doors, and men shouted with glee. They had Kane caged like an animal in a pit!

Cheng would view his prize after he went into Ben's computer. He hadn't taken courses for nothing, and all he needed was the code. Now he had it. But Ben had removed the hard drive that contained the Hunter's messages. Cheng could not bring them back. Angry and frustrated, Cheng hurled the tiny laptop across the floor. It bounced on the floor and made one last noise before it spewed its mechanism out before his eyes. But Vau Cheng was intelligent enough to know that Kane Branson had to have a contact…somewhere. If he couldn't find it by computer then he's find it out by force. He still had agents Branson and Gray. He rose up from his desk and took one of his men and left his office. But now, he had Kane Branson.

Kane awoke. He was battered and bleeding, but he was still alive. He figured he'd been out a while. Sunlight filtered through the hinges on either side of the steel doors that topped off the pit. He could hardly see anything around him. He lay still assessing what damage had been done to him, moving his fingers at he did. One hand moved, the other didn't. He felt his lips. They were cracked and bleeding. His hand searched his rib cage. One maybe two ribs were broken. He set his hand down on the floor. Cold moist dirt greeted him.

"Fuck!"

He was stripped of all weapons, boots, cell-phone, and clothes except for his fatigue pants.

"Nice of them to leave me those," he quipped, and as he smiled his mouth cracked some more.

Suddenly above him, the doors opened and light streamed in. Kane's eyes squinted in the brilliant morning light. A head peered over the top of the open doors. And then another one. A fatter face looked down at him.

"At last, Agent Branson, you are awake. We brought you in yesterday, and we were getting concerned for you. You have to die…but not just yet. Not till we find out exactly who you are. You are a worthy opponent, unlike the others in here. But, I do not see hell when I look at you. Your friend said hell was coming and I don't see it yet." Cheng paused and thought for a moment. Almost as an after thought, he continued, "Oh and I would suggest you do not move too far. There is a partition that separates you and my little pets. Deadly vipers and cobras surround you, and they are probably hungry by now. They haven't been fed today. Yesterday they had a good meal. If you turn your head you can see for yourself. You friend was both lunch and dinner for my little babies." Cheng was talking like the psychopathic killer that he was.

Kane turned and had it not have been that Cheng was watching he would have thrown up. What was left of Alex's body was covered in snakes.

"You bloody bastard," whispered Kane. "You will pay with your life."

"I don't think you are in much of a position for threats. All I have to do is to release them from the chamber behind you. See?" and Cheng was as good as his word.

The partition was raised just slightly and hissing filled Kane's ears. Kane wasn't frightened of anything… except snakes. He shrank away from the dividing glass partition and the writhing mass of death.

"Well, well. The great Kane Branson is afraid of snakes? Don't know if your friend was or not. He was dead before he ever met with them." Vau Cheng laughed long and lingering. He allowed the partition to drop a little lower. Then his tone changed. "Agent Branson, I have something else that belongs to you."

Kane could hear a woman shouting above the hissing noise of the snakes. Two men lifted a struggling Kelly over the top of the pit and held her there. Through blurry eyes Kane tried to focus on her. He stared at her and her face became the reality he had thought about.

"Your wife, I believe. And Genna Ingram is here also. She is Simon Harris' daughter. She also told me you would be coming to close us down."

That was the last piece of the puzzle. Not one, but two of his team were on the wrong side of the law, each for a different reason. Kane was trapped… not only in a pit, but also in a web of intrigue.

"Kelly," yelled Kane. "Did they hurt you, baby?"

"No," she lied. And she dropped her head forward so Kane would not see her lying eyes.

"Let her go," Kane hissed. "It's not her you need to deal with. It's me."

"She is my guest, along with Agent Gray. Miss Ingram is, shall we say, my house guest." He mumbled something in Chinese and one man slipped inside the stone building.

Kelly twisted in the strong grip. She could not break free but she could see who Cheng's men brought out. Genna was ushered out of Cheng's quarters. She stood like a statue, not sure who was on her side.

"You!" Kelly screamed at Genna. "I'd like to kill you right now." She pulled hard in the Chinese hands. They set her on the ground, still holding her tightly between them, and out of sight of her husband.

"Now that would be an interesting spectacle. Go get Agent Gray so he can watch also." Cheng peered back down the pit. "How about some sport before breakfast, Mr. Branson?" He turned to his men. "Get him out of there," he barked in Chinese.

The men uncoiled a rope ladder, and it dropped down into the pit.

Even one-handed Kane climbed the ladder. He twisted his legs around the rope and pulled with his hand. Arms reached down and pulled him the rest of way out of the cavernous prison. He sat on one of the hot metal doors, watching Kelly every moment. Kelly could see his body. It was bruised and bleeding. His hair was caked with dirt and grime, and hung in clumps under the bandana.

As Kane tried to stand, one of Cheng's men hit him in the stomach with a rifle-butt. Kelly watched as Kane doubled over and immediately tried to get back on his feet. In anger, Kane lashed out at the guard, and as he did another of Cheng's men hit Kane from behind, and he fell forward onto the ground.

"Kane," screamed Kelly. "Kane!"

He shook his head and pulled himself up onto his hands. The pain in his fingers was unbearable but to show Cheng that his hand was broken would be a mistake. And Kane had made enough mistakes in the last few days.

"Agent Kelly Branson," Cheng turned to Kelly, "You are going to get your wish. Miss Ingram here is not the hotshot we thought she was." He turned back towards Kane's direction. "Make sure his hands are secured. Then tether his neck to the tree. We want to make sure he can clearly see his wife, though."

Kane was grabbed roughly from all directions, and they pulled him to the nearest tree. Binding his hands and tethering his neck, Kane was trapped yet again. He coughed as the band tightened round his throat.

"Why'd you do that? You didn't have to do that." Kelly was in reaching distance of Cheng, even though a guard held her, and she lunged at him.

She failed with her blow, and Cheng laughed.

"Fiery. I like that in a woman. She as good in bed, Mr. Branson? She must be. You didn't marry Lilia. Then again, you didn't love her. But she gave you a son. Pity you didn't know about him years ago. I wanted to marry her. But you were the only man she loved. Some honor. I shall personally take you on, Agent Kane Branson... when the ladies have finished."

"Ladies? I only see one," Kane mumbled. He turned his gaze away from Kelly towards Genna. "Pity I didn't rape you. At least you'd have died happy."

Kelly laughed. "She couldn't let you, Kane. Oh, she wanted you to take her, but she was wired. That's how they knew where we were at any given time."

"That true, Genna?" whispered Kane, his eyes piercing hers.

A woman with a cracked and bloody nose looked back at him. "Yes, I was wired," she muttered. "Where's Giles?"

"You mean you didn't kill him? Which one of you murdered Ty? What did he ever do to you? He was just a kid. I know you killed Paul and you could have saved Blair. But she was in your way. You thought I'd pick her over you, which I would have. Instead I put my own wife in the line of fire. Just what you people wanted. When did you finally take up with Giles? After the temple episode? Kelly was in your way though, wasn't she? I warned her about you. By the way, Genna, Kelly is much smarter than you." And then Kane heaped the final blow to Genna's pride. "And having to pretend an attempt to fuck you was the hardest thing I ever had to do."

Genna lunged at Kane and hit him hard across the face. He spat at her. She wiped it slowly away with her fingers, and Kane could see tears in her eyes. She looked at him with a venomous hatred he would never forget, but also he saw a flicker of something else. For one fleeting second in time a look passed between them.

"Giles is probably dead by now. I hope so, anyway," Kane sneered.

Genna turned away, and faced Cheng. "Let *Mrs. Branson* go." Then turning back to Kane, she boasted, "Say goodbye to your wife, *sir*."

"Kelly… no. Don't do this," yelled Ben. "Kelly!" He had watched from the sidelines, not daring to say a word. But prompted by the hostility and Kane's bluntness, he had sprung back into life.

She didn't hear. The look on Genna's face attracted her like a bull to a red flag.

"You want me, Mrs. Branson? Then, come get me. And, by the way, your husband did succeed. Why do you think I told you? I know how good your husband is." Genna egged Kelly on.

Kane was Kelly's chink also.

"You're lying! I know you are. I know Kane. I do," and tried to break away.

"You so sure of that?" yelled Genna. "You absolutely sure I'm lying…"

It was time to let Kelly go. Cheng ordered her release and Kelly charged. Genna was ready and ducked under her blow.

"She is lying, Kelly!" screamed Kane. "Kelly….."

But Kelly couldn't hear. The furious rushing noise in her ears was too great. Genna swung around and caught Kelly with a violent thump in the middle of her back. Kelly fell forward. She'd been in many fights before, but Genna was tough and fought with her brains. Kelly stood up, dusted the dirt from her body, and looked Genna in the face.

"He never would have taken you," Kelly hissed.

Kelly swung again and the flat of her hand made contact with Genna's face. She grabbed for Genna's clothes and the two girls fell to the ground. They rolled in the dust and grime of Fan Lau Fort. Kelly fought with all the streetwise moves she knew. Genna was stronger than Kelly anticipated, and Genna could take it as well as Kelly. Both the girls were taking some punishment.

"Kelly," yelled Kane. "Kelly, the baby!"

Something inside Cheng stirred. "Stop them." The two girls were separated by Cheng's men. "She is pregnant?"

"Keep out of this, Kane. I will kill her," screamed Kelly. She crouched ready to attack Genna again. "She deserves it…" but the Chinese guard held her tight.

"Kelly, please…" yelled Kane. The rope pulled on his neck and movement was difficult. His ribs ached and his muscles felt like they had been stamped on. "Kelly, stop…"

"There is no baby, Kane! This bitch killed it," Kelly was almost hysterical.

"She what?" The taught rope made his neck bleed.

"You heard me. She killed our baby, Kane," and Kelly fell back against her captor.

"Dear God. Why Genna? You hate me that much?" Kane pleaded.

Genna stared at Kelly, and then she laughed loud and long. She had finally taken something from Kelly. But somehow inside she felt sad. It was Kane's child. Genna turned her face towards him, her eyes cold and unforgiving. Kane stared at her. Ben never moved, standing like a statue frozen in time.

"Kelly. I'll fight Cheng. Help is on the way, baby. I know it." His mind was in turmoil.

"How do you know it? All your people are here," responded Cheng. He pondered a moment. "Except Giles and we all know which side he is on. Your young agent sent out e-mails…to whom? That's who you are expecting?"

"Yeah, that's right," he lied. "Actually, he's already here," he muttered. He needed his new toy, but he needed to get Kelly and Ben out of there first. Especially Kelly.

Cheng didn't appear to hear his last comment.

Kelly clutched her stomach. The pain had stopped. Kane's yelling had finally got through the hate in her head. She had promised him she would not lose this child, and she had. She had broken her promise and now one would pay. It was Genna who broke the silence.

"This is not the end. Giles will come for me. My uncle will come."

"Your what?" a man's voice sneered.

No one noticed the person that had strolled through the gate was Kane's once trusted friend.

Sam had gained control of the situation in the car. He drove the car to the other side of the fort with an unconscious Giles in the seat beside him. He hoped he'd killed him. Sam had tried hard enough. He'd tried to choke him to death. But Giles had practiced playing dead many times before. He waited until the time was right and from under his jacket he produced his .38, and shot Sam Cheng in the chest. He shot Cheng's nephew, and Kane's son, the double agent.

"What did you say?" repeated Giles.

Genna turned in slow motion. Giles viewed the situation. He saw Kane tied by the throat. Pity he wasn't hanging from the tree. That created a better picture for him. Kelly stood bruised and battered, and Giles felt for her. But what had Genna said?

"My uncle. Simon Harris is my father. Your brother is my father." Genna started to cry.

"Think that's gonna work on a man like Giles?" asked Kane.

Giles walked over to Kane and peered onto his face. He patted Kane on the side of his cheek, gently, then much harder. "I've hated you all my adult life. You always took and never gave. And seems it never stops." He turned to Genna. "Only one thing wrong with this story. My brother was barren. He could never have children."

"The colonel says Simon is my father," replied Genna. "They have been working together all this time. Colonel Cheng told me so."

"That's what he said? Cheng and Simon? Then it must be right. But that would be a little difficult. Simon died three years ago. Seems every-

one has been lying to everyone else. Simon Harris cannot be your father…
because I am."

No one said a word. Not even Cheng. Giles' laughter roared around
the courtyard and echoed down a thousand cannons.

"Simon told you that on purpose, Cheng, all those years ago. It was his
cover. He enlisted your help to get back at Kane. He hated him so much.
Simon and I both knew Genna's mother. We went to a party one night.
We were all pretty drunk. She and I ended up in bed together. I actually
had someone else's woman for a change." He glanced at Kane, then back
at Genna. "Simon, your mother, Genna, and I agreed not to tell anyone.
He took responsibility for supporting you. He gave your mother anything
she needed. When the chance came to send you over here to train, we
jumped on it. While you were gone, Simon died. The correspondence you
had, Colonel Cheng, came from me. No one knew. Not Buchanan, not
anyone. You thought you were hanging Sam's parentage over Buchanan.
He knew, of course he knew. He didn't tell Kane on purpose. Buchanan
knew Kane would be on the next plane out here. Good, honorable Kane,
always responsible for his actions. It was all a scam. We had you, Kane,
believing there was a double agent. I used the whole of this mission as
a cover for shipping the heroin into Australia. There was a double agent,
but not the kind you thought. I just assumed the code word and took
over from Simon. You see, Mr. Branson, *sir*, I was playing both sides, but
not in the way you were thinking. Colonel Cheng, I let you think you
ran this operation. You are not in charge here. I am. You notice no one
stopped me at the gate? Drop your gun, colonel…now!" Giles aimed his
.38 at Cheng, and a dozen other guns did the same. "This has been my
operation for some time. You were just running it for me, oh, and your
step- nephew, Colonel Cheng, and your son, Kane, is lying out there in
a pool of blood."

Kane fell back against the tree. He knew it was Giles, but not that
he was playing two roles. Or even three. Now, he understood why Giles
couldn't sleep with Genna and why he was so worried that he had. Giles
had loved someone all right - his own daughter. But Sam wasn't dead.
That couldn't be. Sam Cheng was too experienced an agent for that. But,
then again, he didn't know the real Giles until that second.

Kane needed his new toy at that moment, the blade that carried more
than death in its handle. It carried a homing device for Chow's men. Was
it still working? Would they find them before it was too late? He couldn't

take that chance. With all the strength he had left, Kane pulled on the silken bamboo rope that tethered him to the tree. It cut deeply into his throat but it snapped from his weight. Genna was standing in his path. Kane sprang forward, pushed the man holding Genna out of the way, and pulled his bound wrists over Genna's head. He pulled tight on her neck.

"No one move, and I mean no one, Giles. I'll kill this bitch with my bare hands. I swear I will. Especially after she killed my child." Kane's face was one of total hate for Genna and Giles. He twisted his bindings tighter, and Genna gagged.

"She did what?" Giles looked horrified at Genna.

"Yeah, Giles. Take a good look at Genna. Then look at Kelly. You hated her having my child. Well you got your wish. Kelly lost the baby."

Giles face was ashen. "Kelly…I…" He didn't know what to say to the women he was in love with.

Kelly took all her strength and spat in his face. Giles closed his eyes and wiped the spit from his face. He deserved that.

Kane continued. "When did you enlist Genna? Pity you didn't bother to tell her she was your daughter. But that certainly would have impeded her feelings for you. How sick can you be? All those suggestions about the ice maiden. How the fuck would you know? And Buchanan. You knew he was straight, just being blackmailed. You helped. He didn't let the China white in…you and your contacts did! All he was guilty of was protecting me. And you let your own daughter kill people. Fucking hell, man, how you must hate me."

Giles raised his head and glared at Kane, and spoke with venom. "Hate is not the start of the sentence. Look at you and look at me. You had Lilia, then Sage Jay, a daughter, an inheritance, that great big house in Australia; a career that you know will take you to the top. You have everything. Even down to a son…and you have Kelly."

"At last we have the truth. You may have a drug ring going nicely for you, but it's not enough, is it?" Kane faced Giles still clutching Genna in between the two of them. "You want my lifestyle, too. Except you can never have it. I have it all. But you have one thing that I have."

"Being?" Giles snarled.

"Me. Hell has arrived, and so has the Hunter. You have me." He watched Giles expression. He didn't know. He really didn't.

Giles stared at Kane. He had the Hunter with him the whole time. If he'd taken Kane out, the whole mission would have been destroyed. But he'd wanted Kane alive till this moment. Now, Kane had his daughter. Giles hesitated. He could grab Kelly. But Kane would strangle Genna before he had chance to hurt Kelly. And Giles didn't want to hurt Kelly any more than she already had been. He looked at her face, at her cut and bleeding lips, and at the sadness in her eyes for her child.

"What do you want?" Giles asked Kane in a quiet tone.

"Let Kelly and Ben go in exchange for me. And I won't kill Genna."

"No, Kane!" and Kelly pulled in the Chinese guards arms.

"Kel, it's the only way! He won't hurt you. The man's in love with you. He has been since Alice Springs," Kane said as he faced his wife.

"You fucking son-of-a-bitch, Kane Branson. You bastard…" hissed Giles. All the years of hate rising in him at one go.

"Kelly's not just the weak link in my armor…but yours also. Let her go. Let them both go and I'll stay," pleaded Kane.

Giles thought for a moment. He looked at Kelly. Kane was right. She was his broken link. He had to let her go.

"Let her through," yelled Giles. He motioned the guards. "Go, Kelly Branson, unless you want to see your husband die." Giles raised the .38 and pointed it at Kane.

"No, Giles…" Kelly begged, tears streaming down her face.

"Run, Kelly. Run and don't look back," screamed Kane. He knew he couldn't hold Genna much longer. His broken fingers were crumbling fast.

Kelly backed down the path, tears blurring her vision, and then she turned and fled. She looked back once to see Ben running right behind her. They took off down the road toward the south gate.

Giles smiled at Kane and then spun around to face the path.

"Never promised I wouldn't kill the geek," and Giles opened fire.

Ben dropped to the ground with a sickening thud. Kelly heard him groan as he hit the floor. She never looked back. She kept on running right into dead men walking. Or what should have been. Kelly stopped abruptly as she collided with the oncoming figure. He held onto her as she tried to wriggle free. She raised her eyes and looked up at the blonde Sam Cheng.

"You're dead! You're dead! Giles said he shot you," Kelly screamed.

"He did." Sam gently let go of her and opened his shirt. A bulletproof vest stared back at her. "Your husband thought it a good idea and he was right. He is…my father is a good man. He fights for what he believes in. Kane said he would get you out at any cost, even that of his own life."

Kelly gasped and turned to run back to her husband. Kane had foreseen a situation like this one. Sam grabbed her by the arms.

"You cannot do that. Then all would be in vain. We will get him out of there. You, me, and Inspector Chow. He is on his way by chopper. But there should be more of you. Where are the others?" Sam peered around her.

"Alex is dead, and Ben is back just a little back up the road. Giles shot him in the back."

Poor Ben. He followed Kane's orders to the last.

"It will be okay, Kelly."

Gently he took his stepmother in his arms, a woman younger than he was by several years. This was a woman he didn't know, and one who belonged to a father he was just beginning to understand.

"Very brave, Kane. Then you always did have a penchant for the heroics. You can let my daughter go now."

"Now she's your daughter, Giles? What's with this paternal instinct? You let her think you were falling for her, for God's sake. What kind of man does that? And you," he pulled Genna tighter to him, "you killed Paul. How did you do it? Come up behind him and hit him with something? Would you have killed Blair also to get here in her place? And all the time you were being used; by everyone it seems. The authorities can deal with you. For now, you're my insurance, the only thing I have to bargain with. And believe me that's all that is saving you. I would keep tightening these ropes around your neck till you were hanging from them if it would bring my baby back." Kane's eyes were fierce and almost like a man who had lost control. Kane paused to regain composure. "And look at Colonel Cheng. Looks like his damn dream went down the toilet. Who took it away, Cheng? Not me, but this fucker you were working with. Giles Harris doubled-crossed you, too."

Cheng hadn't said a word the whole time. He watched. This was the Hunter. This was the man he had waited for. The man he wanted to kill. This was the man whom Lilia had loved, and Sam's father. How he hated him, but how he hated Giles Harris more. Giles Harris had used him the whole time. Now Giles had degraded him in front of his own men whom he had worked with for months. He stared at Giles.

Giles was too busy with Kane to notice.

"Yeah, so what?" Giles yelled. "You did a whole bunch of double-crossing. You faked Alex's death and hid good old Ben away. And I thought all the time that old Cheng here had fixed them. Did they follow us the whole way, or just part of it?"

"Let's just say that Alex saw my Oscar-winning performance with your daughter. Alex always doubted you. Said you were too eager to volunteer. He faked his own death and whisked Ben away before Cheng here got to him through Genna. But you didn't know that because you had no contact with Cheng. You were arrogant enough to believe you didn't need it. Only Genna had contact with Cheng, and she only relayed what she wanted him to hear. You couldn't discuss the truth with Genna, even though she could have communicated it straight to Cheng for you. You, Paul and Genna were the ones we suspected. Obviously wasn't Paul. Genna was picked on purpose to come on the mission. There was a year missing in her file that no one could account for. And several years missing for you. Blair was a decoy. She was never in the running, and you guys made sure she wasn't, all for nothing. When the car blew up, I thought at first it was some of Sam's work. Then I realized that both you and Genna had hung back in the doorway. Ty told me you pulled her back in the club. No one was meant to die though, were they? It was a scare tactic. You dropped your red herrings in the sea along with mine." As Kane spoke he let his hands slide down the front of Genna's pants.

She gasped for air. But Giles saw something else on her face.

"Where'd you hide it, Genna? Had my hand in your pants before and didn't feel anything except moisture." He tugged hard on the pants and pulled them down from the front of her stomach. Kane pulled her back against him. His fingers searched the top of the pants. Not there. He slid his hand up under her vest and found what he was looking for. He pulled the tape and bug from between her breasts. "Very neat…I should have raped you. Would have saved my child's life!" He tossed the bug on the floor and stamped it out like he did his cigarettes.

Giles saw a look of want on the girl's face.

"You're good, Kane. I never doubted that. But your son showing up was a bonus. He did his best not to let me hear what he said in Wang Po. He succeeded. Remember I also speak Chinese and one of his men mentioned Sam was playing both ends of the scale. I knew then you wouldn't trust me." Giles turned to Vau. "You do know that Sam is working for Branson's country? Or do you? Did anyone bother to tell you that?"

The colonel shook his head. No one had really told him. He had begun to figure it out. He had lost everything: Lilia, his nephew, and his position in the compound. His men were pointing guns at him. All he had left was his life. And right now that didn't seem worth a whole lot. He started to move to the building.

"Where you think you're going, Cheng?" asked Giles.

"Just to get my things from my office. You seem to be the gentleman in charge now. Apparently you always have been. You and your brother. Am I to go or stay?"

"Up to you, mate. You can work for me, not with me. You'd make a pretty good manager here. At least I'd know where you were," said Giles with indifference.

"Then I'll stay. I'll be back." Cheng disappeared inside.

Giles was too full of his own importance to even notice. All he wanted was revenge on Kane Branson.

"Let her go. Your life for Kelly's, remember? You cannot win. You or your government," laughed Giles.

"It used to be your government," muttered Kane.

"There is no one left to save you. I'll find Kelly and…"

"Over my dead body," Kane hissed.

"That can be arranged," snapped Giles.

"I don't think so." Vau Cheng emerged from his office. He had Kane's new toy in his hand. "Homing device, right, Mr. Branson? And if that fails, I am sure now that your son would also have called for Chow. That's why you are so confident."

"And who said you were stupid, Colonel Cheng?" laughed Kane. "Perhaps you should have looked better at it yesterday. Inspector Chow is on his way, one way or another." Cheng held onto the object. "None of us have a chance. Chow will bring many men with him. Of course, Mr. Harris, you can always shoot your daughter to get at Mr. Branson, and run for cover. And you probably would."

"Why the sudden submission, Cheng? You always give up this easily?" replied Giles.

"You took everything away from me. He only took Lilia. And everything is too much to lose. Besides, Mr. Branson is the only one that you're afraid of." Cheng knew it was over.

"Are you, Giles? Are you afraid of me? Have you always been?" retorted Kane, his eyes narrowed when he spoke.

"How can I be afraid with a force like this around me?" Giles pointed to the men standing around him. Guns still pointed at Cheng and Kane.

"Because they will turn at the slightest change in the wind. Whichever person is the strongest, they will follow. Look how they changed sides from Cheng to you. Think about it. They will leave you in a heartbeat."

"You wish, Kane. And you, Cheng, do you think he would let you live after you killed Lilia? She was the mother of his only son," added Giles.

Cheng had forgotten that. But he still figured his chances of staying alive were better by surrendering. Kane and Chow, at least, would go by the law. Giles Harris was insane. Even his daughter knew it. Through all of this she had watched him. She had worked for the Chinese because she was paid well to do it and it gave her a sense of power that Genna needed. Giles did it for revenge.

In the skies the shrill cry of the eagle distracted them all. It swooped low above their heads.

"Fucking bird," and Giles looked up and shot wildly in the air.

Genna tried to break from Kane's grasp. He held his arms around her waist, pulling her against his body. She could feel his muscles taught and relentless.

"Not that easy to escape me, Genna. Not unless I want you to," Kane whispered in her ear. "I can still kill you. I can crush your ribcage right here and now."

He felt her tense against him. She did feel something after all. Slowly she raised her head and looked at her father.

"Why don't you just shoot him? He's not going to kill me. Kane Branson doesn't hurt or kill women. He already tried and failed."

"Did he fail, Genna? What would have happened if you hadn't been wired? That's the problem with Kane. He never fails and he didn't this time."

Giles raised his .38 and pointed it in the girl's and Kane's direction.

"She's going back to stand trial, just like Cheng will. This isn't a kangaroo court. We aren't judge and jury. I'm no saint, and I'm not in any position to save the government some money, much as I would like to. It would be so easy to rid the world of fucking shit like you three. Inspector Chow will be here anytime now. Even Cheng knows that."

"Shut the hell up, Kane. I don't believe all that. It's just a ploy. Like that stuff you were listening to back in Sydney about the explosives. All games to you people. I saw those explosives. I helped load them into the car before I killed your precious son." He pulled the hammer back on his gun. "Now let her go before I do just shoot her. At this range, the bullet will hit you too."

"Go ahead, man. Do it. You don't have the guts," encouraged Kane. "Do it, you gutless fucking wonder!"

"You'd pull the trigger and not think twice. You don't have emotions," whispered Giles.

"Never said I didn't have them, I just don't show them." As Kane glanced across the compound he saw the flashes of light in the sun. Choppers were coming in.

Sam saw the lights too.

"Stay out here, Kelly. If we have you to worry about, Kane in particular can't concentrate. Why do you think he got you out?" Sam adjusted the gun tucked in his shirt.

"But I can help. You can't go in there on your own. Cheng has to know by now that you're working with Kane. Can't I do something useful?" she begged.

Sam looked at this woman, her long blood-stained hair that had danced in the sun. Her face was dusty and her lip split open. Blood seeped from the wound. Clothes torn and the butterfly seemed to be dancing on her breast. It was easy to see why his father had married her. She was a magnet for Kane, and he had picked her well.

"Like I said, you stay here." Sam handed her a .38. "You have your weapon back. If you see anyone other than Chow… open fire."

She pouted. "Sam, take care of Kane for me. He is my life."

"I know that, and you are his," Sam agreed, and he was gone.

And so was Kelly.

Giles couldn't see the choppers coming in behind him.

Kane held his ground. "Shoot, you fucking bastard. Shoot." He wanted to unsettle Giles, and he wanted to do it before Chow got there.

Genna wriggled in Kane's grasp. She didn't want to die.

"Cheng, you can have half the profits… Help me out here. He really wants me to do it." Giles was losing his nerve. He turned. And he saw the choppers looming over the trees like giant vultures waiting for the slaughtered carcass. The noise got louder, louder till the deafening roar of the fleet of Chinese Police hovered above the gates of Fan Lau Fort. But that's not all he saw.

At the gate stood Sam Cheng. Arrogant and blonde he stood there, a carbon copy of Kane with 'made in China' stamped on him. Vau Cheng watched this man; a super soldier fighting on the right side of the law, just like his father. Lilia had indeed taught him well. There was no doubt he was Kane's son in more ways aside than just the blonde color of his hair.

As the choppers landed, swarms of policemen poured out. Without a second thought, the guards laid down their guns for Chow's men.

Giles stared in horror to see the man he had shot walking brand-new. Sam crossed over to where Cheng stood. Still Giles clutched his gun aimed at Kane. If he dropped it now, he was a dead man.

"I killed you! I shot you!" yelled Giles with a look of complete denial on his face.

"Apparently not," and Sam moved to Kane's side.

From his belt Sam produced a knife. He slit the rope on Kane's bonds.

"You want the knife, sir?" Sam asked of Kane.

"What I want to do, I can do with my bare hands," replied Kane curtly.

Sam laid his hand on Cheng's shoulder. "Colonel Cheng, we are here to take you back to stand trial for the murder of Lilia Cheng. You will go back to Australia for the other crimes…"

"How quickly you became a Branson," murmured Vau Cheng.

"I was born one," and Sam led Cheng away from the group without any opposition.

Giles Harris knew he was doomed. He moved forward towards Kane and the girl.

"Stop. Don't take a step closer," Kane said with force. "Put your gun down, Giles. It is over."

But Giles kept on going. Kane could see the look in his eyes. It was one of sadness and despair. He had never taken the time to know his daughter, and now he never could. Giles raised the gun higher.

"He did succeed, Genna, whether you knew it or not. He did. You fell for him, and I, well I wanted his wife. Then I would have had it all. Kane Branson never fails, he never has." His aim was steady.

Genna watched her father aiming at Kane's head, not at her. She twisted in Kane's grasp. Kane let her go. Genna screamed, and ran forward to kill the man she now knew as her father. Genna was still protecting the man she loved. But the AFP needed Giles alive. She grabbed the barrel of the gun and wrestled with her father. Suddenly it was free and Genna had the gun in her hands. Whether he let it go or she grabbed it, no-one knew. She made the mistake of turning. She was turning to hand it to Kane. It was then Genna saw the figure standing several feet behind Kane, and she was blinded by hate.

"If I can't have him…" Genna raised the gun and pulled the trigger.

A shot rang out, and the bullet ripped through Genna's chest, sending her body tumbling to the earth. Kelly stood there, the gun still smoking in her outstretched hands. Kelly never did as she was told.

She'd found a different route back inside the fort, scrambling over a crumbling wall to reach the man she loved. Kane spun around. Kelly stood there, arms still raised. She'd shot Genna dead.

"Kelly. Kel, give me the gun. It's over, baby."

Kane walked to her, prying the .38 from Kelly's fingers, and clutched it to his side. He kicked Genna's gun away from her body.

Giles stared at his feet to where his daughter lay. Then he looked up.

"You killed my daughter, Kane," he yelled. "Oh, your wife pulled the trigger, but you killed her. Now we are equal. One child for another. You and your morals. That's the motto you live and die by. So die by it." Giles moved forward and lunged at him.

Giles knocked the gun from Kane's broken hand. They locked arms. Both powerful men. Kane pushed him to the ground with a sickening thud. He turned Giles under him and rubbed his face in the dust. Kelly watched as Kane hit Giles again and again, first to his ribs, then to his back. Giles lay motionless on the ground. Kane pulled himself up into a sitting position. He glanced away just for a second to look at Kelly and Giles grabbed him from behind. He pulled Kane backwards trying to choke him. Kane brought his broken fingers up and tried to free himself. They cracked even more. He was choking.

Kelly grabbed one of the guns from the ground. She pointed it at Giles.

"Let him go, you bastard. Let him go now!" Kelly screamed.

Giles let go on Kane just barely. Kelly squeezed the trigger. The gun was empty. She had grabbed the gun Genna had aimed at her. Genna's father had used the bullets. It was all the distraction Kane needed. He turned and slammed his fist into Giles' face. Now there was no stopping Kane. He wanted Giles dead.

The gunshot had alerted Sam. He handed his uncle to Chow, and then sprinted away from the choppers and back towards his father.

But Giles wasn't ready to die. "I have always hated you and I will kill you! Die, you bastard, die."

"Not today, my friend."

Kane reared up with all the strength he had left and with one powerful blow smashed his fist into Giles' face.

"You fucking son-of-a-bitch!" spluttered Giles', grabbing his broken nose, and he hit back violently.

"Kane, no…" yelled Sam. "We need him alive…"

The two men rolled dangerously near the pit. Cheng had left the partition just slightly raised. Kelly ran forward with a shrill cry.

"No, Kane, don't…" Kelly screamed.

But her cry came too late. Giles made the mistake of looking up at Kelly. Kane brought his failing fist down one more time and knocked Giles to the edge. Below him the snakes hissed vehemently. Kane pushed Giles to the edge. Both men lay on the steaming metal doors, and Kane looked over. He could see the snakes sliding under the partition and he could hear the noise they made. He had no intention of going over the side. Instinctively his hands pushed harder. Giles turned in Kane's grasp.

"Sam, stop them…" begged Kelly.

In slow motion Giles looked down into the hissing mass, and then he turned his gaze to Kelly. He held onto the sod for as long as he could. Kane was too strong for him. For Giles Harris, there was no way out. He took a last look at Kelly running toward Kane, and one last look into Kane's thunderous eyes. Giles watched Kane's fist come down for the last time and he felt himself fall. It was over in seconds, the fear and the pain. Sam caught Kelly in mid-flight as her husband crawled to the edge and looked down.

"It didn't have to end like this." Kane bowed his head. "It didn't!"

"Let me go, Sam. He needs me," Kelly cried, struggling in his grasp.

"No, he has one more thing to do. Then you get your husband back and maybe, just maybe, I will gain a father. Who knows?" He let her go and Kelly stood strangely still.

Kane stood up bedraggled and bleeding. He walked across the mighty battlefield of the fort till he reached the chopper. Chow stood with Cheng securely handcuffed to the helicopter.

"My name…" he cleared his mind and his throat, and wiped his bloodied face with his arm. "My name is Federal Agent Kane Branson. Under the authority vested in me by the Australian Federal Police and the law enforcement of Hong Kong, I arrest you Colonel Vau Cheng for crimes committed against the people of Australia. You will return with me to Australia for the murder of Agent Alex Powers, conspiring to commit murder, conspiracy to traffic drugs between the two continents, and all crimes against the people thereof this the 13 day of July 2001." Kane paused and took a deep breath. "You will also stand trial on your own soil for the murder of Lilia Cheng." Kane stared at Cheng with eyes so full of hatred that Cheng drew back against the chopper. All Kane wanted to do was kill Vau Cheng right where he stood. Aside from Lilia Cheng, Vau Cheng had killed his friend.

Chow saw it. "Government will be proud of you, Mitter Brandon." Chow looked at Kane and his hand rested gently on Kane Branson's shoulder.

"Whose?" replied Kane, and wiped more blood from his face with his hand.

Kane stood on the bloodied earth. He waited for his wife and Sam to join him. He watched the choppers take off into the skies like giant silver birds of prey. Only Chow's chopper remained.

Kelly ran to Kane and threw her arms around him. She buried her head in his chest and cried.

"It's gonna be okay, baby. Gonna be okay. We're goin' home, just like I promised you. You'll be fine. I promise you," and he wiped the blood and sweat from his eyes, and stroked his wife's hair.

Sam stood by and watched. Maybe he did like Kane after all. He wasn't sure, only time would tell.

"You wanna ride some place?" asked Kane.

"I have the car…" Sam pointed back into the brush.

"That's right, you have the car."

There was an awkward silence. Sam shuffled his boots in the earth.

"You'll have to testify against your… against Colonel Cheng," muttered Kane.

"I know. I'll be there." Sam paused. "I'll see you both then…"

"Right, mate…in Australia. Sydney, Australia. We're in the AFP book," Kane laughed. "Did you put the ONC where I told you too?"

"Yes." Sam handed Kane the detonator. "So I'll be going, Mr. Branson…"

"Right… chopper's gonna leave anyway. You better get away from the fort… you know big bang…"

"Yes, sir…"

Kane let go of Kelly. He stretched his hand out to Sam. Sam slid his hand into Kane's. Kane went to turn away, then swung back and grabbed Sam by the shoulders and hugged his son to him.

"You're a fine agent, Sam …" Kane paused. "Whatever the fuck your name is."

"Yes, sir. Thank you, sir."

Kane let go of Sam and pushed Kelly into the waiting chopper. Kane turned one more time and looked toward his son.

"Sam, take this," and Kane untied the bandana from his head.

He dropped the piece of war into his son's hands. Sam was speechless. Kane jumped into the chopper, and raised his hand in salute to Sam.

The blades started to turn and the wind whipped around the ground. Sam ran back to the safety of the trees.

"My name… my name is Sam Branson. And we will meet again. You can bank on that," and Sam clutched the bandana to him.

Chopper blades blew the dust around the tainted earth, and the helicopter climbed higher into the air.

"Mitter Brandon, the Hunter…"

"Inspector Chow, you missed him. The Hunter has been and gone. He has claimed his own," Kane said with finality.

Kelly whispered in Kane's ear. "I'm sorry that I…"

He put his broken fingers to her lips. "There is nothing to be sorry about. When we get back I'll file the report, then we'll take time for us. I'll talk with Buchanan. He did it for my sake, but it was still wrong. He was guilty of one crime, protecting his own, just as you and I did."

"How can you speak up for Buchanan? Who are you Kane?"

"The Hunter. You know that, baby."

"Who are you really?"

"I'm hell, Kelly. Hell was here, Kel. The Hunter had always been my ultimate goal. It put me over Buchanan. I have been the Hunter for a long time. Buchanan was working for me on this mission. I told him recently my exact position in the AFP. They did promote me over him. I discovered he was being blackmailed about the same time I learned about Sam. " He glanced at his surprised wife. "The evening you happened to over-hear us talking, I knew you had heard about the Hunter operation. But we decided to let you go on thinking what you did. I didn't want you to know the real truth."

"I had no idea, Kane," and she snuggled in beside him. "No idea," she murmured.

"There is just one thing left to do, baby."

As the chopper gained its proper height, Kane looked across the bronzed hill. Slowly, as the sun dipped its head Kane reached for the det-onator that Sam had handed him.

"All your men out of there, Chow?" Kane yelled across the craft.

"Yes, sir, Mitter Brandon, what you…"

Kane's finger hovered on the button. He looked through the window. He could see the dust of a car doing zero to seventy away from the fort. Sam had placed the explosives around the walls. Kane pressed the button and the cannons of Fan Lau Fort would see no more action. Fiery red dust rose into the skies. At last they were going home from the fires of hell, and the making of China white. It wouldn't stop the trade, but it had made a dent.

Beneath them the fiery clouds dispersed. The chopper hovered and took off in the evening skies. Kane rested his broken hand on Kelly's legs. And he looked out the helicopter window. He saw the eagle fly across the fading sun, gliding on the air. It screamed above the chopper engines, and for two seconds, he felt at one with the bird of prey. He understood its thoughts and its motives. It was still searching for the thing that he at last had found. The bird swooped and disappeared over the mountains of Lantau. And as the Hong Kong mist settled in for the night, Kane's Hundredth mission was over, and justice for his friends prevailed.

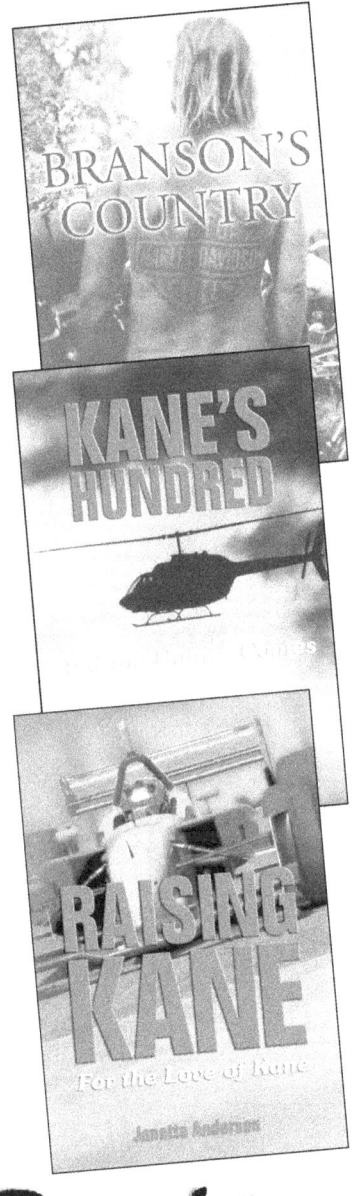

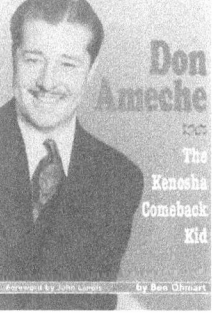

www.ingramcontent.com/pod-product-compliance
Lightning Source LLC
Chambersburg PA
CBHW072354030726
47505CB00014B/1814